SNAKE WATER

Alan Williams

SNAKE WATER

Published by Sapere Books.

20 Windermere Drive, Leeds, England, LS17 7UZ,
United Kingdom

saperebooks.com

ISBN: 978-1-80055-151-0

For P.E., D.G., R.K., and D.S.

CHAPTER ONE: MAN ON THE LOOSE

Ben Morris leaned against the deck rail, his mouth turned down at the corners, and watched the lights winking at him across the bay. The shore lay perhaps half a mile off, perhaps a mile — it was hard to calculate in the tropical twilight. The engines had slowed to a thud, and he listened to the water lapping against the hull. His cabin had been cleared and locked, his suitcase and canvas briefcase stowed at the head of the gangway. All he could do now was wait for the pilot boat to come out and guide them into port. From then on, he was alone.

There were steep mountains beyond the shore and storm clouds that curled in the dusk, settling darkly over the town. He could smell rain and felt his skin prickling under his shirt. Even the scrubbed deck rail was moist.

There was almost no sound on board. The other passengers would probably be in the wardroom now, playing Scrabble or gin rummy. He doubted whether any of them would ask to go ashore tonight. He was the only one leaving the ship here: the rest were booked on the round trip back to London.

She was a slow freighter that ran cargoes around the west coast of Africa, down to Central and South America, with accommodation for six passengers. Ben's companions were two English couples in their fifties and a widower who drank up to three bottles of rum a day and was prone to fall over every time the ship rolled. They took their meals at a table with the captain and chief engineer, two gloomy Scots who usually ate in silence, chewing steadily as though to batten down their boredom.

The voyage had lasted nearly four weeks, with calls at Casablanca and Dakar. The first couple of days, as they steamed down the Channel into the Bay of Biscay, he had spent on his bunk with the porthole screwed down, sweating. The other passengers had been seasick; he had not. He had lain in silent battle with himself, fighting down the fear and loneliness that had been attacking him ever since he had awakened two months ago in that hospital in Bordeaux.

At night he relied on sleeping pills; sometimes they worked; often they didn't. He would drop off for an hour or two, then lie awake till the steward came in the gray of the morning with tea and biscuits. He had had no appetite in those first days; had drunk warily and talked to almost no one. He had done a lot of reading: *David Copperfield* and *A Tale of Two Cities* for the second time; the Richard Hannay adventures by Buchan; a stack of paperback thrillers, H. L. Mencken's essays, a Spanish phrase book.

After Dakar came the muggy crossing of the tropics when the physical limits of his life had been as confining as those of a man in prison. There were the deck, the wardroom, dining room and his spartan cabin with its steel basin and single bunk; and gradually the monotony of each day had brought him a numbed peace, until, like a man trying to postpone a dreaded reality, he had wished the voyage would last six months, even a year.

A door opened beside him and a man stepped from a lighted cabin onto the deck. Ben recognized the captain; he was wearing a white shirt without jacket or tie, his face mauve with blood pressure. 'Evenin', Mister Morris.' He spoke with a strong Lowland accent.

'Good evening, Captain.' They paused, peering through the dusk for a glimpse of the pilot boat. 'So ye're goin' ashore here, are ye?' the captain said, without turning his head.

'That's right.' Ben felt a stab of panic. After so long on the open sea the stillness of the ship filled him with an irrational anxiety.

The captain was breathing heavily beside him. He was not an easy man to talk to. On their last night in Dakar he had come on board drunk and called Ben into his cabin, confessing savagely that he hated the sea: the tedium and hard work and poor pay, with less than three months at home in the year: telling Ben he was a lucky lad to be free to travel halfway round the world. Free as air — scowling into his cup of gin and tepid water. *Free!* Ben thought. Oh, he was free all right. He'd escaped. He had absolutely nothing now, except his suitcase and briefcase, and £330 in traveler's checks and 170 dollars in cash — all the money he had in the world, now buttoned down in the breast pockets of his bush-shirt, the one with the label 'Genuine Safari Bush-Shirt Guaranteed to Fade'. He had tried to plan how long the money would last: perhaps as long as his six-month visa, if he avoided the big hotels and clip joints and whorehouses. There was a single-line railway through the mountains to the inland capital of Parataxín in the south. He planned to take the first train out. He had nothing to hold him now: no responsibilities to anyone. He was free.

The captain growled beside him: 'Ye must be mad stoppin' here! The dairtiest port on the coast.'

'What's the matter with it?'

'Pure bloody hell!' the captain cried, in a sudden fluting voice. 'If the dear Lord wished to give the world an enema, he'd know just where to insert the tube. Guadaigil!' He nodded at the lights ahead. 'Why don't you come t' Rio? There's a city for ye! This place has nothing.' A bell clanked somewhere above them in the darkness. That'll be the pilot boat.' He turned toward his cabin. 'Come t' Rio, mon,' he muttered again, without looking back.

'Rio's too far,' said Ben. 'This is as far as my ticket goes, and this is where I get off.'

The captain moved away without answering, slamming the cabin door behind him.

Pure bloody hell he'd said it was, Ben thought, looking at the dipping waterfront. And the captain ought to know — he did this run twice a year.

Ben walked down the quay toward the Customs shed, his suitcase in one hand and briefcase in the other. The night was black and sticky, and the sweat was already itching down his face and under his collar. In his case were a couple of bottles of Johnnie Walker, bought duty-free on the ship, which he had decided to declare.

Two men sat inside the shed drinking coffee under a fan. One was a Negro with a face pitted like anthracite. The other was an officer; he had white piping on his shoulders and wore sunglasses, a holster and supple black boots. He snapped his fingers at Ben without standing up: 'Passport!' One hand flicked at a black nailbrush mustache while the other turned the pages of the passport, taking its time.

'You speak Spanish?'

'A little.'

'How long are you staying in Guadaigil?'

'I'm going to Parataxín by train.'

'The first train is tomorrow at eight. How much money have you?'

Ben told him. The man's fingers snapped again: 'Show me.'

Ben unbuttoned his breast pocket and took out the billfold of traveler's checks and the 170 dollars in cash.

'You have pesos?' the officer asked.

'No.'

The sunglasses watched him blankly for several seconds. 'All money must be changed by the proper authorities,' he said at last. 'It is illegal to import pesos from abroad.' He paused meaningfully: 'Black-market activities are severely punished in this country. You understand?'

'I understand,' said Ben. 'I have no pesos.' He looked up at the framed photograph of a heavy-faced man in military uniform, with the inscription: *President of the Republic for the Glory of God, Dr. Isodor Romolo.* Doctor of what? Ben wondered. The Negro yawned and went on sipping his coffee. Ben said: 'Where can I change money?'

The officer put out his hand again: 'Give me the dollars. I change them.'

Ben gave him a single ten-dollar bill, the lowest denomination he had. The officer spread it on his knee and studied it, then opened a drawer in the table beside him. He counted out fifteen dog-eared notes, each worth one peso, and thrust them at Ben.

Ben hesitated.

'Fifteen pesos,' the officer said.

Ben knew from the list of exchange rates given to him with his traveler's checks that the peso stood at 3s. 6d. — almost exactly half a dollar. He had been short-changed by 25 percent. The man could have made a mistake. Ben gave him a false smile: 'I am sorry, Señor — ten dollars is twenty pesos.'

The officer slipped the bill inside his tunic. 'Fifteen pesos,' he said, and opened the passport again. Ben took out his check folder, pointing at the exchange rates. The values were given against sterling only and the officer did not seem interested; he reached out for a rubber stamp.

Ben felt hot and exhausted. The currency value could have changed since he had left England. This was not, after all, one of the world's most stable states. He watched the officer stamp his passport and write down its number with his name in a ledger beside him. Then he pointed at the suitcase and briefcase. 'Open!' He examined both thoroughly, again taking his time. When he came to the Scotch he lifted the two bottles out and stood them on the table. 'Eight pesos,' he said.

Ben took out his money again and peeled off eight notes, but the officer shook his head: 'I change ten more dollars.'

'But I have pesos now.'

'Not enough. For one night in Guadaigil you will need at least fifteen pesos. You pay eight for import tax — you have seven left. Yes?'

'Yes,' said Ben, with sudden helplessness. He gave him another ten-dollar bill and the officer gave him seven pesos change. Ben put the Scotch back in the bag. 'I want a receipt, please.'

The sunglasses stared at him.

'*Recibo*,' Ben repeated.

'It is not necessary,' the officer said and handed the passport back.

Ben's color was rising. He took a step forward: 'It is necessary! I want a receipt for eight pesos!'

The Negro shifted in his chair and put down his coffee cup. The officer did not move. He said: 'If it is necessary, then I will tell you. You will go now.' He made a motion with his hand and the Negro stood up and stepped over beside Ben.

For a moment he was filled with a wild fury; he had been cheated and humiliated: short-changed by nearly two pounds;

and no doubt the eight pesos on the Scotch would go to buying the officer cigars. But Ben had chosen to come to this country, and this was the way it worked. He picked up his bags and went outside, through the port gates where a band of scrawny Indian porters came whimpering round him like dogs after a bone. He ignored them and after a few yards they slunk away into the darkness.

He began walking down a dirt road into the town, past stunted palm trees that reminded him of pineapples. Further on there were huts and warehouses with lights hung at long intervals. An oil tanker out in the bay groaned suddenly like some great beast in pain. Otherwise there was no sound. He felt a horrible loneliness. The incident with the officer had depressed him and put him on the defensive. *The next person who tries to hustle me*, he thought, *is going to regret it.* He came into a street of white houses with wooden verandas, and noticed that the ground everywhere was covered in a powdery gray dust which in places had drifted into heaps up to a foot high.

A man with a gun sat in the door of a wine shop, chuckling to himself. He yelled something at Ben, who hurried on, into a brighter street where there was a little yellow church and a row of bars murmuring with *mariachis*. Insects began humming around him, sticking to his hair and the sweat on his face. Ahead, he saw lightning flashes up in the mountains.

A couple of taxis stood near the church door, their drivers dozing inside. A young man in a baseball cap was lounging against one of the hoods. He started up when he saw Ben and came forward smiling: 'Hey, mister, wanna hotel?'

Ben walked on, and the young man began walking beside him. 'You American? O.K., what you are?' He was still smiling.

'I can find a hotel. Thank you!'

'You go to Pez Espada Hotel,' the young man said, keeping in careful step with him. He made no attempt to carry Ben's bags, and at the end of the street he said: 'C'mon — this way!'

Ben began to get angry. 'Listen, I don't want to go that way. I can find my own hotel. Understand?'

The man smiled: 'Down there, Hotel Pez Espada.' Ben looked and saw there was only one way to go — the way the man was pointing. The street led into a plaza with arcades and a dry fountain. As soon as he started off again, the young man fell in behind him.

The hotel was a two-story house in the Spanish colonial style, with a stuffed swordfish over the entrance. 'Hotel Pez Espada!' the young man cried, skipping up beside him, grinning. Ben clamped his jaws shut and said nothing. He started up the steps and the young man was beside him at once, touching his sleeve: 'One peso please mister!'

'Go to hell!' Ben said without turning round. He took another step and the man was in front of him. He was not smiling now. He had black glassy eyes that looked too old for his face. 'One peso mister.'

Ben felt his pulse quicken. *Don't push it*, he thought: *I'm in a nasty mood. I've been in a nasty mood for a long time. I may try taking it out on somebody.* He stepped round him and took another step, and the man shouted something in Spanish which Ben didn't catch. A big sad-faced man in a striped pajama top came out of the hotel foyer and looked down at them. He had a long nightstick clipped to his belt. *'Qué pasa?'* he said quietly.

The man in the baseball cap began talking rapid Spanish. Ben shook his arm free and spoke to the big man: 'I want a room for the night!'

The man stared at him: he had a drooping mustache on a face the color of a dead leaf. 'You pay him one peso,' he said, nodding at the young man.

Ben put down his bags. For a moment he stood with arms tensed, his heart beginning to race. It was a long time since he had hit anybody: not since the night in a Soho restaurant when a drunk had called his wife 'a stuck-up little deb.' The man had had to be helped out into a taxi afterward.

'Shit!' he said in English, and the big man repeated in Spanish: 'You pay one peso.'

'Why?'

'Commission,' the man said quietly, his hands hanging motionless at his side. It would take a couple of seconds to unclip the nightstick, Ben thought. On the other hand, one of them might have a knife; and even if he won, the police would probably throw him in jail and fine him fifty times what this was going to cost.

He took out a one-peso note, avoiding the young man's eyes. 'You're a thieving little bastard!' he said as he gave it to him, and the man waved, grinning: 'Bye! Bye! Mister!'

Ben went up the steps, past the big man in the pajama top, and thought bitterly: *I'm letting them get away with it. Twelve pesos, or nearly two quid, in half an hour. I'm a coward.* He said: 'I want a room for one night.'

The big man nodded and went behind the desk.

It was a poky room on the ground floor with a humpbacked bed, a basin and iron bidet. He put his case on the bed, took out one of the bottles of whisky, went over to the basin and saw there was no water glass. He tried the tap; it coughed and spat out a dead insect. He took a deep breath and looked at himself in the mirror. His face was tauter than when he had left

England and he looked more than twenty-nine. It was a broad face with short pepper-brown hair and a nose that had been badly broken twice — first at the age of five when a door had been opened against him in a game of hide-and-seek, and again during a boxing match at Aberystwyth University. Apart from the nose it was a good face; the nose gave it a hint of brutality.

He went into the passage and shouted for the big man to bring him a glass and bottle of mineral water. As he got back the rain started. It came in a roar, splashing through the shutters against the mosquito net which had shrunk and split away from the frame. He threw the shutters open and let the water bounce onto his face.

Then he noticed the dust on the ledge. It was the same as he had seen in the street outside — about half an inch deep, like a layer of cigar ash. The rain was already swilling it into a gray slime. He ran his finger through a corner that was still dry and it did not feel like ordinary dust: it was hard and gritty, and oddly sinister.

Somebody knocked on the door. A woman came in carrying a tray with the glass and mineral water. He watched her put it down and noticed that her legs were shaped like Indian clubs, tapering down from low heavy hips formed by generations of women used to carrying loads on their heads. She was the first girl he had seen since Dakar, nearly a month ago.

She hurried out of the room, her eyes away from him. He waited till she had closed the door, then poured the tumbler full with equal measures of Scotch and water, pulled the suitcase to the floor and flung himself down on the bed, sipping his drink and staring at the ceiling.

He began to think of Laura. He tried to avoid her, fight her off, but her memory crept up on him, as it always did at about this time, and as always it was more a physical pain than a mental process. She had been very beautiful; but after that he could not really remember what she had looked like. She had been twenty-two when he first met her — almost exactly two years ago, while she was working in a West End bookshop and he was in his sixth year of a good dull job with a firm of City architects. He had married her five months later. There had been a big wedding down at her parents' house near Cirencester in Gloucestershire. He remembered that part well: the marquee in the garden, presided over by Laura's father — a hard-drinking, Jaguar-driving tycoon with a wife who sat on the magistrates' bench. They had not been too sure about Ben at first. His background was not imposing: born in Fishguard, West Wales, where his father was a librarian. But they had finally accepted him, and her father had furnished a flat for them both in Camden Town, and also paid for the honeymoon in Marrakesh.

They had been married for eleven months, seven days and almost exactly two hours — making the adjustment from French to British Summer Time. It had been that holiday in France — driving down to Biarritz in a brand-new convertible. The pain of memory was spreading. He blinked at the light in the middle of the ceiling and noticed that the bulb was freckled with flies. It was past nine o'clock. He had had no dinner, but was not hungry. He poured another whisky, with less water this time, and lay listening to the rain. He wondered if he'd be able to sleep without a pill. It had been getting a little better on the ship. In the first weeks after getting back from France it had been very bad indeed — when he'd nearly cracked up and had had to take six-months leave from his job, which really meant that he would never return, and had moved in with Tom Clay, a former sportswriter on the *Daily Worker*, who was now in the drawing office of Ben's firm. It was Clay who got him

17

through those first weeks when he could scarcely sleep three hours a night and would pace the floor from corner to corner till Clay woke and made him hot whisky-and-lemon and talked him back to marginal sanity.

He emptied his second drink and closed his eyes. Perhaps he wouldn't need that pill after all.

Outside it was still raining. He had dozed off and it was now nearly midnight. He sat up listening to a muffled sound that seemed to be coming from under the floor. After a moment he recognized the thump of music.

He had a headache and his mouth tasted sour after the whisky. He went over to the basin, cleaned his teeth and gargled with what was left of the mineral water, put on a tie and went into the passage. The music was coming from somewhere at the back of the hotel. He groped his way round corners and came to a purple neon sign burning out the name CLUB MOCAMBA BAR, pushed open a swing door and went down a flight of steps into darkness that smelt of disinfectant and cigar smoke.

The music came from a loudspeaker behind the bar. The barman was a young Negro with a white jacket over a cotton singlet. A couple of girls with low-cut blouses and metal teeth sat on stools opposite him, sipping Coca-Cola. The floor and a few tables round the walls were empty, and a fan swung round from the ceiling, stirring up the stale air. Ben sat down at a stool at the far end of the bar. The two girls immediately slipped from their stools and moved toward him. The young Negro flashed him a smile and said, '*Quieres whisky?*'

'One beer,' said Ben.

The smile set for a moment, enamel-white in the darkness. 'Whisky?' he said again, hopefully.

'Beer,' said Ben. '*Cerveza. Una.*'

One of the girls purred close to his ear: 'You buy me whisky, mister!'

Her companion was slimmer and prettier — an Indian girl with small features. The barman put a glass down in front of Ben and poured it full of a yellow liquid with a head like soapsuds. Ben looked at the label: it was a local brew called 'Merrybeer'. 'One peso,' said the barman, still smiling. *They were great smilers*, Ben thought: *they'd be smiling as they lifted your wallet and slipped a knife in your ribs.* He counted what was left of the twenty dollars he'd changed. The room had cost nine pesos, paid in advance, and with the whisky duty and the hotel tout he was now left with only twelve pesos. The two girls watched as he paid the barman. 'You buy me whisky?' the first one said again, touching his arm. The younger girl was gazing at him with parted lips.

The barman said in English: 'You wanna buy these girls whisky?'

'No.'

The barman chuckled: 'You American?'

'No. British.' He felt rather stupid saying it. Perhaps he ought to have said 'Welsh' — that would have confused them. The barman said, 'Ah, *Inglés!*' and seemed to lose interest. Ben sipped his beer and wondered what he would do when he got to Parataxín. It had been Clay's idea that he come to South America; there had been no stronger reason than the fact that he spoke enough Spanish to get by. One morning Clay had just said: 'Ben, you must go away — a long way across the sea. South America. Go and see how lucky you are not to have been born one of the great unwashed. Be miserable with everyone else. It won't cost you much.'

Perhaps Clay had been a little optimistic there. Ben rapped his glass and called for another beer. The girls sat patiently beside him with the Coca-Colas, listening to the music. Perhaps after a few days he'd move down to Rio, as the captain had advised. He looked round at the younger of the women, and found himself wondering what her body would be like under the shabby frock. Silky brown buttocks, thin legs and sharp black nipples. He thought how it might be fun on his first night ashore to have both girls, all rolled up together in the grubby humpbacked bed, with the rain outside and the springs creaking. The young one would be the best. He wondered how much she would cost, and realized he was staring at her. She began to smile, murmuring: 'Whisky?'

The barman chimed in in a musical bass: 'You buy the girl whisky?'

Ben shook his head and asked for a third beer, wishing he had Tom Clay to talk to — anyone to talk to. Laura more than anyone else. The sight of the girl beside him had made him think of Laura, and start comparing her with Laura. There was no comparison, and he knew, with a familiar spasm of terror, that no girl would ever be like her again. Clay had warned him to keep off girls for a bit. They'd only depress him. Keep on the move, Clay had said: Keep a diary, write a book, visit the Aztec ruins.

But he'd be out of here by tomorrow morning. He might as well enjoy himself. He said to the girl: 'You want a whisky?'

She nodded eagerly and slipped into the empty stool between them. Ben said to the barman: 'Give her a whisky. One!' He turned to the girl and touched her cheek and she grinned and rubbed her face against his hand like a cat. '*Habla Inglés?*' he said.

She giggled: '*Español.*'

He watched the barman pour the whisky under the bar. 'Show me the bottle,' he said. The Negro brought up an old Haig bottle. Ben took it and sniffed. It had a harsh oily smell, but if the girl was happy thinking it was whisky perhaps it didn't matter. She looked at him and cried, '*Bueno?*'

'*Bueno!*' said the barman, grinning. He gave her a thimbleful, and said to Ben: 'Three pesos.'

Ben lifted his beer to the girl and touched her glass. They both drank, and the barman said again: 'Three pesos.' He waved a hand at him: 'Pay you later.' He put his hand on the girl's knee and felt her wriggle closer, pressing her thigh against his, her head leaning sideways so that he caught the brittle smell of her hair. He began to think of something else: the straight fast road down from Bordeaux to Bayonne: sun flashing between the pines. Sand under the pine and Citroëns screaming past at a hundred miles an hour on the crown of the road. Back seats piled with children. *Bloody maniacs*, he thought, and turned, looking wildly about the bar, gripping his beer glass so hard it was about to crack.

The door swung open and three men came in. One of them was the officer from the Customs shed. He took off his peaked cap and sat down with the other two, who wore dark suits.

Ben turned back and heard the girl calling to him in a sparrow voice: '*Tienes cigarillos, por favor?*'

He told her he didn't smoke cigarettes. She showed him her empty glass: '*Un whisky?*'

The Negro was already refilling her glass. She mewed happily beside Ben, who leaned out and squeezed her thigh; it felt firm, without slip or garters. He watched her tip back her drink, a little too fast. He held his own glass up to the barman, and she immediately held hers up too, chanting: '*Un whisky!*'

The barman poured her another thimbleful and Ben closed his eyes. That damned officer was there in the corner. *Ten pesos he owes me*, he thought. *When the girl's finished her drink, I'll ask her to leave with me.*

The barman tapped a cool black finger on Ben's hand. 'Twelve pesos,' he said.

Ben looked at him and blinked. The Negro's smile was only a few inches away. For some reason Ben smiled back. Perhaps the man would listen. He leaned across the bar and said, in his most careful Spanish: 'Listen to me. I wish you to listen to me. I killed my wife.'

'Twelve pesos,' the Negro said in English.

Ben nodded: nearly two pounds for a few bad beers and three shots of Latin-American Special. But he didn't want to argue. He had no quarrel with the barman. He smiled again at the Negro, then turned to the girl. She had finished her third drink and now sat with her back to him, smiling at the officer and the two men in the corner.

Ben took her arm and repeated slowly in Spanish: 'Listen to me. I killed my wife.' She looked quickly round at him, then at the barman, who repeated: 'Twelve pesos.'

He fumbled with his buttoned-down pocket, trying to remember how many beers he'd already paid for. He was growing muzzy and careless; he didn't have many pesos left now. He'd have to start all over again changing more dollars.

He got the roll of dollars out and dropped them on the floor. As he went down, groping under the stool, he began rehearsing his Spanish for telling the girl exactly what had happened. How the pines had raced past: Nationale Dix striped with sunlight and shadow, and Laura's hair flowing in the wind, sweeping across her eyes. He had been driving, lulled by the swift hum of the tires, and suddenly there had been a milk truck in the middle of the road. It had stopped. Everything had stopped, except for the wail of a siren and the milk churns clanging round him, and the whole road flowing with milk. He had been lying on the sandy verge under the pines, and Laura had been there beside him covered with a blanket, kicking. He remembered watching her with an odd detachment, wondering why she was kicking like that. A man in blue overalls was standing over him, and there was a policeman in a white crash helmet, and cars were passing, slowing down, and another policeman was out in the road, whistling them on. And all the time Laura just lay there beside him under the blanket, and after a while the kicking stopped; and when he came around later in hospital they told him she was dead.

As he picked up his money off the floor, he became aware of a pair of boots by the girl's stool. The man was still wearing his holster and sunglasses, smiling at her under his nailbrush mustache. He glanced at Ben, as though he hardly recognized him, and went on talking to the girl. Ben saw her smile and the officer snapped an order to the barman, who bowed and brought out the Haig bottle.

Ben sat down and wondered what to do. As he listened to the officer's voice, soft and coaxing in the girl's ear, he felt a hot rage beginning to pound through his head. He was gripping the roll of dollars in front of him, when the barman said again: 'Twelve pesos.'

Ben paused. He looked around at the officer, then at the girl, and neither of them took any notice of him. He took hold of the girl's wrist and tugged, not very gently. 'Come,' he said in Spanish, 'we go and drink whisky. Real whisky. We leave here.'

She looked at him vacantly and began to withdraw her arm. He said loudly again: 'Come and drink whisky. Upstairs!'

She pulled her arm away and looked round at the officer, who pointed at the barman and said to Ben: 'You do what the man says. Twelve pesos.'

'You owe me ten pesos!' Ben shouted and put the dollars back in his pocket.

The officer stiffened and moved back from the girl's stool. 'You make trouble?'

'You owe me ten pesos,' Ben said again. 'And leave this girl alone. She's with me.'

The officer hesitated, muttered something to the girl who just shrugged, then turned back to Ben: 'You pay the money and you go. We not want you here. This is a nice place.'

'This is a bloody clip joint!' Ben shouted in English, and slid down off his stool, his face throbbing with excitement. 'You get out of here yourself! Who the hell are you coming in here and telling me what to do…?'

The barman had lifted the hatch, and at the same moment the officer slammed his hand down on his holster. It was then that Ben hit him. He was surprised afterward that he did it with such precision. He kept thinking, *I mustn't break his glasses: I must concentrate on the lower part of his face and his body.* He gave him a straight left-handed punch to his jaw and felt the man's head snap back, while he followed in with two quick jabs, a right and a left to the ribs, and a last swinging blow with the back of his right arm that caught the man just below the ear, spun him around and threw him with a crash against the wall, where he slithered down and lay still.

The girls were screaming. The barman had stopped, with the hatch up, his eyes and mouth big. Ben had one free second to realize that it is not wise to hit an armed police officer in a banana republic.

As he started toward the door the whole room broke into pandemonium. The two men in the corner loomed across the dance floor. The barman slammed down the bar hatch behind him and leaped after Ben, who was through the door, up the stone steps in the dark, hearing the shouts behind him, thinking quickly: *I must somehow get my luggage — get out of the hotel, get to the ship*. He wondered if the big man in the pajama top was still on duty at the desk.

They were coming after him up the steps, and he thought: *I hope I knocked the bastard out! If I didn't he'll be after me with the gun.*

At the top of the stairs he turned left, trying to remember where his room was. The shouting and pounding of feet were hard behind him and his eyesight seemed to be growing blurred. It was very dark. He tried to steady himself against the walls of the passage — first one hand, then the other — zigzagging up to the corner where he slipped and went down with a smack and stab of pain in his knee.

He stumbled to his feet and saw the big man in the pajama top coming toward him. He was holding the nightstick in both hands, advancing slowly, feet apart, his body silhouetted against the light from the reception desk.

Ben hesitated just a fraction of a second. The man was between him and his room. Behind were at least three men — and perhaps a fourth who was armed. Ben decided to take the big man. He felt controlled and tense, remembering that a man who chooses to fight with a stick is like a man with a knife — or a gun with only one shot. He has to win the first round, or he's in trouble. Ben would make him strike first. He didn't have much time: perhaps five seconds before the others caught up.

He put his hands out at his sides, the fingers stiffened, lowered his head slightly and charged, straight at the man's belly, his eyes watching the swing of the stick as it came up — just a little too late — reaching the height of its parabola at the moment Ben's fingers struck the man just beneath his rib cage, sinking into a fold of stomach fat and thrusting upward under the ridge of bone, pulling the man's body against him, his lowered forehead cracking into the center of his face. He heard something crunch, and the man shrieked and brought the nightstick down in a wild flaying movement, hitting the wall, then trying to raise it again and swing it around at Ben's head. Ben jerked his knee up into the man's groin. He thought: *I'm in so deep I'd better use every trick there is. One blow in the right place with that stick and he'll kill me.*

He watched the stick go up again and heard the man groaning, beginning to crumple with pain. The barman and the two other men were running down the passage toward them. Ben pushed the big man against the wall, slipped around him and threw him backward against the barman. The nightstick clattered onto the linoleum. Ben grabbed it and swung it over his head. The big man was kneeling on the floor, holding his stomach. The barman stood beside him, his face wide with terror, eyes rolling with the swing of the stick. Behind him the other two were beginning to back away down the passage.

There was no sign of the officer. Ben shouted out to the barman: 'Back or I'll smash your brains out!' The stick was solid wood with a handle wrapped in Scotch tape. He swung it again, taking a step forward, and the barman muttered: '*Sí vámonos!*' — and stepped back after the others.

Ben turned with the nightstick in his hands and ran. He looked vainly for his room. He turned left and saw a door leading into a patio. He was sweating now, beginning to panic. He started back down the passage. Ahead he could hear a subdued, excited chattering. At the corner of the passage he turned left, cursing himself for not remembering his room. He thought of what he would have to leave there: one and a half bottles of Johnnie Walker, a lightweight suit, shirts and sweaters, changes of socks and underwear, shaving case — and the briefcase, of course. Perhaps he regretted that most of all.

A hush had fallen over the hotel. He thought: *The bastards are creeping up on me*. He reached the end of the passage, slowing at the corner, expecting them to jump out on him.

The passage beyond was empty. At the end lay the reception desk and the door into the Plaza where the rain slanted down in flashing spears. There was no one at the desk. He ran out and down the steps, slipping on the gray slime that was everywhere — creeping in greasy rivulets between the paving stones and along the gutters. The Plaza was full of steaming puddles blistered with rain. He began to make for the arcades, past a man lying propped against the wall, his head nodding forward under a sombrero. Ben could not see whether he was asleep or drunk. He reached the arcades and began to run round the Plaza away from the hotel, trying to work out some plan. The only thing would be to try and reach the ship. He wondered what the legal position would be. Could they force the captain to hand him over? The old man would probably put up some sort of fight for him: he didn't like foreigners. After all, what had Ben done? Just started a little brawl in a clip joint.

Above the rain he heard shouts and feet clattering down the hotel steps. He shrank back against one of the arcades and peered out. A man was at the bottom of the steps, splashing across the Plaza in the direction of the arcades where Ben was standing. His head and shoulders were hunched against the rain, and he was holding a pistol against his stomach. It was the officer — still wearing his sunglasses.

This is it! Ben thought: *I should be able to outrun him even if he does try shooting. An ordinary pistol isn't accurate at much over ten yards, and that officer can't be in too good shape for either running or shooting.* He didn't know about the other two men; they had looked a mean pair. He hoped his wind would hold out.

He was still carrying the nightstick, running desperately with the blood throbbing in his head, his lungs aching. There was no one in front of him. He came to the corner and started out from the shelter of the arcade, into the warm rain. He heard the shouting start up again behind, and ran on with his feet throwing up great splashes of mud; and noticed that the rain on his hands was mixed with a black powder like soot. It was also staining his shirt and trousers.

He glanced over his shoulder and saw two men coming after him. He turned into the street down toward the yellow church. It was deserted, and when he next looked back he saw no one. He slowed, catching his breath, his ears roaring, then flung the nightstick away and started off again toward the port gates.

He ran on past the little yellow church with the two taxis standing in a spreading lake of mud; and he realized that he had not thought about Laura for at least twenty minutes. Perhaps this was the antidote: Ben Morris out on a limb, deprived of all worldly goods, running for his life. At least it helped clean his liver out.

A single steel guitar wailed above the roar of the rain. He turned into the street between the huts and warehouses. The port gates and the Customs shed loomed up at the end. The shed was in darkness, the gates closed and bolted with double padlocks. He stumbled up to them, ankle-deep in water, and saw far down the quayside the lights of the ship. The gates were at least fifteen feet high, with no foothold, and topped with a roll of barbed wire that extended the length of the seawall. He seized hold of the bars and shook them for a moment in desperation. The padlocks clanked dismally.

Then he remembered the taxis by the church. They would be his only chance now, unless he could find a way round the seawall. But that would be the first place they'd look. He'd get a taxi out through the mountains to Parataxín, one hundred and eighty kilometers away. Pay the driver in dollars — all his dollars, if necessary. And sleep in the taxi. Get dry and warm and sleep.

He turned and started off again, back toward the church. He was almost there when he heard the siren screaming at him out of the darkness. Then he saw the jeep, a blue light swinging round on its roof, careering toward him with four helmeted police inside. He flung himself flat, the mud squelching through his fingers, and listened to it howl past. Then he was up again and running.

The two taxis had all their windows up, the drivers asleep under rugs on the front seats. He climbed into the first and shook the driver awake, already pulling out the sodden dollar bills from his shirt pocket. The man stared suspiciously. 'Parataxín!' Ben shouted. 'Take me to Parataxín!'

The driver began to speak, but his voice was drowned by the drumming of rain. Ben counted out thirty dollars and shouted: 'Parataxín!'

Get on with it! he thought: *Start her up! That jeep's going to be back any second now.* The driver was fingering the notes, his eyes beginning to think. 'Fifty dollars,' he said.

Ben counted out another twenty. '*Vámonos*,' he cried, 'Parataxín!'

'Parataxín is very far,' the man said in Spanish. 'It is five hours.'

'O.K., five hours,' Ben said, and the driver switched on the ignition. The flywheel whirred feebly, failing to catch. Ben clutched his knees, listening for the police siren. The driver tried again and the engine gave a groan, and came to life. There was a fierce splashing as the car began to skid sideways. The driver scowled at him: 'There is much water.'

'Quickly!' said Ben. 'Get it out of here!'

The man put it into second and the car jerked forward a little, sliding round in a half-circle. At that moment Ben heard the police siren. It was still some way off. He tried to keep calm, telling the driver, 'When you get to Parataxín I give you twenty dollars more!'

The driver nodded without expression and began to turn the car round. The siren was approaching rapidly. Ben looked back, watching for the revolving blue light to come up through the rear window. The taxi swung over and turned down a side street, edging along between walls without doors or windows. Behind them Ben heard the siren scream past and saw the glow of the jeep's headlights sway for a moment over the walls of the church, then vanish. The driver gave him a dark stare: '*Policía!*'

Ben swallowed and grinned: 'Somebody in trouble, eh?'

'*Claro*,' said the driver. They began bouncing along a rutted track, away from the center of town. Ben could see very little through the windows where the wipers were plowing aside a thickening layer of black smut that splashed down with the rain.

'How much gas do we have?'

'We buy gas here,' the driver murmured, waving ahead.

Ben tried to calculate how long it would take to trace him to the taxi, then the road up through the mountains to Parataxín. It might be a matter of hours — or minutes, if the other driver had seen them leave. He looked at the fuel gauge. The needle was below the empty mark. He said angrily: 'There's no gas!'

'It is broken,' the driver said, as they turned into a steep bend. Ben was quiet for a moment. It was nearly two o'clock and he was beginning to feel cold; the caked black mud on his hands was burning his raw knuckles.

The car crawled upward for several minutes, then suddenly pulled over and stopped. The driver opened the door and shouted something. Ben had his door open in the same second, leaping out into the rain.

He was tensed, ready to run or fight; instead, he took a deep breath and climbed back in. They were in a clearing between palm trees with a gasoline pump and a hut. A light went on inside the hut and an old woman appeared wearing a chimney-pot hat. He watched her, his teeth chattering, as she hobbled over to the pump, unlocked the hose, carried it to the back of the taxi, returned to the pump and began working the wooden handle back and forth as though she were drawing water. Very slowly a glass jar at the top of the pump filled with gasoline.

When it was full she stopped and waited for it to run down through the hose. Then she began all over again. She seemed to take even longer this time. Ben got out, took the handle from her, muttering '*Dispénseme!*' and began pumping with frenzy, every few seconds glancing down toward the town. There were no lights coming up the road.

When the fifth jar had been drained into the taxi he pulled the hose out, stuffed a ten-dollar bill into the woman's hand and jumped back in. They started up the road again, the engine creaking to less than fifteen miles an hour. 'Can't you go faster?' he cried.

The driver shrugged: 'It is the mountains. Very high, very slow.'

Ben looked out of the rear window; but there was only a dull wet blackness behind, and he shivered. He remembered a recurrent dream he had had since childhood — half-dream, half-nightmare — that took the form of a chase. The details varied, but the formula was always the same: he was being hunted by some superior and dangerous enemy over a great expanse of country; sometimes it was day, sometimes night; and he always had a lead on his pursuers, but they were catching up on him, and always, just before the end, he could see them coming up behind him, far below, on a mountain road or across a plain. Then he woke. And the odd thing was that he was somehow disappointed — he felt he had been cheated, as though the chase were a special pleasure in its own right.

He now realized, with a chill of excitement, that the dream was true — that as he looked back out of the taxi a tiny part of his mind was wanting to see the headlights of the police jeep, and felt a perverse disappointment when all he saw was the darkness slashed with rain.

He had no intention of being caught. What he wanted was the challenge of being hunted — and of being able to outrun the hunter. But if the hunter wasn't there, he just became a tired, wet man without luggage, spending a lot of money taking a taxi across the mountains in the middle of the night.

They drove in silence. Outside, the layer of smut brought down by the rain was growing thicker. After a while he pulled off his soaking shirt and borrowed the driver's blanket, wrapping it round his shoulders and hunching himself against the door.

They were climbing hard. It was going to be a long night.

CHAPTER TWO: MAN ON THE RUN

He awoke feeling cold and cramped. It took him a few seconds to realize where he was. It had stopped raining and a dirty light was creeping up over the mountains where clouds hung in dips of jungle.

They were still climbing, round a narrow road washed with black mud, and he saw that the hood and the edges of the windshield were still covered with that curious powdery dirt that seemed to lie everywhere like some blight.

It was almost six o'clock. They had been going for more than four hours. The driver sat impassively smoking a foul-smelling cheroot shaped like a dog's turd. 'Where are we?' said Ben.

'We come near Xatopetl.'

'Where's that?'

'Pueblo in the mountains. We are very high.'

Ben nodded. 'What's this dirt everywhere?' He pointed at the windshield.

'It is the Marapi,' the driver said. 'She is exploding thirty kilometers away.' He waved ahead toward the mountains disappearing into dark cloud.

'Marapi?' said Ben.

'Big volcano. She has been exploding now since five days. Everywhere it is black.'

Ben wondered what they were doing back in Guadaigil: they'd have had time by now to find that one of the taxis had left town. *Another five hours to Parataxín*, he thought: *a jeep could do it in a good deal less.*

Once in Parataxín he would take the first plane out of the country. He'd have to risk being picked up at the airport. But perhaps in Parataxín they didn't care much about what happened in a little port like Guadaigil. If they did decide to follow him up the road, though, he knew he didn't have a chance. He wondered how many other roads there were out of Guadaigil. Would they search them all?

They were driving into a steep pass full of decayed crucifixes sprouting from the rocks on either side. The car was still doing less than fifteen miles an hour.

'How much further to Parataxín?' he asked.

'Five hours.'

'But you said it was five hours from Guadaigil!'

The driver tapped a wedge of ash from his cheroot on to his trousers. 'The road is very bad,' he explained simply.

Ben cursed. Five hours was as good as *mañana*. He couldn't even remember exactly where Parataxín was on the map; and his own map was back in the hotel with everything else.

The car squelched on up the road, out of the pass into a sloping valley with the cloud closing round them, hanging down in a dark canopy from the sides of the mountains. A few miles on they came into a village — a single street of mud-and-wattle huts with corrugated-iron roofs, and a two-story wooden building with a hand-painted sign over the porch saying HOTEL BAR TEJA.

The only signs of life were a number of athletic black pigs that scampered away through the mud as the car drove past. Ben could now distinguish the fine particles of ash drifting down out of the cloud. Fat tropical fruit hung from the trees behind the huts, and he caught the dank smell of jungle, as though the mountains were sweating.

Just beyond the village they ran into a couple of Indians in the middle of the road, waving at them. The driver stopped, and they began talking to him in a language Ben did not understand, pointing up the road. The driver nodded gravely.

'What are they saying?' asked Ben.

'They say the rains have destroyed the road. The car will not go through.'

He felt a tightening in his stomach: 'What do we do?'

The driver put the car into reverse. 'We must return.' They began to roll down backward until they reached the Hotel Teja. A crowd of Indians had come out onto the porch. One was carrying a machete knife. They closed round the taxi, talking together in the same strange language and looked at Ben as they began to raise their voices, angry and excited. He turned to the driver: 'What do they say?'

'We must return to Guadaigil. You are not welcome here.'

Ben looked at the faces outside the window: flat, closed faces, their eyes sullen and button-black, switched off from all human contact. He looked back at the driver: 'What's happened?'

'They say you are not to come to Xatopetl. You are an American.'

'I'm not an American!' he cried.

The faces outside the car had not moved. The driver added: 'They tell me to take you back to Guadaigil.'

Ben thought, with desperate simplicity: *I must get out and reason with them. They're ignorant people — they distrust strangers. It's a question of reassuring them.* He opened the door and said boldly: 'You speak Spanish?'

The man with the machete growled the single word: '*Gringo!*'

Oh hell! thought Ben, and said: 'I am an English tourist — I am going to Parataxín.'

The Indian shook his head ominously.

'What is the matter?' said Ben. As he spoke a stout man with glistening black hair parted in the middle came out of the door, pushed his way through to the car and spoke to him in Spanish, jabbing his thumb back at the hotel: 'You are a friend of the American?'

'What American?'

'He has been here in the hotel for three days.' He tapped his forehead: 'He is a madman. You are not his friend?'

'No. I know no Americans here.'

The man paused as though taking a grave decision. Finally he said: 'You must go back to Guadaigil.'

'I cannot go back to Guadaigil,' said Ben. He turned to the driver. 'I have paid you to take me to Parataxín.'

The man shrugged: 'It is not possible.'

'I will pay you fifty dollars more,' Ben said. 'I must be in Parataxín tonight.'

The driver shook his head and repeated: 'It is not possible. The rains and the Marapi have destroyed the road.'

'How do you know?'

'These men here tell me.'

Ben looked at the Indians, standing there in their wide black hats, saying nothing. He told the driver: 'If you will not take me to Parataxín, you must pay me back twenty dollars!'

The man took out the wad of dollars and paid him. Ben was suddenly disconcerted: he felt the Indian eyes watching every movement. 'Are you going back to Guadaigil now?' he asked.

The driver nodded and moved away toward the taxi. Ben thought: *It'll take him less time to get back down — two and a half hours at the most, and another two for the jeep to come up after me.* He had no clear plan, except to delay that moment as long as possible.

'I invite you to a drink,' he said, nodding at both the driver and the stout man.

They all went into a dark wooden room with benches round the walls and an iron stove that leaked smoke. Two women sat on a rug in the corner, picking at a bowl of black fruit. Ben sat down on a bench near the door while the stout man brought a bottle of tequila and three metal mugs. They swallowed their drinks together, and there was a heavy pause. The other Indians were crowded against the wall, muttering. It was the stout man who spoke at last, addressing Ben: 'Señor, why do you wish to go to Parataxín?'

'I am a tourist. I arrived in Guadaigil last night.'

'But you have no baggage.'

'My baggage has been stolen.'

The stout man nodded grimly: 'That is what the American says. He says the people here steal his baggage. He makes great trouble for us. This morning he ran out of the hotel and killed a pig.'

'A pig?'

The man nodded: 'The people here have had enough. The American will be punished.'

'Where is this American?'

'He is here in the Hotel Teja.'

The Indians by the wall had stopped talking; the man with the machete was fingering it delicately.

'What are you going to do with him?' Ben asked, taking a deep drink.

'He will be punished,' said the stout man. 'He has killed a good pig, and in this pueblo the people are poor.'

'Have you called the police?'

The man stared into his tequila. 'Here we have one police guard, but he is sick with eating the coca plant.'

Ben finished his drink in a gulp and said, as casually as he could manage: 'How will you punish this American?'

But before the man could reply there came a series of crashes from above, followed by a muffled yell and the sound of breaking glass. The Indians cowered back with their eyes on the ceiling, while the stout man leaned forward with his mouth open, listening. The only sound now was the dripping from the roof.

The taxi driver stood up and made for the door. Ben motioned upward: 'The American? I'd like to talk to him. Which way is he?'

The man did not move. 'You go upstairs?' he cried incredulously: 'He will kill you!'

'I don't think he will,' said Ben. 'Show me the way.'

The man pointed to a door at the back of the room, leading into a muddy patio where a woman was bent over a cauldron stirring a heap of steaming rags. On Ben's left an open staircase led to a wooden gallery around the top of the patio, past a row of doors. The place smelt of charcoal and lavatories. As he started up the stairs there came another crash and a bellow like a wounded animal. He continued more cautiously.

A voice now called out in English: 'Oh, for the love of Moses, get out! Get out! Get out! Get away, away! Away! Away!' The words collapsed in a broken sob, and there was the sound of a door being kicked. It came from the end of the gallery facing the stairs.

As Ben walked toward it he had only one idea in his head: to find himself an ally — somebody to help him get out of Xatopetl before the police arrived.

There was silence when he reached the door. Below him a row of faces peered up at him from the entrance to the patio; the man with the machete was in front. Ben turned and rapped on the door. It was answered by a terrible yell, less than two feet away: 'Get out, you bleeding dago!'

'I'm not a bleeding dago,' said Ben. 'I'm a Welshman. Now open this door!'

Silence; then a bolt slammed. The door opened a couple of inches and a yellow eye glared at him for a moment out of a hooked face which lurched back and disappeared. Ben pushed the door open and walked in.

The man was crouched on a bed against the wall, panting. An empty bottle was rolling about near his feet, and there was broken glass all over the floor. He looked at Ben and grinned: 'I'm drunk.' He spoke in a clipped accent that was not American. 'You're not a dago, are you?' he added, still grinning. 'You're a policeman! Ha! A Welsh policeman!'

He was lean and black haired, with a faintly greenish complexion that was quite beardless, although he had apparently been here several days. He wore chukka boots, a dark corduroy suit and khaki shirt. The room had a musty smell. Ben took a step forward: 'Who are you?'

The man cackled: 'An African. I'm a bleeding African!'

'Be sensible. What are you doing here?'

'Doing here! I'm going off my bloody head, that's what I'm doing here! You don't believe me. I'm an African! A white African Jew — Samuel David Ryderbeit, of Salisbury, Rhodesia!' He began rocking back and forth with his head in his hands.

'What are you doing here?' Ben asked again, careful to keep his distance in case Ryderbeit should run amok.

'Came from Parataxín three days ago,' the man said, his voice beginning to slur. 'Had a car. Got blocked by the volcano. I was stripped down like a bloody whore and put me to bed with a bottle of tequila, and I woke up skint.' He peered miserably at Ben and belched. 'Skint!' he said again. Took every bleeding thing I had. Three cameras — five hundred dollars' worth. Wallet — case — the lot!' He suddenly lunged at the door, flinging it open and roaring out on to the gallery: 'Filthy bleeding dagos! Come on up and get me!' Ben just had time to see the row of faces flit back inside the door. Only the old woman stayed in the patio, stirring her pot of rags. Ryderbeit leaned against the balustrade and began to laugh. 'They're scared of me, soldier! Bloody terrified!'

Ben said: 'It's you who should be scared, Ryderbeit. Now listen. You're in trouble. They're ganging up on you down there. They say you killed one of their pigs.'

'Pigs!' The man put his hand to his belt and drew a sheath knife, holding up the dirty brown blade. 'Pig's blood!' he said, leering cunningly.

'Why did you kill it?'

'Didn't like the look of it.'

Ben nodded: 'Well, downstairs they don't like the look of you. They're going to kill you.'

Ryderbeit came inside and stood for a moment thinking; then he raised his head and yelled, 'Let 'em come up and kill me! Up and at me!'

'Shut up,' said Ben. 'You're not waiting for anybody. You're getting out of here with me — now!' He looked round the darkened room. In the back wall was a shuttered window with a wire mosquito mesh. He went over and opened the shutter about an inch; through the chink he could see a patch of mud leading under a wall. He turned. Ryderbeit was sitting on the bed again, mournfully inspecting his feet. 'Do you know any way out of this town — except the one down to Guadaigil?' Ben asked.

Ryderbeit gave him a bloodshot stare. 'No way out!' he croaked. 'Bloody volcano blocked everything. Get some tequila and let's have a drink!'

Ben pushed the shutters wide open. Almost directly below stood a big mud-splashed car, its wheels sunk up to the axles. A couple of faces peered at him from the corner of the wall. He swung round: 'What sort of car have you got, Ryderbeit?'

'I got nothing. Stolen.'

'What sort of car was it?'

'Hired job,' he moaned. 'Get something to drink, for Christ's sake!'

Ben tried to be patient: 'Was it a brown sedan?'

'That's right. Brown Chevvy. Costs me twenty-five pesos a day.'

Ben nodded: 'It's out there under the window. Where are the keys?'

Ryderbeit sat squinting at him, his face beginning to disintegrate almost visibly. 'What? What yer say?'

'Keys!' cried Ben: 'Come on, the keys for the car down there.'

'Keys?' Ryderbeit began to cackle: 'You said keys? Can't hear, soldier. It's like a bloody silent film in here — I can see you, but I can't hear you!'

Ben came closer, working hard to keep calm. 'Easy now. We don't have much time. Just look in your pockets and see if you've got the keys.'

Ryderbeit shook his head. 'Screw the keys! It's the cameras I want. Bastards took the lot!'

'When did it happen?'

Ryderbeit looked at his watch. It was a black Rolex Oyster Perpetual which told the date as well as the time. 'Left Parataxín three days ago,' he muttered.

'If they robbed you, why didn't they take your car and your watch?'

Ryderbeit's eyes glared red at the edges: 'You ask a lot of bloody questions, don't you? Who the hell are you? What are yer doing busting in here? Get out! Get away!' He stood up, his face split in a dreadful snarl. Ben took another step forward: 'Don't be a bloody idiot!'

'That's right — bloody idiot!' Ryderbeit yelled, and reached again for the sheath knife. Ben sprang at him, grabbed his wrist and hit him on the jaw. The man sagged down till he was kneeling. 'Who the hell are you?' he croaked again, and began to weep, fists in his eyes like a child.

'Come on, get up,' said Ben. He pulled him to his feet, taking the knife out of his hand. Ryderbeit turned his yellow eyes to him, no longer angry but feeble and imploring: 'Who the hell are you?'

'Don't worry about who I am. You worry about getting out of here. Just try to think straight. Where did you lose your wallet and cameras?'

'Didn't lose 'em! I was rolled.'

'All right — so you were rolled. Now empty your pockets.'

To his amazement Ryderbeit obeyed this time without a murmur. There was nothing in his pockets except a khaki handkerchief, an empty billfold and three fifty-centavo pieces. He flung the coins viciously across the room.

Ben went back to the window. There were now three Indians standing at the corner. He said: 'We're going to jump for it. With luck we may get the car started without the keys.'

Ryderbeit shambled across from the bed and hauled his long body up onto the sill. The moment the Indians saw him they vanished behind the wall, and he dropped into the mud just beside the Chevrolet. Ben had more trouble, squeezing his broad shoulders between the frame, lowering himself with both hands. As he fell he could hear voices very close. He ran to the driver's door. It was unlocked. He climbed in, while Ryderbeit loped round and got in the other side, muttering, 'So they didn't take the bloody car!'

'Where's the catch for the hood?' said Ben.

'Eh?'

'To open the thing!'

Ryderbeit leaned over and picked something up from under the mat at Ben's feet. It was a ring of keys.

'So you knew they were there all the time?' Ben cried.

'What?'

Ben put one of the keys in the ignition, and Ryderbeit shook his head: 'Sorry, soldier, I'm a bit confused.'

'Think nothing of it,' said Ben. It was a big comfortable car with automatic transmission. He turned on the ignition and the fuel gauge flicked up to just below half. As he pushed the starter he looked up through the ash-caked windshield and saw Indians gathering silently as though from nowhere, like crows on a telegraph wire. The engine roared to life first time, without any choke. He could feel the body of the car rocking and straining in the mud. The Indians were beginning to creep forward toward them. He leaned over and locked all four doors. His skin was crawling with sweat. He didn't know what the Indians planned, and he didn't much want to know. He stepped gently on the gas pedal again, and the car suddenly sprang away, wheels churning. Some of the Indians scattered in panic.

Ben turned out into the road in front of the hotel. Here the mud was less bad. The Indians were shouting and running; but there were others closing in on them just ahead.

'Run the bastards down!' Ryderbeit cried.

Ben swerved and accelerated. There were bamboo trees ahead, gray with volcanic ash. A last group of Indians tried to wave him down, then leaped out of his way and he was past them, driving up under the trees. Ryderbeit began to cackle: 'Lovely, soldier! I like what you just done!'

'Do you know where we are?'

'Up the spout.'

'You got a map?'

'Got nothing. Cleaned out.'

'Have you done this road before?'

He shook his head, then shouted miserably: 'No bloody way out!'

'How do you know? How far did you get?'

'Don't remember.'

Ben decided to leave him alone: there was nothing to be got out of him in his present state. He prayed the road would stay open.

They were driving up under huge trees, their branches gray and slimy like the arms of a petrified forest. The cloud was thickening with a stench of sulfur fumes that seeped through the closed windows, making their eyes smart. Ryderbeit sat hunched forward, wheezing noisily.

'You all right?' said Ben.

'I'm sick. Been on the bottle for three days.'

Ben nodded.

'Don't recall exactly where I was. I got to the hotel and grabbed a few bottles of tequila and got happy!'

'What were you doing back there?'

'Came down from Parataxín to do a photo story on the rainforest for an American magazine. Then the volcano started throwing up.' He began choking with an asthmatic cough. 'What the hell are *you* doing here? — you damned Welshman!'

'I'm going to Parataxín.'

'Why?'

'Running away from the Guadaigil police.'

'Oh, yes! What d'yer do? Something funny?'

'I hit a policeman.'

Ryderbeit cackled with pleasure: 'Oh that's nice, soldier! That's really gorgeous. I've got a lovely traveling companion. No wonder you were in such a hurry to get a ride in my car!'

Ben said nothing. He hoped desperately that Ryderbeit would go to sleep.

For a few minutes they drove on in silence. The road was twisting out over a wide valley that sliced down between the walls of rainforest. Then Ryderbeit started again: 'You're pretty fit, aren't you? Smart with your fists.'

Ben still said nothing. 'I'm sick on the tequila,' Ryderbeit went on, 'otherwise I'd have fixed you just now. Nobody thumps Sammy Ryderbeit and gets away with it.'

'When we get to Parataxín,' said Ben, 'I'll buy you a big glass of tequila. '

'Poisonous piss! What made you come out to this death hole, anyway? Woman trouble?'

'In a way,' said Ben quietly.

'Not worth it, soldier. I had troubles, too. First wife — walked out on me. Second wife, two children — walked out on me. All up the bloody spout.'

'I'm sorry,' Ben murmured.

'Don't be sorry! I'm not. The only thing that matters in this life is money. People say money doesn't buy happiness. Well those people are bloody liars. I haven't got any money. If I'd sent off my photos from Parataxín the New York bureau was going to pay fifteen hundred dollars. Now I haven't got anything. Now I just feel sick.'

'You're all right,' said Ben.

'You got any money, soldier?'

'A bit.' Ben thought it better not to elaborate.

'A bit's nothing. I know a scheme that could make a couple of jolly rogers like us a million dollars each.'

'That's right,' said Ben. 'Strike oil. Start a gold rush. Happens every day.'

'Bloody cynic,' Ryderbeit muttered without bitterness. 'You get woman trouble, come out here and hit a policeman, then go whimpering off into the mountains. You know what that makes you? It makes you a bum. A poor white bum.'

'All right, all right,' said Ben.

'What yer want out here?' Ryderbeit persisted. 'You want adventure?'

'I want to be left alone.'

'Ah, screw it! You want a woman, that's what you want.'

Ben held the steering wheel very tightly and spoke without looking at Ryderbeit: 'Why don't you try and go to sleep? You're putting me in a bad mood. That police officer in Guadaigil put me in a bad mood too.'

Ryderbeit eyed him narrowly, suddenly alert: 'You threatening me?'

'I'm warning you. You're boring me.'

'Hah! So what do I do? I'm trying to make pleasant conversation!'

'Don't,' said Ben. 'I got you out of trouble back in that village. I'm riding in your car and that's the only favor I'm asking.'

Ryderbeit frowned. 'I'm not ungrateful, believe me! I was going to do *you* a favor. Help you make a million dollars.'

Ben said nothing. Ryderbeit went on: 'You got woman trouble, I got woman trouble. We're just two idlers, you and me. I know a professor in Mexico City — a bright boy, economist. Once ran the government for three whole days before they kicked him out. Now lives in one room and does his own laundry. He told me that any man who can stick the sight of the same woman for more than six months has something radically wrong with him.'

'How old is this bright boy?'

'Seventy-two.'

'And how old are you?'

'I'm thirty-four and I have the mind of a young child.' He gave another cackle, then fell silent for a moment, while they drove around the shoulder of the mountain, with the sulfur fumes growing stronger, into a smutty yellow fog that clung like cobwebs to the trees and rocks.

'You mustn't misunderstand me, soldier,' he said suddenly. 'I wouldn't like that. A lot of people have misunderstood me. I had all the advantages, you know. My old father made a couple of fortunes in Africa before he was sixty and lost them both. But he gave me a good private education. Started me off at the very top, and from there I went to the very bottom!' He gave his joyless laugh: 'The perverse Jew! So I went down to South Africa to make good. But somehow I got a bit misunderstood down there. I'm a qualified mining engineer. Started work in a diamond mine near Jo'burg. Got a pilot's license. Did a lot of hunting too.' He looked eagerly at Ben for approval.

Ben nodded: 'Big game?'

'Anything. You name it! I can hit a man in the head with a rifle from half a mile.'

'That's very good. Ever done it?'

'Sure — up in the Congo. That was afterward, though. After I married my first bloody wife. I was twenty-three — she was nineteen. Sued me for divorce after five months. Grounds of exceptional cruelty.'

Ben was steering through the fog with the mud growing perilous. Ryderbeit went on:

'Well, for about five years after that I did a good deal o' wandering. Back to Rhodesia, up in Kenya. But I always finished up in South Africa. I like their technique. You a liberal?'

'Not to you,' said Ben.

Ryderbeit laughed: 'You're all right, soldier! Anyway, I got another job in Jo'burg three years ago and met an English girl. A real rich bitch, as it turned out. Daddy was a big diamond magnate. I was all right. She went for me — loved me to distraction! I have a peculiar appeal, you know — quite a swordsman when the chips are down. Big Daddy gave me a job in his corporation at £4,000 a year with a car and a house and a load o' servants. I was fine. Wife gave me two kids. Want me to go on? This drive's bloody boring.'

'Go on,' said Ben.

Ryderbeit groaned: 'God, I'd like a drink! I don't know quite how it happened. I like a drink or two, you see. She went for me one day — said a few things I didn't much like, about being a Jew and a no-good and that sort o' thing. So I took a pair o' scissors and snipped off one of her lovely tits.'

Ben turned and blinked at him. Ryderbeit leered: 'Nasty business, eh? Jo'burg police thought so, too. Pulled me in and gave me a good working over. I was let out on bail, and when I got back home I found the doors locked and the bird had flown, and taken both the kids with her. So I go round to Big Daddy's place to find her, and the bastard calls the cops and I'm back inside — in for the high jump. All because I want my legal bloody wife back!'

He rolled down the window and spat into the cloud. 'I got a year inside. Divorced again — again for exceptional cruelty. And Big Daddy gives me the push and cuts me off without a farthing. Even took back the Alfa Romeo. Nice people.'

Ben drove on feeling very tired.

'So what d'yer think?' said Ryderbeit.

'I don't think you're the marrying type,' said Ben.

Ryderbeit bent forward, laughing soundlessly: 'Oh you're good, soldier! I'm glad I found you. You make me happy!'

Ben glanced at him uneasily.

'Want me to go on?' said Ryderbeit. 'I've had an amusing life. After I came out I got a job with the Union Minière in Katanga, then when all the trouble started I became a fighter pilot for Tshombe's Air Force. Two hundred quid a week and no tax. That was a big laugh. I used to practice flying at tree level down the main streets of African towns. Then one day I made a mistake. I'd been having a few stingers with the other Mercenaries in E'ville and my judgment wasn't too good. I put the plane down on top of an African market — killed five bastards and walked out with a busted bone in my foot. So you see — unlucky in love, lucky in death. You never think you're

49

going to die, you never do. It's the careful ones who get it, and I don't care anymore. Do you care?'

'Not much,' said Ben. The road ahead had almost disappeared in fog and mud. He kept the car crawling at walking pace. 'So what happened then?'

'Well, then the U.N. threw me out — the pious bastards — so I reckoned Africa had had it for me. The whites are packing it in everywhere, except Southern Rhodesia which is too small — and in South Africa the name of Samuel D. Ryderbeit is by now something of a dirty word. So I tried South America. I make a living — from time to time. Any halfwit can aim a loaded camera.'

'What are you going to do now?'

'Make a million dollars. You and me, soldier. Honestly — I could help you. Just wait till we get to Parataxín.'

'Why don't you try to get some sleep,' said Ben. 'You're going to have to do some driving soon.' He was beginning to wonder just how, if they ever did reach Parataxín, he was going to get rid of Ryderbeit. He knew that if he stayed with him, sooner or later Ryderbeit would land him in trouble.

'Now this million dollars,' Ryderbeit was saying: 'It might be a million — it might be more. How do you feel about it?'

'Let's get something to eat,' said Ben.

They had crossed the hump of the mountains and come down out of the fog and sulfur fumes into a little village at the edge of a plateau where the rainforest had given way to swelling flowers — hibiscus and acacias and brilliant mimosa shrubs bursting from the brown earth. In the last three hours they had driven through small landslides of mud and ash which would certainly have stopped the under-powered taxi from Guadaigil. Ben wondered, however, if they would be enough to deter a police patrol.

He and Ryderbeit were sitting outside a little café with Coca-Cola signs and wooden chairs set out on the veranda. The only other client was a puffy-eyed *pistolero* who sat alone under a leather hat, watching them.

The rains had stopped and the sun burned out of a clear sky, drying the plaza in front of the café. Behind them the mountains were hidden under white towers of cumulus clouds that reached into the stratosphere, a barrier closing off everything beyond, both in space and time: the chase, the hotel, the ship, London, his job — even Laura. And as he gazed up at the clouds he began to wonder how he had ever got through.

They sat eating tortillas and maize and bowls of bean soup, washed down with sour black coffee. Ryderbeit's complexion had turned the color of porridge and his eyes were dull jellies staring unhappily across the plaza at the purple and white houses and the plateau beyond. Parataxín lay somewhere out there, about fifty miles away.

Ben glanced across the veranda at the *pistolero*. The man was still watching them. He wore knee boots and a holster with a belt of ammunition. 'Who is that guy?' he murmured.

Ryderbeit stared at the man, who stared back, licking his lips. 'Country cop,' he said idly. 'Harmless.'

'Do you think the Guadaigil police can get word down here?'

'Not unless they got radio in this place — which I doubt. There's no telephone here.' He grinned: 'You scared?'

'I'll be happier when we get to Parataxín.'

'You certainly will. You just let Sammy Ryderbeit look after you. You know, I like you, soldier! You're a bit of a desperado in your gloomy way. I like desperadoes. I think we could make something of you. Me and old Captain Leonard Stopes. The Captain's looking for somebody like you.'

'What the hell are you talking about?' said Ben. He felt very, very tired.

'I'm talking about how the old Captain might explain to us both how we can all make a million dollars.'

Ben nodded wearily: 'Marvelous. Who is the Captain?'

'Compatriot o' yours. A living corpse. Came out here after the war as some sort of attaché to the British Consulate in Parataxín. Got fired a few years ago for having his finger stuck in a few matters Her Majesty's Government didn't approve of.'

'Like what?'

Ryderbeit shook his head: 'Sh! That might be telling! As a matter of fact, I don't quite know. It appears old Britain was trying to get some mineral concession over here, and Stopes was involved and double-crossed his mother country.'

'What's this got to do with me?'

'Just this. About two months ago Stopes went off on an expedition across the Hiarra Mountains in the south into the swamp country. He asked me to go with him, but I had an assignment in Rio. He wouldn't tell me what it was all about until I finally agreed to join him — which shows how much we all trust each other in this beautiful place.

'Well, I couldn't go, so the Captain found someone else — a young Kraut called Hitzi Leiter. I never met him. I never will now, either. He's dead. I heard the whole story five days ago just before I came down on this jaunt. I happened to run into Stopes in a club. He was pretty stoned and gave me a wild tale. How he and Hitzi Leiter had gone over the mountains into the Xatu country — mostly jungle and swamp — and one night this poor bloody Kraut forgot to cover himself with insect repellent, and within ten minutes he had a few thousand mosquito bites all over him which drove him crazy, and he stuck a pistol in his mouth and blew his head off.

'So old Stopes had to make it back alone. But the expedition hadn't been a complete failure. He said he'd found something down in the swamp. Something that could make him a million dollars — perhaps more.'

'He still didn't tell you what it was?'

'No. He's a cagey old bird, even with half a bottle of booze inside him. Said he'd talk about it with me in more detail when I got back and had more time. You see, Stopes wants to return to that swamp, but next time it's got to be better organized. He wants more than just one person to go with him. Safety in numbers, he said. I thought I might mention your name. What d'yer say?'

'What can I say? It sounds to me like an alcoholic fantasy. Anyway, let's think about getting to Parataxín first. I still don't much like the look of that guy over there with the gun.'

CHAPTER THREE: CASA SPHINX

That evening Ben sat out under the deep sky in a café on the Plaza Mayor of Parataxín, watching the girls stroll past in their thin dresses, and waited for Ryderbeit.

It was nearly half-past nine. Ryderbeit had promised to be back at eight, and Ben had come to rely on him. Since arriving in the capital that afternoon the Rhodesian had become more clear-headed, and had gravely assured Ben that he had only to check into any hotel in the city to have the police round in five minutes. Guadaigil would certainly inform the capital of the Englishman who had savaged one of their colleagues. He had then tried to reassure Ben with promises that he could find him somewhere safe to stay — murmuring more about Captain Stopes and his million dollars. Ben was left confused and exhausted; but Ryderbeit had said he would be back, and Ben had decided to wait.

He felt clean and more rested now; he had had a long soap-down in the Municipal Baths, been shaved, bought himself a cotton shirt and a hideous seersucker suit — for a total of just under fifty dollars — and was now enjoying his fifth *café con leche*.

Earlier in the evening a man had come round the tables with a peculiar box-like machine with metal handles. Occasionally someone would leap out and pay him fifty centavos to hold on to the handles for a few seconds before letting go again. Ben had tried it and received a mildly invigorating electric shock, presumably meant to shake off the torpors of the day's heat. The incident seemed to sum up his whole predicament: the sharp pain of adventure was better than his private, gnawing misery.

A Negro with no legs was pushing himself up and down the pavement on a trolley, trying to sell lottery tickets. Across the square, near the gloomy mass of the cathedral, a neon sign flashed out an advertisement for Panagra. It reminded him that he was left with just over sixty dollars and a few pesos in cash. His traveler's checks might now prove awkward to change. He had nowhere to stay; and Ryderbeit had not returned.

There was always the British Consul, of course. If it had been a few years ago it might have been Captain Leonard Stopes he could have gone to see. The idea seemed to be some sort of omen — of what he was not sure.

The Panagra sign went on winking seductively at him in a curious rhythm with the cries of the crippled lottery vendor. He wondered how much it would cost to fly to Caracas or Rio; but it would take at least a day to get visas, and by then it might be too late.

At a quarter to ten Ryderbeit had still not returned. Ben paid for the coffees and began to wander across the Plaza, past a procession of pigtailed Indians carrying sandwich boards for a nightclub. Round the sides of the Plaza the police patrolled in pairs, some with Sten guns at the hip. There were two of them near the Panagra building. Ben recognized the familiar white piping on their shoulders, as he hurried through the plate-glass doors into the air-conditioned hall. At the end stood another policeman filing his fingernails.

Ben ran his eye over the female receptionists sitting behind their white telephones, and chose the prettiest — a light-haired, fair-skinned girl with a wide face and straight nose. He went up and asked in his groping Spanish: 'I desire to leave Parataxín as soon as possible.'

She smiled: 'Shall I speak English?'

For a moment he stood and gaped at her. 'You're English too?' he said stupidly, with delight.

'Yes.'

'Thank God!'

She smiled again, politely. 'Where do you want to go?'

'Anywhere I can. At once.'

'I see.' She tilted her nose a little, and he felt she was summing him up. He glanced past her, at another framed photograph of Dr. Isodor Romolo, jowls and black eyes over white tie and carnation. There was nothing comforting about that face; it seemed to warn him: *You hit one of my men, Mister Morris — you better get out of my country double-quick!*

The girl said: 'There's a TWA flight to Caracas at eleven tonight. The bus leaves the terminal in Calle Iqal in about ten minutes. If you've got your luggage you can just make it.'

'I haven't got any luggage,' he said, 'and I haven't got a Venezuelan visa.'

'Oh.' Her face had a flat, deadpan expression. 'You have to go tonight?'

'Yes.'

She bowed her head to consult a flight schedule and he saw there was bronze in her pale hair. She looked up and said, 'Sorry, there's nothing else tonight. Tomorrow we've got a Panagra flight to Kingston, Jamaica, then on to London.'

'What's the fare?'

'Just a moment.' She took a ledger from under the desk. 'You're paying in traveler's checks? It's forty-seven pounds single to Kingston, then a hundred and thirty pounds, eight shillings to London.'

'I've just come from London.'

'I see.' She held him for a moment with her wide flat stare. 'You can still go to Jamaica,' she added.

'What time does it leave?'

'Three o'clock in the afternoon. I'll have to check there's a seat. Is it just for one?'

He nodded, not concentrating properly. Nice English girl who had renounced gum boots and gymkhanas to travel the world and enjoy the bright lights. But why choose a remote landlocked city like Parataxín? He had a sudden curiosity to take her outside, buy her a drink and hear her whole story. She was saying: 'Do you want to book now, sir?'

'When do you close?'

'Ten.' The clock on the wall said three minutes to. The hall was beginning to empty. 'The terminal in Calle Iqal's open till three,' she added.

'All right. Book it.'

She picked up a telephone. 'You'll have to pay now, I'm afraid. It's one of the regulations.'

He began to reach for his traveler's checks and knew he was being watched. He slid his eyes round, up the hall to where the policeman still stood — no longer filing his nails, but staring straight at him. Ben felt it was not a good time to be taking out English traveler's checks. He turned quickly to the girl: 'Listen, I'll come in and book tomorrow,' — adding on an impulse: 'Why not come for a drink when you close?'

'Yes — why not?' Her voice expressed no surprise, only a vaguely unsettling complacency. The telephone purred by her arm: 'Can you hang on a minute?'

He thought again: *What the hell is she doing in a place like this?* Perhaps she was wondering the same about him? She must have a lover here. She was talking fluent Spanish into the telephone. Without even turning to look, Ben knew that the policeman was coming down the hall toward him. He could hear his boots creaking across the marble. They were almost the only people left in the hall now.

The girl put down the receiver. 'All right. I'll just go and tidy up.'

The policeman stopped beside him and touched his arm. '*Por favor, Señor!*' He was a hard-eyed man with a trim, close-shaven face and was saying something that Ben scarcely heard. The girl answered with a smile, and the man saluted and moved off toward the door. 'They're closing the place up,' she said. 'Can you wait for me outside?' She paused: 'Are you feeling all right?'

'Fine,' he said. 'I need a drink. I'll meet you outside.'

I don't look English, he thought, as he waited for her on the pavement. *At least, not the Latin-American idea of an Englishman. Seersucker suit, bush-shirt, broken nose. But I've still got to get out of here. A pity, though. She was a good-looking girl; she'd moved well when she stood up: long legs and high hips and an air of cool authority A cool girl altogether*, he thought: *perhaps even cold. The sort of girl who can do without makeup and mend a fuse.*

'Well, where shall we go?' she said, standing beside him.

'There's a café across the square. I was supposed to meet somebody there earlier.'

'All right,' she said, 'let's go!'

They began to walk under the arcades round the Plaza. 'What brought you to Parataxín?' he asked.

'Well, I was offered this job with Panagra while I was up in Acapulco,' she said. They reached the first of the police patrols on the pavement, and Ben tried to hurry her past, as she continued in her clear English: 'I'd got through most of my money and couldn't find a decent job in Mexico, so I accepted.'

They were past the police now; Ben found he was breathing fast.

'How long are you staying here?'

She shrugged: 'Until I get fed up, I suppose, then I'll go somewhere else — up to the States probably.'

They reached the café he had been in earlier and he saw that Ryderbeit had still not arrived. He was not sure whether he was pleased or not. The girl was probably a more dependable ally — and might even have a spurious influence with someone in authority. He chose a table under the colonnades where the legless Negro was still propelling himself up and down on his trolley. Nobody seemed to be buying his tickets.

'I'll have a Cuba Libre,' she said, even before he had had time to ask her. He ordered a tequila for himself and there was an awkward pause. He looked round to see if anyone had noticed them. The café was full of the same men in limp white suits sitting watching the girls go by. There were no police here.

She suddenly leaned across the table and said: 'Is something the matter?'

He looked quickly at her. 'No! Why?'

She smiled. 'When that policeman spoke to you back there I thought you were going to pass out. You're not in any sort of trouble, are you?'

He thought, *there's no reason why she should give me away.* 'Yes, as matter of fact I am,' he said, watching the waiter put down the drinks; the tequila was served here in the traditional Mexican style, with salt and lemon. 'I had a spot of trouble down in Guadaigil.' He pinched some salt onto the back of his hand, squeezed lemon on it and licked it down, swallowing the tequila after it. 'I hit a police officer. He had cheated me of some money and I was a bit drunk and lost my temper.'

'Oh Lord!' She smothered a giggle. 'Did you hurt him?'

'I knocked him down. I don't know whether I hurt him. I got away, though.'

'Yes, but not far. I happen to know that about the only efficient people in this country are the police — and they're very efficient! Do they know you're English?'

'I'm afraid so. The man I hit had checked my passport at immigration.'

She nodded: 'The only thing you can do is get on that plane tomorrow! Although I can't promise there'll be a seat. It's very crowded to Jamaica.'

'There'll have to be a seat.' The drink had begun to relax him; he called for another. 'Now, I've told you everything about myself. What about you?'

'You haven't told me anything. Except that you got drunk and biffed a copper.'

'What else do you want to know?'

'Your name, for instance?'

'Ben Morris. And yours?'

'Mel — short for Melanie. MacDougall is my married name,' she said smiling. 'We've parted company. Are you married?'

'My wife was killed in a car smash four months ago.'

She looked dutifully solemn. 'How awful. And it's hard luck getting yourself in such a jam just now.'

'To hell with that! It's a distraction.'

She shook her head: 'You won't think that if they catch you. You know what they say that charming slob Doctor Romolo does to people he doesn't like? He doesn't just lock them up or shoot them — he puts them in a plane and flies them out over the Xatu country behind the mountains and drops them into the swamps. The place is full of Indians — and Xatu Indians don't like white people. If they get you, they do nasty things before they kill you.'

Ben was thinking: *Ryderbeit in his ramblings during the day had mentioned the Xatu swamps: where Captain Stopes had gone off in search of a million dollars with a German who shot himself.* Ben said: 'You supposed the Doctor would think of dropping me over this swamp?'

She grinned: 'He might.'

'With a parachute?'

'Oh, no. The plane flies very low, so you usually just break a leg and can't get away. Then either the snakes get you, or the Indians.'

He put back his second tequila. 'It sounds a lovely country, this! What made you come here?'

'Oh, to get out of London — just get away, anywhere. I admit this is a pretty horrible country — in fact, it must be one of the worst-governed countries in the world. Perhaps that's why I like it.' She smiled to herself, sucking her rum-and-Coke through a straw. 'I'm not a very law-abiding person, I'm afraid. And of course the climate's marvelous here on the plateau. Anything's marvelous after a whole winter spent cooped up in a basement flat with two other girls in Warwick Gardens!'

'What happened in London?'

'You want to hear?'

'I'm fascinated.' He was not being sarcastic.

'Well, there's not much. My mother's dead and my father has a farm near Canterbury. I lived there till I went to London to learn ballet. Actually, I was quite good — good enough to get into Sadler's Wells School for a year, till I gave it up because they said I was too tall. Then I got the usual secretarial jobs, and finished up as secretary to the secretary of a television program manager. That was good fun — lots of rushing about and parties and meeting TV personalities and that sort of stuff. Then I got married — to a scriptwriter. It was pretty sudden, actually. We'd been going around for about a year, and one day he took me out to buy a hat and put me in a taxi to Kensington Registry Office, and that was that.' She paused. 'Can I have another drink?'

He signalled the waiter. 'So it didn't work out?'

'No.'

They were interrupted by a high-pitched cackle from behind Ben's chair. Ryderbeit was standing there, dressed in a pitch-black suit that looked as though it had been cut out of carbon paper. His hair was oiled and combed, and his eyes were shining clear yellow. 'I said half past eight, soldier!' he cried, jabbing a rolled newspaper at Ben as though it were a weapon.

'You did,' said Ben, 'and I waited till a quarter to ten.' He introduced Mel. Ryderbeit inclined his hooked face toward her and smiled beautifully, pulling up a chair between her and Ben. 'Some people have all the luck!' he said, not moving his eyes from her: 'I leave Morris for a few hours in a strange city, and what does he do but turn up with a piece of Junoesque statuary,' — he thrust his head forward, peering at her more closely — 'early eighteenth century, I should say. But I don't blame you, soldier. You'd better enjoy yourself. Read this!' He thrust the newspaper into Ben's lap.

The paragraph was in a boxed panel on the front page: *'Englishman assaults Government official in Guadaigil.'* The report was vague: a sailor, B. Mors, off a British ship in Guadaigil, had become drunk and attacked a Government official of honor, causing him to be gravely injured. The criminal had fled into the Santos Mountains. The police and the population were determined that the foreigner should be apprehended and suffer the rigors of justice. The police were alert and the population vigilant.

Ryderbeit tapped him on the arm: 'Fame, my boy, fame!'

Ben put down the paper. 'They might have got my name right! I suppose that officer copied it down wrong. Anyway, just as well I'm leaving tomorrow!'

'You're not, you know,' said Ryderbeit.

'What do you mean?'

Ryderbeit bent forward with a chuckle: 'I mean simply that you're not leaving tomorrow — nor the day after, nor the day after that.'

'And who's going to stop me?'

Ryderbeit gave a slow grin: 'All right, so you want to leave tomorrow on a plane?'

'If there's a seat.'

'And how far do you think you'll get? You've got your passport in the name of Ben Morris, or B. Mors — it doesn't make much difference. You might get past the departure desk. But then there'd be passport control — immigration officers. That's where you tripped up before, wasn't it?'

Ben felt a prickle at the back of his neck. He looked at Mel but her expression told him nothing: she reminded him of one of those Holbein portraits of girls staring out from behind varnish.

He looked at Ryderbeit: 'So what do I do? Go to the British Consul? Give myself up?'

'Neither. I just spoke to Captain Stopes on the 'phone. He's very sympathetic to your problem. Might even talk over a little business with you. Interested?'

'I don't seem to have much choice, do I?'

'You don't!'

Mel stood up suddenly. 'Well, if you've got business to talk over, I'll be off.'

Ryderbeit flashed her his crooked smile: 'Come along too! Business with pleasure! Besides, the business is all with Morris here.'

They all stood up, Ryderbeit leaping around to pull Mel's chair back, and Ben detected more in his eyes than just gallantry. Like the photograph of Dr. Romolo, there was very little about Ryderbeit's face that was comforting.

He began looking for a taxi. Ben asked: 'What happened to the car?'

'Turned it in. Needed the money back on the deposit.'

Mel said: 'It's all right, I've got a car. Over the other side of the square.'

Ryderbeit stared at her: 'A car! A lovely English rose in Parataxín with a car? That can't be right.'

'It's rather beat-up, I'm afraid. I got it very second-hand in Mexico. But it moves.' She began to lead the way back across the Plaza.

Ryderbeit shook his head, his greenish pallor intensified by the yellow glare in his eyes: 'Holy Moses!' he muttered, watching her walk ahead: 'All woman!' He lowered his voice into the sound of traffic: 'Who is she, soldier? Some joyrider?'

Ben explained briefly, and Ryderbeit seemed impressed; he wanted to know more, but Ben had other things to think about. He could still try the Consulate, but there wouldn't be much they could do if he'd assaulted a policeman; and after the newspaper story, the airport was probably the most dangerous place of all. That left him with Ryderbeit and the improbable Captain Stopes. Still, he might as well see what the evening had to offer; he had nothing to lose.

Mel had stopped in a side street beside a big dusty Ford convertible with the top down. A few loafers on the pavement leered and hooted as the three of them climbed in, Ryderbeit in the middle. 'O.K.,' she said. 'Where to?'

'Down to San José, then on the road to Tajas,' said Ryderbeit. 'I'll tell you where to turn off.'

She eased the car into the traffic around the Plaza. 'Where exactly are we going?'

'A little surprise, my darling!'

She shrugged, with a glance across at Ben: 'Is he always like this?'

Ryderbeit gave his wild cackle. 'Like the Almighty, Samuel David Ryderbeit moves in mysterious ways!' he cried, and started to put his arm round her shoulder, but she flinched slightly, and he withdrew it, grinning to himself, as the lights swept past, gathering speed. She drove fast and cleverly, with a blaring of the triple horn, along a palm-lined avenue that led suddenly into open country, up on to a six-laned highway curving out over the dominoes of lights below, through orange groves scattered with villas where — according to Ryderbeit — the playboys of Parataxín could wake up in the morning and roll out of bed into swimming pools under their balcony windows.

They rode without speaking, the chill night air of the plateau howling past them in the slipstream. Ahead a pair of winking red and green lights drifted down across the sky. A moment later a sign swooped into the headlights: AEROPUERTO DE TAJAS — 2 KMS. Ben shouted at Ryderbeit: 'We're not going to the airport, are we?'

'All right, relax!'

Mel cried: 'Where *are* we going? I can't get on a plane just like that!'

Ryderbeit bared his teeth. 'Turn right here!' he yelled, as the car reached a dirt track that left the road, bumping along between lanes of orange trees. 'We're not going on any plane,' he said gently, now that the slipstream had dropped. 'From now on you just leave it to me. We're going to a very cozy place where we can all enjoy ourselves.'

'I've never been down here before,' said Mel.

'I didn't think you had,' said Ryderbeit.

About half a mile on they came to a clearing in front of a green-tiled villa with Moorish arches and a row of cars on the gravel courtyard. As Mel drew up, a Negro stepped out of the shadows and saluted, giving her a sidelong look as he held open the door on her side. A slant-eyed Indian in a tuxedo had appeared from the villa, bowing them under the arches, through a nail-studded door into a foyer where a woman sat behind a grille next to a curtain. The Indian stood in front of the curtain with his feet apart, his loose white jacket reminding Ben of a judo costume.

Ryderbeit took Ben by the arm: 'Listen, I'm a little short of funds. The old Captain's inside and the evening's on him — but there's a house rule here that customers pay an entrance fee.'

'How much is it?'

'Fifty dollars.'

'*What!* For an entrance fee? Ah, come off it! — I haven't got that money to throw around.'

'You'll get it back. Fifty dollars for three people — it's cheap at the price.'

'What is?'

'You'll see. Don't let me down, soldier. I'm your only chance.'

Ben realized he was in a poor position to argue. Reluctantly he counted out five ten-dollar bills, leaving him only one left of his original hundred and seventy.

Ryderbeit said, 'You'll get it all back — a thousand times over!' — as he pushed the notes through the grille at the woman, who handed him three black plaques inscribed in gilt, *Casa Sphinx*.

The Indian skipped aside, holding back the curtains, and Ryderbeit led the way into a long dim room decorated in a chaos of Moorish, Polynesian and Victorian styles. An all-steel band was warming up on a dais in the far corner. A man in a dinner jacket was dancing with a young mulatto girl, and there was a crowd of girls along the bar down one side of the room where another Indian in a tuxedo was serving a couple of men in uniform who looked like high-ranking army officers.

Along the other wall, behind pillars of plaster arabesques, were alcoves with red velvet couches and red lanterns. In one of them, sitting alone over a knee-high table, a man was drinking from a hollow coconut, his face turned down, eyes concealed by green-tinted glasses that curved round his head like ski goggles. He gave no indication of having seen them.

Ryderbeit leaned out and cried: 'All right. I got 'im!' He turned: 'I want you to meet Captain Leonard Stopes.' He introduced them both formally and the man rose, bobbing his head. They sat down.

He was a small man with yellowish-gray hair meticulously parted. The upper half of his face was lined and sunken, and the lower half had that damp, rubbery look of a man who needs five pink gins before lunch. With Captain Stopes it was probably cheap tequila. His gray-flannel suit needed pressing; he wore a boiled shirt and dark tie with a silver stripe.

When he spoke his voice had a scaly intonation that belonged to no definable class or region: it was the accent of the expatriate who rarely has the opportunity of speaking his own language.

'I'm glad you could come. It's a bit quiet here at the moment. Should get a bit more lively later on.' He looked into his coconut. Another Indian had slid up and Ryderbeit snapped the order. '*Cuatro wahines!*' The man bowed and vanished.

'A *wahine*,' Ryderbeit explained, 'is the house speciality — ancient Polynesian cup made out of vodka and Bacardi. The principle of the Casa Sphinx is very decent. Right, Captain?'

Stopes did not seem to be listening; he was clasping his coconut with hands of a papery whiteness on which the veins stood out like worms. Ryderbeit winked: 'The Captain's a bit ashamed of the Casa Sphinx. But the principle is still to be admired. You pay fifteen dollars a head, plus tip, and get one drink and any girl at that bar you want. Then for a hundred dollars you can have as many drinks, and theoretically as many girls as you want. Which is very subtle of the management, because after a few of these *wahines* you can't even manage one girl.'

Mel was looking at the bar: 'They're very pretty, I must say.'

'All of 'em not a day over fifteen,' said Ryderbeit, 'and untouched by human hand!'

The Indian had returned with four coconuts stuffed with slices of fruit and a frothy liquid that tasted like lemonade. As Ben lifted his drink he saw a man coming through the door. His appearance was startling. He was dressed in a mustard-colored suit, and although quite young his hair was chalk white, growing in a crew cut from a head as round as a football that looked too big for his body.

Stopes was sitting with his back to the door and did not see him; but the man could see Stopes, and as soon as he did he stopped and ducked into one of the adjoining alcoves. His movement was so sudden that Ben was about to mention it, when he realized that Stopes was speaking to him: 'I heard you had a spot of trouble after you got here?'

'A hell of a bit of trouble. Ryderbeit told you?'

'Yes, Sammy has told me a lot about you. I'm quite impressed.'

'Oh?'

'Yes — with the way you gave the police the slip, as well as helping Sammy out of his own little trouble. You haven't, of course, thought of going to the Consulate about your difficulties?'

Ben shrugged: 'Yes, I've thought of it.'

'Well don't. The Consul could do nothing for you if the police preferred charges against you — which they certainly will if they catch you. On the other hand, I think perhaps I can help you. That is, if you're prepared to be helped.'

Ben said: 'I'm not fussy about help, Captain. I've just paid fifty dollars for the three of us, apparently just to have the privilege of meeting you.'

Stopes nodded: 'Perhaps we can have a little chat somewhere? There are private rooms through the back.' He was already standing up. 'You can bring your drink.'

Ben looked at Ryderbeit, then at Mel. 'I'll see you both later then?'

She smiled, her eyes shining like mirrors: 'Enjoy yourself!' Ryderbeit just sat and gave his crooked grin and a thumb's-up sign, as Ben followed Stopes out of the alcove toward a door at the back of the room behind the bar, through which he had already noticed a discreet movement of girls passing in and out with their clients. As he reached it he glanced back down the room. The young man in the mustard-colored suit was watching them, his round white head lurking in the alcove. Stopes pushed the door open and led Ben into a corridor lighted with blue bulbs. The door had a padded frame that closed with a hiss, shutting out all sound the other side.

There were doors down both sides, all without handles. A fat woman in a shawl came padding toward them with a ring of keys. She growled something and unlocked one of the doors, leading them into what looked at first like a dim cave. There were no windows and the only light came from another blue bulb in the ceiling. It was very small and smelt of sweat and cigars. There were two chairs and a table, and a couch piled with cushions along the back wall. The woman pulled from under her shawl a packet of photographs which she began to show Ben, before Stopes waved her away. She shuffled out and they heard the key turn in the lock.

The silence was sudden and unnatural. 'Sit down, please,' Stopes said.

'Why are we locked in?'

'So we are not disturbed.' He sat down and unhooked his spectacles, peering at Ben with rheumy eyes crinkled at the edges.

'But why choose a brothel?' said Ben.

Stopes began studying his fingernails. 'Because I work here, Mr. Morris. It's not a very dignified occupation, perhaps, but one has to live. I do a little publicity — PRO work — contacting visitors to Parataxín — businessmen, diplomats — you know the sort of thing. It's a perfectly respectable establishment. It has a government license and all that.' He paused, shaking his head: 'Life is not easy here, Mr. Morris. You must understand that. Such a lot of chiseling, double-dealing. No sense of loyalty at all — no such thing as blokes getting onto a good thing and sticking together. That's why it's good to find another Englishman. I think we can trust each other, can't we?'

'What is this business proposition, Captain? You're not going to offer me a job here, are you?'

Stopes made a sucking sound in his throat that might have been a chuckle: 'No, no, Mr. Morris! I have something quite different in mind.' He leant across the table and said with intensity: 'I have the means and the knowledge, Mr. Morris, of helping you make a very large amount of money.'

Ben took a drink and said nothing.

Stopes went on: 'Sammy told me about you as soon as he got back today. He said you are a good man, damned tough — the sort of man who'll take a few risks. That you wouldn't mind too much, perhaps, if you did something here which was not quite within the law.'

'I never said that,' said Ben.

'Yes, yes, I know, but you're wanted by the police?'

'That was an unfortunate incident. I was drunk.'

'But you're still wanted by the police.'

'All right — so how does that help me?'

'It helps me, Mr. Morris. It assures me that you won't cheat me.'

Ben took another drink. Stopes continued: 'I have a scheme which has immense possibilities, but it requires my placing absolute trust in you. I go so far as to say that if I even suspected that you might break that trust I would not hesitate in handing you over to the police.'

Ben smiled: 'You make yourself clear, Captain.'

'On the other hand, Sammy and I cannot proceed safely with this scheme without at least one more man. Sammy has recommended you. We would both prefer we worked with another Englishman than with one of the locals. They can never be trusted.'

'Thank you.' Ben pursed his lips and looked Stopes in the eye: 'Sammy talked to me yesterday about something you found out in the swamp country — you and a young German who killed himself.'

Stopes nodded: 'He told you that much, did he?'

'It was all he told me. He didn't say what you'd found. He said he didn't know.'

'He knows now,' Stopes said softly. 'I told him this afternoon.' He paused, flicking out a pink tongue and licking his lips. 'It now depends on you, Mr. Morris. Firstly, how much money do you have?'

Ben hesitated: 'It's all in traveler's checks. They'll be difficult to change.'

'We'll find a way. How much do you have?'

'Three hundred and twenty pounds.'

'That will do very nicely. The money you put into the enterprise will be a business investment. There will be plenty of risk — not only financial but physical, too. But I shall be coming to that in a moment. Now, can you shoot?'

'I did some in my National Service. The usual rifle-range stuff.'

'With a .303?' said Stopes, nodding. 'Well, I hope we can find something a little more maneuverable for you. Sporting rifle perhaps.'

'And who'll we be shooting, Captain?'

'Oh, nobody, I hope! But the country we'll be crossing can be very dangerous. Most of it's not even mapped.'

'Xatu country? Where Doctor Romolo drops people he doesn't like into the swampland?'

'It's a rumor that goes round. But you know a lot for someone who's only been here a couple of days, Mr. Morris.'

'That English girl we came in with told me.'

Stopes frowned: 'I see. Who is that girl? A friend of Sammy's? He never told me about her.'

'He wouldn't have. I only met her this evening.'

'Why did you bring her here?'

'Sammy asked her. He suggested we all came along together.' Stopes sat stroking his lower lip, his eyes cast down into his drink. 'Sammy fools around too much,' he said slowly. 'Has he told this girl anything?'

'Not that I know. He hasn't had much chance. Is it important?'

'Of course it is. She might be working for someone — some organization.'

'What organization? She works for Panagra.'

'Maybe. A pretty girl would be an ideal person to use. How did she meet you, Mr. Morris?'

'I met her — in the Panagra office. Look, what the hell is this all about?'

Stopes lifted his head suddenly, focusing his watery pupils on a point just above Ben's ear. 'Very well, Mr. Morris, I'll explain. I'll take the risk, and you'll take it with me — or be sorry.' He put his hand in his inside pocket and drew out a buff envelope with a pressure-sticking flap which he peeled open, shaking into his hand a brown pebble about the size of his fingernail. 'You know what this is? Rough bort diamond. Low grade, industrial quality. It's worth between fifty and eighty pounds, depending on the market.'

He closed his palm like a clam, dropped the pebble back in the envelope and slipped it away again inside his jacket. Ben controlled his excitement, saying nothing. Stopes seemed faintly annoyed: 'You don't want to know how I came by it?'

'You tell me.'

Stopes lifted his coconut with both hands, emptying it in one swallow, and when he lowered it, his eyes held a sly glitter: 'You know anything about diamonds, Mr. Morris?'

'They cost money.'

Stopes laughed like a dog barking. 'They damn well do! But do you know where they come from?'

'From deep down, Captain.' Ben finished his drink, listening with an easy sense of unreality as Stopes talked on, more excited now: 'They come from blue clay — extreme heat concentrating on carbon deposits. We all know that — schoolboy stuff. You can read up on it in any encyclopedia.'

'Go on,' said Ben, 'I'm an ignorant person.'

'But they don't always come from mines. There are places where you can pick them up off the ground. You've heard of the diamond fields along the southwest coast of Africa? — or down off Venezuela? Some of the most heavily guarded territory in the world. If you and I were to walk down those beaches on a Sunday afternoon we could pick up diamonds like seashells. And if all the stuff on those beaches were to go out on the world market a diamond would be worth about as much as a lump of crystal.' He paused, breathing loudly.

'Go on,' said Ben.

'If I told you that I knew of a place where you and I and Sammy could go for a walk and pick up thousands of diamonds, just like the one in my pocket, what would you say?'

'I'd want to know why you were working here in a brothel — or the Parataxín Officers' Club, or whatever it is — and not out there on that beach now, Captain.'

'I'll be coming to that in a minute. Now, do you know much about the geography of this country? Just imagine you're running south from here across the plateau. In four hundred miles you come to the Cordillera Hiarra, a volcanic range that goes up to ten thousand feet. On the other side lies one of the smallest and hottest deserts in the world, the Kirau Desert — called by the Indians the "Devil's Spoon" because that's what it's shaped like — about forty miles long and twenty miles wide, with temperatures going up into the hundred and thirties. If you want to get to the other side alive, you have to go round the edge at night — about thirty miles in all.

'Then you come to the Chinluca Wall, a cliff barrier round the side of the Spoon which leads you on to a massif that eventually drops down into the swamps of the Xatu country. A hundred miles of mangrove swamp running out to the ocean, and always believed to be impenetrable. And through the middle of it there's a kind of river. Not an ordinary river — it's really no more than a channel, half water, half mud, clogged with jungle and mangrove trees.

'But in fact it's not at all like that. To the north, as you come down from the Devil's Spoon, there's an extinct volcano. It was last active in prehistoric times, but the ancient lava flows spread a long way. Some of them even reached the river. Here it stops being just stagnant bog water — there are beaches and banks and a solid bed.

'The official maps don't show any of this. The only reason I happen to know about it is because a few years ago the British Government did a good deal of mineral prospecting in that area. They were after nickel more to the north, which they didn't find, but they made a number of aerial survey maps, and several of them covered the volcano and the river.

'I had a good deal of opportunity to study those maps. They didn't tell me anything conclusive — like showing a route through the swamp to the river. But they did tell me there was a river there, and they told me there should be a way through, following the old lava shelf.

'It was later, looking through the Consulate files, that I came on something much more important. Among the geological data picked up during the surveys, there was evidence of blue clay. Again nothing conclusive. But I'm a trained geologist, Mr. Morris. It was part of my job with the Consulate to keep an eye open for mineral possibilities here.'

'What did you do when you found there was blue clay?' said Ben.

'I didn't do anything — at first. I certainly didn't tell H.M.'s Government. I got the push from the Service soon after — but that was for something else.

'I had the information I needed. Then I began to work on the history of the area. There was a lot of guesswork involved — but then half mineral prospecting is guesswork. One of the things I found was evidence of extensive volcanic activity over the whole area, dating back thousands of years. Some of the Conquistadores mention it in their writings, but only second-hand. Indian folklore was full of references to volcanoes, and much of their religion has been influenced by them — about their being the mouths of Hell, and so forth.

'There was a mass of other technical detail to support my theory — some of it hard evidence, some circumstantial — but taken altogether it gradually began to add up to the almost perfect conditions for producing diamonds. Low grade — but diamonds all the same.'

He was sitting forward, his white fingers locked round his empty coconut, his upper lip sweating big drops that trembled as he spoke:

'The really big question was whether they were accessible without immensely complicated equipment. If they hadn't been washed down on the upper beaches of the river, they were no good to me.

'So about two months ago I got together enough money to finance an expedition. It was a very small outfit — far too small, as it turned out. Sammy was busy taking photographs, and the only person I found I could trust was this young German engineer called Hitzi Leiter. I used to meet him in the billiard hall off the Plaza Mayor, and sometimes he came up here to the club. He'd arrived from the States about a year ago with some construction company that was building bridges. The contract fell through, but he stayed on doing a few odd jobs — worked on a dam project for a bit, but when that was over he began to feel the pinch.

'He didn't know much about minerals, but I tried him out with my diamond theory and he liked it. We fitted ourselves out with a tent and food supplies, and Hitzi had a big telescopic elephant-gun, and we went down to the Hiarra and hired a mule and an Indian guide who was willing to take us as far as the Chinluca Wall. It was heavy going. Took two nights round the Devil's Spoon, sleeping in the tent during the day. It was just bearable.'

'What happened in the swamp?'

Stopes shook his head glumly: 'I didn't make the swamp, I'm afraid. My health's been a bit uncertain recently — nothing serious — but we'd only taken one mule, you see. They're tough beasts, but it couldn't carry more than the equipment. We should have taken at least three of them, of course. I made it to the edge of the swamp, to this extinct volcano I was telling you about, but I couldn't go on. There's a big lake inside the crater with some caves above it, and I stayed there while young Hitzi took the mule and the tent and tried to push on to the river alone. I had a pretty good idea already of the formation of the lava shelf. I gave him the directions and sent him off — and dammit, I was right! He made it, and was back at the volcano five days later. I was more or less back to normal, but he was in a terrible state. You know the story from Sammy?'

Ben nodded: 'He had forgotten to put on mosquito repellent and went mad and committed suicide?'

'That's right. He arrived all blown up like a rubber tire. It had happened the night before, but he was getting worse. I tried to give him quinine, but it only made him delirious. He started screaming and throwing himself around, then suddenly he picked up this damned great elephant-gun of his, ran out to the edge of the lake, stuck the muzzle in his mouth and triggered the thing off with his toe. Horrible mess!'

He paused, the sweat streaming down his rubbery chin.

'And the diamonds?' said Ben.

'He found three. Just where I hoped they'd be — on the shallow beaches where the lava shelf reached the river. I sold two of them last week to raise some cash. I kept this one as proof.'

'But only three?' said Ben. 'I thought you said they were lying around like seashells.'

'They probably are. But it would need a few days to find the rich stretches of beach, and perhaps another couple of weeks, even a month, to get a really big haul. Hitzi didn't have the time or the experience — and he was scared of the Xatus, being alone. As it was, it was the mosquitoes that got him in the end.'

'Does anyone else know about this river?'

Stopes lowered his eyes, making an odd munching movement with his jaws. 'I'm not sure. I don't think so. Certainly no one knows exactly where it is, or how to get there. But these things get around. There've been rumors, I'm afraid. This started soon after the British finished their surveys. There have been rumors, of course, for a long time. Some of the Indians in the Hiarra talk about the El Dorado that lies over the mountains in what they call the "Snake Water".'

'Snake Water?'

'It means "cursed water". The swamp. It's just possible that even before the Conquistadores came some of the ancient tribes knew about diamonds being there.'

Ben said: 'Very well, Captain. It's a fantastic story. I don't know enough about these things to disprove it, but if Hitzi's dead how do you know how to get to the river yourself? Did Hitzi take the trouble to tell you the way before he blew his brains out? You said he was half delirious.'

'He drew a map as he went. Every detail, with compass bearings taken from the volcano. Very efficient, very German.'

'And you've got that map?'

Stopes leveled his eyes at him with a surprisingly sober stare: 'I'm very careful with that map, don't worry.'

'And you think you're up to doing that trip again?'

'For a million dollars one can do a lot, Mr. Morris, I'm not an old man yet. And if we take it easy, with plenty of mules and the proper equipment, we can do it.'

'You and me and Sammy, eh? The Three Musketeers. But why three? Why not just you two? — there'd be less to split at the end.'

'Two's not enough. I found that out with Hitzi. If one of us gets ill or wounded or killed, one man can't get those diamonds by himself. And if the Xatus attack, the more guns we have the better.'

'But why go by mule? If you're not sure about these diamonds, why not charter a helicopter?'

Stopes gave his bark-like laugh: 'Give me the money, Mr. Morris, and I'll hire one tonight! At an hourly rate of two hundred dollars, less fuel, for perhaps three weeks. Work that out!'

Ben nodded. 'All right, so we haven't got the money and we go by mule. But supposing there's someone else who has got the money?'

'What?'

'Enough for that helicopter, Captain.'

'Enough? What?' Stopes peered at him across the dim blue room and licked his lips. 'There's no one else, Mr. Morris.'

'What about the organization — the one you thought that girl might be working for?'

'There is no organization.'

'Then why did you mention it?'

'It was just an idea,' Stopes said hurriedly. 'Nothing definite. Nothing to worry about.'

'But there are other people? People with money who might know about the river?'

'No. No, that's not true! You and Sammy — you're the only two.'

Ben looked hard at Stopes, whose eyes were again sunk down toward his drink. 'I hope that's right, Captain.'

'You'll have to trust me,' Stopes said quietly.

Ben nodded: 'All right. But what happens when we find the diamonds?'

'That's no problem. I know at least two Government officials in this city who buy rough diamonds on the black market for fifty percent of their value — for cash, in foreign currency.'

'It sounds too easy,' said Ben — beginning to wonder, all the same. 'Why not do it legally by selling to a bank or a diamond corporation? Get ten percent and be safe.'

Stopes grinned: 'Yes, Mr Morris. Take your sack of diamonds down to the Bank of England, collect your check and buy gilt-edged — after you've paid tax, of course.' He shook his head sorrowfully: 'But it wouldn't be like that. Not with a man like Dr. Romolo at the top. He'd claim those sacks of uncut diamonds as State property, and that would be the end of it — and probably the end of us too. So we find some junior official who has contacts with an illicit diamond dealer abroad and he just exchanges those sacks for a couple of suitcases full of dollars or Swiss francs — and perhaps his twin-engined plane with hi-fi and cocktail cabinet, which he can afford to give away now — and we all say goodbye and Sammy flies us down to Rio where we put the money in a bank and live happily ever after. Nothing legal or illegal, Mr. Morris — just one corrupt official on the inside, and no tricks — no trying to put the squeeze on by demanding concessions on the river, or anything ambitious like that.'

'Won't this official be scared we'll spill the beans once we're out?'

'Why should he? Another allegation of Government corruption? Everyone here's corrupt, and everyone knows everyone's corrupt. Besides, Castro marches on. Revolution's in the wind. Any sensible man in this country would take his half-million dollars' profit and buy real estate in Florida.'

'He might try to make the whole million by knocking us all off,' Ben suggested.

'Not if he's sensible. There'll be three of us — one of him. And the man I'm thinking of won't make that sort of trouble.'

'What about us? Sammy, for instance? You think he's reliable?'

'Sammy's a bit wild, but he's a good worker, especially when there's money involved.'

'And me?'

'You won't try to cross me up — because if you do I hand you over to the police.'

Ben nodded and sat back and wiped his face. His head was beginning to throb.

'So you are agreeable, Mr. Morris?'

'I'll go along with you.'

Stopes groped in his pocket for his tinted spectacles, put them on and clapped for the old woman to unlock the door.

Back beyond the padded door the nightclub had become very crowded. The band was beating out a drum roll while two dark girls wriggled out of their clothes under a spotlight. No one took any notice of Ben and Stopes as they pressed round the floor to their alcove. The drums crashed to a crescendo, there were a sheen of bluish-brown flesh swelling and shaking through the cigar smoke; the drums stopped, the light cut out. There was a bellow of applause, and Ben found himself looking into an alcove full of army officers. He looked into the next to make sure he hadn't made a mistake. There was no sign of Mel or Ryderbeit. He turned to Stopes who was talking to one of the waiters. The drums started up again. He looked at his watch: ten past midnight; then glanced down the alcoves and all he could see were well-fed faces chewing cigars, and girls who were all eyes and teeth, then he caught another glimpse of the white-haired young man in the mustard-colored suit.

At that moment a tall *mestiza* girl glided on to the floor in a sheath of black satin. She had an astonishingly fine face like an El Greco Madonna. Stopes had moved away again, still talking to the Indian who was now paying him money — presumably his commission on the evening. That reminded Ben that Stopes was supposed to be standing him the entrance fee. He shouted through a wave of applause: 'Sammy and the girl have gone!'

Stopes peered at him through his glasses: 'Yes. They left you this.' He gave him a sheet of notepaper written in a neat sloping hand:

Sorry but I was getting hungry and you seemed busy. So your friend took me off to dinner. See you tomorrow perhaps at the office before twelve. Good luck. Mel.

The bitch, he thought. Someone bumped into him and he felt his temper rise. The applause burst around him again. Out on the floor the girl was caressing her shoulders with graceful El Greco fingers. Ben's head was aching. She began to ease the black satin down over one small breast. The crowd was suddenly quiet. The drums boomed softly. She had a long ivory belly, rounded and dimpled above the strip of lace pants. Her face was grave and absent: there was nothing deliberately erotic about her — she might have been undressing in her own bedroom.

Ben thought: *Damn Ryderbeit, damn Mrs MacDougall! And I'm still owed fifty dollars.* Stopes said in his ear: 'Nice girl, eh?'

He nodded vaguely. With a long slow movement she let the satin slide down her thighs and stepped out of the dress, rolling her hips very slightly, her breasts quite firm, lifting her arms high above her head. The drumbeat quickened suddenly, as a shining Indian in a red loincloth bounded onto the floor, seized her round the waist, whirling her up in the air, and with a snap that sounded even above the drums, ripped the pants from her body and flung them far out into the darkness, then vanished with the spotlight.

Stopes was shouting above the applause: 'I shall have to go now, Mr. Morris!' He was pushing a printed card into Ben's hand: 'I'll leave word with the night porter.'

Ben read in an embossed script: *Señor B. Stopes, Apartamiento 3, Hermosillo 8, Parataxín. Consultor Commercial Business Consultant.* The words held a pathetic boast that suddenly made the prospect of this old man being able to bring back a million dollars from an unmapped river seem as remote as his finding a fortune on the dark side of the moon.

Ben put the card away and said, 'Thank you,' then added with his eyes still on the floor show: 'I paid fifty dollars for the entrance fee, Captain. Sammy said you'd let me have it back…'

The applause broke out again and a crush of spectators knocked Ben to one side. He looked about in the darkness. 'Stopes! Captain Stopes!' A man turned and stared at him. He realized he was shouting in English, and ducked away into the crowd.

The spotlight came on again and there was more applause for a couple of acrobats and a girl in a top hat and sequined corset. He went over and leaned against the bar; the girls were almost all taken up now. He remembered that he still had the right to one of them. He'd like the *mestiza* stripper — she might even worry him enough to take his mind off Laura.

None of the girls at the bar meant much to him. It had been a crazy evening, he thought. That young German lying in a crater, bloated with mosquito poison and blowing his head off — with the chance of picking up a million dollars if he'd lived.

Perhaps the whole story had been an elaborate con: Stopes would get his commission on the fifty dollars, and Ryderbeit had had a free evening, with Mel thrown in. And here was Ben on the run from the police, all on his own in the middle of the night in a brothel packed with half the bigwigs of Parataxín. Yet perhaps there was something to be said for that, after all: like Edgar Allan Poe's idea of hiding the purloined letter in the most obvious place. They'd never think of looking for him here.

He stayed and watched the next couple of acts. They became very obscene, in a coarse, jolly way, with none of the sniggering furtiveness of the London strip clubs he had visited. The audience roared and clapped like a crowd at a football match, and when it was all over they'd probably go back and embezzle a few more million pesos that would keep a few hundred thousand more Indian peasants on the breadline, or beat up another batch of political prisoners, then sleep with their mistresses and wake up to roll into swimming pools under their bedroom windows.

He thought: *Half a million after the discount, cut three ways: more than fifty thousand sterling each. But it could never be. Not with a man like Stopes.*

As he went out toward the courtyard to find a taxi he noticed that the white-haired young man seemed to have gone. He wondered what would make hair go white so early. Freak of nature? Or shock?

It was past one o'clock. He had just enough pesos to get him back into Parataxín.

CHAPTER FOUR: STRANGE BEDFELLOWS

Number 8, Hermosillo, was a grubby stone building in the older part of the city. A *mestizo* in a black apron sat behind the iron gate with a ring of keys in his hand. Ben showed him Stopes' card and the man pointed up a staircase that smelled of cats. Flat 3 was on the first floor; on the door there was a plate engraved with Stopes' name. He knocked and waited. There was no sound from inside. He knocked again harder, then called Stopes' name. Nothing happened. He stood for a moment listening and all he heard was the *mestizo* coughing downstairs.

He began to curse Stopes, remembering the risk he'd run if he tried registering at a hotel. In desperation he tried the door handle. It opened.

It was dark and quiet inside, with a musty smell like an old boarding house. He called again: 'Stopes!' — softly this time, not expecting an answer. The only sound was a clock ticking and a drip of water. He found the light switch. He was in a small sitting room full of ugly black furniture, with a linoleum floor, brown-painted walls and a horsehair sofa. There was one shelf half full of books — mostly Spanish paperbacks — and a couple of grimy lithographs of traditional gypsy scenes. In a kitchenette about the size of a cupboard, set into the corner, were stacks of empty bottles, an empty rucksack, some rusted cooking equipment and a long black oilskin bag that had been dragged partially into the sitting room. On a table in the middle of the floor a bottle of Scotch stood three-quarters empty next to a bowl of moldy bananas. A glass had rolled under the table, but was unbroken. Ben picked it up and sniffed: there was a drop of whisky still at the bottom. He looked at his watch: nearly half-past one. Stopes had been gone from the club an hour and a quarter; it was only a fifteen-minute drive back into the city.

He put the glass on the table and went through a half-open door on his left into a tiny bedroom with a bathroom leading off it. The single bed was unmade, with sheets that did not look quite clean. The only other furniture was a big wardrobe that took up half the room. The curtains were undrawn.

He went into the bathroom. More empty bottles; a laundry bag behind the lavatory; slimy washcloth in the basin and the hot-water tap dripping. He turned it off and picked up a towel from the floor. It was damp.

He went out quickly to the front door and shot the bolt on the inside. The lock did not work by pulling the door shut: it needed a key on both sides. Stopes must have come back, washed and had a drink, then rushed out again — in a hurry it seemed, letting his glass fall under the table and forgetting to lock the door after him. Or perhaps he was just leaving it open for when Ben arrived.

He stood for several seconds in the middle of the floor, and suddenly he knew there was something wrong. Something about the door? The spilled whisky? The empty oilskin bag? Or perhaps it was just the whole flat. There was nothing here that told him anything more about Stopes than he knew already: that he was a middle-aged expatriate who lived alone and drank too much and scraped a living as a pimp in a high-class brothel.

He went over and looked again at the bookshelf. There was a Whitaker's Almanack three years out of date, a couple of volumes on mineralogy and one on contract bridge.

He was beginning to feel very tired; he went into the bedroom, kicked off his shoes and lay down to wait for Stopes.

He thought it rather odd of the man to invite him here for the night, then rush out leaving the door open. But then the whole evening had been pretty odd. Perhaps Stopes had gone off on a binge; perhaps he was out playing bridge. And perhaps that diamond hadn't been a diamond at all — just a brown pebble in an envelope to help Stopes and Ryderbeit con him out of fifty dollars. Only it was hardly a very clever con, because here was Ben lying on Stopes' own bed waiting for him to walk right in.

After a while he turned the light out and lay back with his eyes closed, and in the darkness it was very quiet in the flat, except for the clock ticking by the bed.

He woke and saw a patch of daylight through the window. The clock said a quarter to eight. The room was empty. He jumped up and called 'Stopes!' There was no answer. He went into the bathroom, washed his face in cold water, went back to the bed and leaned down to pick up his shoes.

A nerve jerked in each leg and he leaped back a full two feet, colliding with the wardrobe. He was cold all over; then he began to sweat. He went back slowly, braced himself and looked down. There was a hand under the bed. He looked down further. The head was facing away from him, but he recognized the yellowish-gray hair.

He jumped up and ran into the sitting room, and was a couple of feet from the door when there came a quick double knock.

He stopped dead, sweating hot and wet now under his collar and down the back of his neck. The knock came again and a voice shouted through the door: 'Stopes! Get out o' bed — we got work to do! And you, Morris!'

Ben let his breath go in a hiss; he was shaking all over as he stepped forward and pulled back the bolt. Ryderbeit stood outside leering at him; he was carrying a huge rucksack and was dressed again in his corduroy suit.

'How are yer? Stopes up yet?' He walked in, looked around and said: 'You look sick, soldier.'

Ben nodded. 'Go and look under the bed next door.'

'Huh?' Ryderbeit's face tightened into a frown; he put down the rucksack and walked quickly into the bedroom. Ben didn't move. He heard a few muffled sounds next door, then Ryderbeit came back in, slowly, thinking hard. 'You do this?'

'What do you think?'

'Somebody did. You slept in there?'

Ben nodded.

'Charming. Who let you in?'

'It was open.'

'What time?'

Ben told him.

'Notice anything wrong?'

Ben pointed at the empty glass on the table. 'And I think somebody had had a wash just before I got in,' he added.

'I bet they did! He's got three knife wounds in his back. Hasn't bled much. Whoever did it must have just walked right in while he was having his nightcap, put his arms round him and slipped it in — if you'll pardon the expression.'

Ben wiped his brow and sat down. 'Christ!' he muttered.

'Ever seen a dead man before?' said Ryderbeit.

'Not like that.'

'Happens all the time out here.' He went over to the kitchenette and picked up the long oilskin bag: 'This is what

Stopes used to wrap Hitzi Leiter's elephant-gun in — he showed it me last week, just before I went up north and met you. There was also a compass here and a splendid pair of German U-boat day-and-night binoculars.'

'And the map?'

Ryderbeit nodded: 'The Captain had it on him. It's gone — along with his wallet and the diamond.'

'You think it was an ordinary robbery?'

Let's leave the police to worry about that. They probably won't find him for a couple of days, and then I don't suppose they'll work their arses off to solve it. Who was Stopes anyway? A drunk, a broken-down no-good white bum — God rest him. Come on, let's get out o' here!'

Ben followed him out to the dark stairway. *Ryderbeit was a callous bastard*, he thought: *Stopes had been his friend, after all.*

'Did the porter let you in downstairs?' Ryderbeit asked, as they started down.

Ben nodded.

'He must have let the killer in, too. But I don't think we'd better risk asking him any questions now. He might remember you enough to give your description to the police.'

'That's all I need,' said Ben feebly. The iron gate into the street was open and the *mestizo* porter had gone.

'Come on,' said Ryderbeit cheerfully. 'You look as though you could do with a drink.'

'It was somebody who's after those diamonds, that's for sure,' Ryderbeit was saying; 'but that leaves a wide range of candidates. The old Captain had a lot of friends — or let's say, contacts. People he did little deals with — currency fiddles, false declarations for the Customs — using the good old British passport as a cover. Like the Old School Tie. It still works wonders out here.' He smiled crookedly, leaning across the marble-topped bar table, while Ben chewed a lump of salted ham on a toothpick. 'Only this time,' Ryderbeit went on, 'it was a bit more than just a quick deal in bonded whisky.'

'But how could the murderer have known about the diamonds?'

Ryderbeit shrugged: 'The old Captain liked a drink every now and again — say every couple of hours — and when he was really hitting it, he liked to talk, and sometimes he talked too bloody much!'

Ben nodded: 'He talked all right last night.'

Ryderbeit looked up sharply: 'Well sure! He was filling you in. What d'yer mean, he talked?'

'He talked about a gang,' said Ben: 'an organization with money that might try to reach the river with a helicopter. Does that make sense?'

Ryderbeit's eyes narrowed: 'He told you that?'

'He thought Mel might be some sort of spy for them. He said it was nothing definite — nothing to worry about.'

Ryderbeit took a drink of raw local brandy and breathed deeply. 'If it was anything serious the Captain would have told me. Still, it's a possibility — and not a pretty one. We've enough stacked against us, as it is. We've lost the map, the gun, the night glasses, and five hundred dollars Stopes got from selling his two diamonds. So now we've got to start from scratch — and you, Morris, are going to help me.'

'You're not still thinking of going after the diamonds?'

'Damn right I am! Listen, I used to work in diamonds. And when Stopes told me the whole story yesterday before I saw you, I knew it all matched up. The Captain was a bright boy. The big corporations pay their geologists top salaries to make deductions like his.'

'But how do we go after them without the map?'

'If Hitzi Leiter could find that river, so can we — even if we have to take six months doing it. The big snag is money. If we're going to do this properly, we're going to need at least five hundred quid plus.'

'All mine's in traveler's checks,' Ben reminded him.

Ryderbeit smiled: 'And you know who's going to change 'em, don't you? Our sweet friend Mrs MacDougall. Don't look so surprised. The lady's very interested in our situation.'

'You told her about it?'

'Not everything. But enough to find out from her that she has a nice little bank account in this city to the tune of some seven hundred odd dollars. Which is just about what we need.'

'What do you plan to do? Forge her checks?'

Ryderbeit grinned: 'The morning's not your best time, is it? Perhaps sleeping on top of a dead man all night does funny things to the intellect.'

Ben said slowly: 'If I'm thinking what you're thinking, Sammy, and if Stopes wasn't exaggerating, that part of the world's no place for walking around in stockings and high heels.'

Ryderbeit sat twirling his glass between finger and thumb. 'She has a car — with foreign touring plates. The police rarely stop tourist cars.'

'Unless they're looking for me.'

Ryderbeit shrugged: 'That's a risk we'll have to take. We'll need a car, whatever happens, to carry our equipment across the plateau. It's over three hundred miles to the Hiarra Mountains, and a hired car with local registration plates would risk being stopped at a routine police check — there's a lot of them out on the main roads to control the movement of Indians. It won't matter so much going in, but coming out we may have a few sacks of diamonds on us. We'll stand a hundred percent better chance in an American car with foreign registration, driven by a pretty English girl. No policeman's going to think of looking for diamonds in that.'

'We hope,' said Ben. He called for another brandy. The whole fantastic scheme was beginning to assume a certain improbable logic of its own. 'You think she'll be crazy enough to come?'

'I do. Any girl who comes running out alone to a country like this is already half crazy. Maybe completely crazy. But for the moment I'd just hazard she's in the mood to try anything once.'

'You seem to have forgotten one thing,' said Ben. 'Whoever murdered Stopes now knows exactly where that river is, and he — or they — aren't going to waste time getting there. They've probably started already.'

'I hadn't forgotten at all. Because if we can't find that river on our own, Stopes' killer, or killers, are going to find it for us. They're going to lead us there. There aren't many people who try to cross the Devil's Spoon into the Xatu swamps, and there's only one known route to take. Don't worry, soldier, we'll find that river. Only we're going to have to hurry.'

Mel leaned back against the bamboo screen and sat for a long time staring at the ceiling, her pale hair stirring under the fans. Outside, beyond the striped awning of the restaurant, the hum of traffic was dying down, the shutters closing against the noon heat.

'When are you thinking of leaving?' she said at last, her eyes still on the ceiling.

'Tomorrow at dawn,' said Ryderbeit.

She nodded slowly: 'Pretty short notice.'

'It is. Stopes' killer saw to that.'

She nodded again, untroubled, then sat forward and sipped her coffee. 'I must say, it's rather an exciting idea. It might be fun.'

'Not fun,' said Ryderbeit: 'Profitable!'

She smiled: 'Yes, I hadn't forgotten. We'll be away a month you think? Well, I suppose I can always tell them at the office that my father's died. I might as well try to keep the job open in case we never find any diamonds.'

Ryderbeit grinned and tried again to put his arm round her shoulder, but she drew carefully away and began to study the list of supplies that Ben and Ryderbeit had already bought that morning, after putting the plan to her while she arranged through her office to have Ben's traveler's checks changed without anyone seeing his passport.

She had then asked for a couple of hours to 'think about it'.

The list in front of her included a tent of double-lined white cotton with sewn-in ground sheets and mosquito nets; three sleeping bags (the third one bought on the bold assumption that she would accept); cooking equipment, marine compass, a pair of second-hand 12 x 30 binoculars with glare-shields, six four-liter plastic water cans, four liters of kerosene, a Tilley lamp, powerful flashlight, and a set of large-scale cloth-backed contour maps of the Cordillera Hiarra, starting at the town of Benisalem at the end of the plateau and covering part of the Devil's Spoon.

Throughout the morning Ryderbeit had worked with a dedicated efficiency, quite alien to the demented drunk Ben had met only two days ago in Xatopetl. He now said to Mel: 'There's still a lot o' shopping left. Food. Clothing. Medical supplies. Guns.'

She nodded: 'I can't get any of my money out until the banks open again at four. Will there be time?'

'We'll make time. Ben and I'll concentrate on clothing — light shirts, plenty of string underwear, sweaters, windbreakers, caps with earflaps, snow goggles. It can get bloody cold up in those mountains. By the way, what size boots do you take?'

'Sevens. Another reason I couldn't become a ballet dancer.'

Ryderbeit wagged his head: 'Never mind, my darling, you'll soon be richer than Margot Fonteyn and them all put together!' He paused, checking the list, and Ben just watched and waited and felt a quickening of the pulse — not from fear or anxiety this time, but a pure pleasurable excitement chasing out all the pain and loneliness of the last few months, until he suddenly realized he was happy.

Ryderbeit was saying to Mel: 'The food's your province — tinned supplies for a month. We won't be able to afford a very varied menu, but don't let's stint ourselves. Lots o' soups and corned beef, and throw in a few delicacies. I'll take care of the drinking side — a dozen bottles of imported Scotch I can get through someone I know at the Paradiso Club at ten dollars a bottle. Extravagant, I know, but we must have our little luxuries.'

Ben was not sure he liked this turn of the planning. He said: 'Why not take something cheap like wine?'

'You're not quibbling over a few dollars, are you!' Ryderbeit cried. 'In a month's time we'll be thinking in terms of a million.'

'We haven't got that million yet,' said Ben. 'Anyway, why whisky?'

'Because I like whisky. Any objections?'

'Only that I and Mel will be paying for it.'

Ryderbeit winked at her: 'I think old Morris is getting mean! You're not going to get mean, are you, soldier? Whisky's nothing! It's the guns that are going to be the big expense. You don't grudge us a few guns, do you?'

'What sort of guns?'

'Rifles. We can pick up a good second-hand Winchester for about a hundred dollars. They're available without a license for people who want to go after anything from condors and hyenas to bandits and unfaithful wives.' He turned to Mel: 'Have you ever shot anything?'

'Only rabbits on my father's farm — with a shotgun.'

'Well done! We'll fit you out with one here — 12-bore, Number One shot. Can kill a man at thirty yards.'

Mel turned again to the list of supplies: 'We need a full camper's first-aid kit with morphine, and plenty of quinine, iodine, aspirins, foot powder, salt tablets, vitamin pills.'

'And mosquito repellent,' Ryderbeit put in: 'We don't want to make that mistake again! And plenty o' laxatives — the heat dries you up fast.'

She nodded: 'And while we're on luxuries, lavatory paper.'

'And cigars,' said Ryderbeit.

'And the airmail edition of the *New Statesman* flown out each week,' said Ben.

Mel asked: 'We've had all the usual shots for typhoid and cholera?' They nodded. 'What about snakebite?'

Ryderbeit laughed: 'If you get bitten by a snake out there, my darling, you bid this world goodnight! There are too many varieties to carry serums for them all. We just keep out o' their way. Snakes are quite reasonable creatures really — they only attack if they're frightened, which is more than can be said for the Xatu Indians, or whoever killed the old Captain last night.' He paused. 'Can you think of anything else?'

'Are we using special boots for the swamp,' asked Ben.

'Ordinary leather knee boots. If we go any deeper into the swamp we'll have had it anyway. We'll be keeping to the lava shelf.'

'What about mules?'

'We'll hire them in Benisalem at the foot of the Hiarra Range.'

'Will mules be able to manage a swamp?' said Mel.

Ryderbeit grinned: 'If you can, darling, so can they. They're scruffy little sexless brutes, but they're tough as hell.' He paused, then shook his head: 'If we were down in Peru we could hire llamas. Ever ridden a llama? Ah, the loveliest animal on earth. Fascinating! Neurotic and primitive, and if you upset them they spit in your face from ten yards away. And their breath smells like the tomb. But they're beautiful! They have the rumps of a Rubens woman covered in hair. They also have congenital syphilis which they're believed to have passed on to Europe via the Conquistadores.' He leered round the table: 'Honest to God! If you try to treat a llama with penicillin it dies. Up in the Andes the Indians love 'em! When they get drunk at fiesta time they sit on the village walls and pull their llamas on like gum boots.'

Mel giggled: 'What a frightful story, Sammy!'

'You want a bet on it, darling? Check with any reputable zoo — or one that isn't so reputable, I'd say!' He gave a shriek of laughter that made one of the waiters stare, then he turned to Ben, suddenly serious:

'Is there anything else you want to know?'

'Yes. Last night Stopes told me he knew of two Government officials here who'd buy diamonds in cash for a fifty percent cut. Do you know them too?'

Ryderbeit shook his head: 'I know someone else who will, though. A fellow called Danny Berck-Millar. I call him Mister Fix. He's involved in some shady company in Venezuela, and after he's paid us in cash here, we go up to Caracas and pay the money into the company, and they can arrange — at a discount, of course — to have it deposited almost anywhere we like. New York, London, Paris.'

'Can't we pay the diamonds straight into the company here?' said Ben.

'No. It doesn't have any connections here — and even if it did, the restrictions on hard currency are too tight. We'd have to bribe half the Government first. It has to be done directly through Venezuela where the company's registered.'

Mel said: 'Couldn't we just smuggle the diamonds direct to Caracas and pay them into the company without changing them into cash at all?'

'You'd lose up to thirty percent of their value. Diamonds are still at a premium here. In Venezuela they're not. And if there was some hitch about the company at the last minute, I'd rather have a suitcase full of dollar bills than a few sacks of uncut diamonds.'

'Have you told this American all about it?' asked Ben.

'Of course not. But I happen to know he did a very similar thing about six months ago in a tin deal with some Cubans. It involved Berck-Millar and a pal of his, who's a director of one of the big Parataxín banks, buying tin concessions below the market price in exchange for U.S. dollars which were paid over in a suitcase. That gives you a fair picture of how the economy of this country works.' He looked round: 'Any last questions?'

'Yes,' said Ben, 'where do I sleep tonight?'

'With me,' said Mel, 'on the sofa in my flat.'

Ryderbeit grinned: 'She's a nice good girl, soldier. Don't forget it!'

Ben sat back in the corner of the sofa and watched her bend down and pour the coffee. He felt alert and excited, and yet at ease. It had been a good evening. The three of them had dined in one of the plushest restaurants in the city; Ryderbeit had laid bare some of the facts of his life in dreadful detail and Mel had eaten impassively through it all and smiled politely at the end. Ben had paid — with almost the last of his pesos — but felt he had been rewarded.

Ryderbeit had gone back to the hotel where he kept a room, and Ben was now sitting in Mel's flat.

It was a nice flat: it had a telephone and Japanese prints and a proper bath under the shower. The bed was big enough for two and let down from the wall in the sitting room. The radio was playing something by Ellington, and there was a bottle of Hine cognac in the cabinet next to the record player. Panagra seemed to treat her well.

He watched her straighten up from the coffee table and waited until she turned with two cups in her hand, then said: 'Why, Mel?'

'Why?'

'Why are you doing it? You must be stark staring bonkers, you realize that?'

'Perhaps.'

'But why?'

She stopped in the middle of the floor, still holding the coffee. 'Because I want to be rich, that's why. Satisfied?'

He smiled: 'And you really think we're going to find diamonds strewn around that river?'

'I don't see why not,' she said, without moving.

'Don't you? Well, all I can say is you have a touching faith. You're being naive, Mel.' He watched her standing there and heard one of the cups rattle on its saucer.

'Why?' she said again, in a small hard voice.

'Because you're a young English girl in a lawless land in a far-off continent and you allow two almost perfect strangers to talk you into giving them your seven hundred dollars' savings — without even a receipt, mind! — as well as commandeer your car, in order to back up some wildly improbable scheme for finding diamonds…'

'Now wait a minute!' She stepped out and thrust one of the coffees under his face: 'First of all, I don't think it is improbable!'

He took the coffee with a mock bow, still sitting, and thanked her through her words which now came fast, with sudden passion: 'If that German chap, Hitzi-whatever-his-name, managed to find diamonds, then so can we! You're just like every other damned Englishman one meets out here. You're so stuffed shirted and terrified of stepping out of line.'

'That's me,' said Ben, 'from the moment I got here two days ago.'

She ignored him, going back and sitting in a cane chair at the other end of the room. 'This isn't like England or Europe, you know. This is a wide-open continent. What Sammy and that old man Stopes said is true. You can find diamonds here — you can find gold — you can make fortunes overnight. And people still do it! And you know how? Because they've got initiative — what you call being stark staring bonkers. How do you think the Conquistadores managed to take most of South America with just over a hundred men and twelve horses?'

'They were fortified by their llamas,' said Ben, drinking his coffee.

'And what about Sammy's father? He was a millionaire before he was twenty-seven — and I don't care if he did lose it all afterward. He started as nothing, then he became something big. He did something!'

Ben nodded: 'It takes all sorts. Rimbaud wrote most of his poems before he was twenty, then became king of an African tribe, and Hitler was a beatnik till he was thirty and never paid any income tax. And I'm an out-of-work architect with no money, up the creek and far from home. Go on.'

'Yes, and I'll tell you something else!' she cried, crossing her legs with a crackle of cane: 'I don't care a hoot how wild this scheme is. I like it and I'm going along with it, and I'll tell you why. Since my marriage broke up and I came down from Mexico I've been bored half out of my mind. I want something to happen to me. I don't want another bloody marriage, or some tatty affair with one of these brilliantined lover-boys — I want some adventure. And when I've had it, I'm going to go back to England and try to start all over again. Do you want some brandy?'

'A big one,' he said smiling, and watched her bend down again and take the Hine from the radio cabinet. Her eyes were shining slightly when she turned and brought him over the cognac in a wineglass, but otherwise her face held that same dead composure. 'Anyway, what's wrong with the scheme?' she said.

'Nothing at all, except that we might all get murdered like Stopes or tortured by the Xatus or die of fever or snakebite — or just not find any diamonds at all.'

She sat down and drank her coffee, and her eyes rested on the darkness beyond the open window. Her voice was softer when she spoke: 'Well, why are *you* coming, Ben?'

He smiled grimly: it seemed a good question. 'Because I don't have much choice, I suppose.'

'Because of the police? That's not the whole reason, is it? Sammy was misleading you a bit yesterday, you know. It's true they may be looking for you at the moment, and it'll probably be risky to try the airport for a few days, but you could always get out of the country if you really wanted to — you could cross by any of the inland roads through the rainforests. But I don't think you do want to.'

He sipped his brandy and stretched back on the sofa and nodded. 'Very well. I'm doing it for the same reason as you. I want excitement. I want adventure. I want to be rich.'

'Ah!' Her face filled with a sudden trusting innocence. 'Yes, let's hope we get rich!'

'But there's one thing,' he said slowly, and rolled the wineglass between his palms as he said it: 'Ryderbeit.'

'Oh? What's the matter with him?'

'I don't trust him.'

She shrugged and sipped her cognac. 'He seems a nice enough fellow to me.'

He smiled sadly: 'Mel, whatever else Sammy Ryderbeit may be, he's certainly not a "nice fellow".'

'Well, I know some of his stories are pretty gruesome, but at least he's frank. Unless he's exaggerating, of course. And he's fun. He gave me a damned good dinner last night. I admit he asked the inevitable question at the end, but he didn't push it particularly. What's wrong with him?'

'He's mad.'

She laughed: 'Oh well, I like people who are mad.'

'What time did he take you home last night?'

She frowned: 'He didn't stay the night, if that's what you mean.'

'It's not what I mean. What time did he say goodnight to you?'

'About midnight. Why?'

'Because I think he may have had something to do with Stopes' death.'

She sat very still for a moment, then stood up and poured herself another coffee from the percolator on the side table, went back to her chair, crossed her legs again and said, with studied calm: 'You think he murdered Stopes?'

'I don't know. But I think he might have had something to do with it.'

'But why an old man like that?'

'Precisely because he was old. Too old to take along on the expedition.'

She sipped her coffee and stared through the window, and might have been as far from thoughts of murder as a girl in a Knightsbridge flower shop. Suddenly she sat up and said: 'Yes, but if he did murder him, it means he'd have the map and the other two diamonds and the gun that were stolen. And he hasn't.'

'He says he hasn't. All he needs is the map and that wouldn't be difficult to hide. And he seems very confident he can find that river.'

He paused gravely, knowing she was not impressed. 'I'm only saying this, Mel, because the three of us are going to be spending a lot of time together in the next few weeks. I don't want you to have any illusions about Sammy. He's a wild man.'

She nodded: 'But we don't know anything for certain, do we?'

'No.' There was a long silence, then she looked up and said: 'You trust *me*, don't you?'

He grinned: 'I think so. You'd be satisfied with a third of a million dollars, wouldn't you? Or would you?'

She put down her cup and stood up. 'It's getting late. I'll make up a bed for you on the sofa.'

He stood up too and came toward her, and for a moment she faced him with her cool mirror-like eyes; then, with an easy, almost unconscious movement, he leaned out and pulled her against him. Her hand fastened round his arm and held it for a moment, her body stiff and straining, while his own body filled with a quick electric excitement.

'It's getting late,' she said, pushing against him. 'We've got to be up by five.'

'That's four hours away. There's no hurry.' He drew her closer, his hand in the small of her back, feeling her tremble.

'Please. Let me go.'

He pulled her hard against him and pressed his mouth against the soft hairs under her ear, and she twisted her head round with a small murmuring sound, her body flinching feebly. 'No, please, Ben.'

But he went on holding her, with a certain detached amusement, curious at first to know what her reactions would be. He kissed her mouth and it was smooth and cold, and he wanted her now with a sudden greedy pain, all detachment gone as he held her close, feeling the length of her body against him, his mouth dry, his blood racing.

She moved her face away from him and said quietly: 'Do you want to sleep with me?'

'Very much.' He let go of her, and she pushed him gently aside and stood for a moment staring again out of the window — at the black shadow of a banana tree. 'I think I'll have a brandy too,' she said, and went over to the cabinet, poured a dribble into one of the wineglasses, sat down again and said,

'Oh God! Don't start, please! Don't go on. We're going to be living in each other's laps for the next few weeks and it's not going to be easy.'

'It's going to be absolute hell,' he said, managing a ghastly grin, and sat down on the edge of the sofa. 'Do you want to sleep with *me?*' he said slowly.

'Not really. I've nothing against you — in fact, I like you a lot — it's just the whole routine. It's the same every time and I don't care. It isn't even as though I felt filthy and depraved at the end of it — that might at least be interesting. It just seems such a waste of time.'

'What happened, Mel?'

'Oh, hell, nothing happened, except that my marriage broke up. It's over a year ago and I've been unfaithful to him about a dozen times.' There was a weariness in her voice now: 'I suppose it sounds pretty silly talking about being unfaithful to him after the way he behaved.'

'What happened?'

She shrugged and swallowed her brandy in a gulp; when she lowered it her face had a solemn heavy look. 'All right, I'm mad. Like Ryderbeit. And so was my husband. Both absolutely bonkers, as you say. We met and had a big fling and I fell for him — every bit of me, so that I used to start shaking when I heard his voice talking in the office corridor, or even on the telephone. I was crazy!'

'And how was he crazy?'

'He started to beat me up — about once a week. For no reason at all. Because he said I didn't smile when I said hello to him, or because he thought I looked moody, and in the end he said it was just that he couldn't get through to me — that being married to me was like bashing his head against a brick wall. I don't know. He was never like that before we were married.

'I stuck it for about a year, but it got worse and worse till I was terrified to have a child by him. I thought he'd probably beat that too. Then one night he got drunk in a restaurant and I walked out, and when he got home he dragged me out of bed and blacked both my eyes and busted my nose, and that was the end. I left him.'

'Damned right. Do you still love him?'

'I suppose so, in a ridiculous way. I don't know. I think about him quite a lot — but I suppose that's because I'm bored with most of the people I meet out here. They're all a lot of spoiled rich children trying to get me into bed to satisfy their ego.'

'At least they don't break your nose every week.'

She smiled faintly, then her eyes met his and became grave again, and there was another silence.

He got up quietly and came toward her and leaned down and kissed her, and she kissed him back, politely.

'Let's go to bed,' he said.

She nodded. 'All right, I suppose. Why not?' She stood up and turned to the foldaway bed in the wall. 'You'll have to give me a hand with this.'

He moved vaguely, even unsteadily, hauling the bed onto the floor, pulling down the striped Mexican rug that was tucked in like a counterpane, watching her pick up the cups and glasses and take them into the little kitchen set off the passage beside the bathroom. He remembered Stopes' flat, and for a moment this one seemed almost as strange, as puzzling. He was even beginning to feel nervous.

He heard her call from the bathroom: 'Can you turn the record player off?'

He switched down the volume and closed the lid. From behind the bathroom door he heard water running. He swallowed hard and his mouth tasted like scuffed leather. He wondered if he had had too much brandy. He went into the kitchen and drank two tumblers of water from the tap, then worried if the water was drinkable.

He went and sat on the bed, Ryderbeit had said she'd come on the trip because she was half crazy — perhaps completely crazy. Ben had known plenty of girls who jumped into bed on the first night and went home when the milk came. But they hadn't been like this girl: they giggled and smudged their makeup and spent their money at the hairdresser's. They didn't run away alone to South America and invest in an expedition to a mangrove swamp after diamonds. This girl wasn't like any of them: even Laura hadn't been like her.

He sat down on the bed and waited. He closed his eyes for a moment and tried to see Laura, but no picture came. Tom Clay had said No. Stick to Aztec ruins. What would he have said about going after diamonds? He was a rational man: he'd have said it was nonsense. He'd have taken Mel to bed, then made his way in the morning to one of the remote inland frontiers across the rainforests.

'All right, you can go in now,' she said, nodding at the bathroom. She was naked except for a pair of flat-soled bedroom sandals and a tiny square wristwatch. She smelled of soap and toothpaste. He held her against him and kissed her and her lips were still cold and scarcely moved. 'Hurry up,' she said, 'it's getting awfully late.'

He undressed quickly in the bathroom, and when he came back she was in bed with the light out. He climbed in beside her and the bed suddenly felt cramped and small under the tight cotton sheet; he heaved it off and heard her mutter something, as he pressed himself against her, hard against her belly and big, cool breasts, her lips and legs opening methodically, moving with him without a murmur as he tasted her skin, touched her hair and the brisk flick of eyelashes. And he knew, even in the darkness, that her eyes were open.

It became very still in the room.

'What's the matter?' she said, in a whisper beside his ear that seemed to roar through his head.

'Nothing.' He kissed her, but she slid her mouth away and tried to move from under him. 'Let's go to sleep now.'

He lay beside her, sweating, shaking a little; wanting her still yet knowing it had all gone wrong, and dreading it. He wanted her and he would go on wanting her; and she'd escaped him. She sat up and pulled up the sheet over them both, and her body felt as cool and clean as when she had come in naked from the bathroom. He thought bitterly again of Laura and suddenly he remembered her very well: warm and wet and humming in the darkness, and chattering afterward, going to sleep with her knee pulled up between his thighs, and how she used to sit beside him and cut the fingernails of his left hand.

'I'm sorry,' said Mel; as she moved her shoulder from under him and turned over. 'It's just I'm so sleepy.'

He didn't say anything; he lay and listened to her breathing, and felt the desire in his body being converted, as though it were some noxious chemical substance, into a sour rage; and for a moment he thought he might understand a little of what her husband had felt. But that was a mean thought. She had loved her husband; it made all the difference, just as the bishops and editorial writers said. Clay was more practical in his advice, but it added up to the same thing in the end. He didn't love this girl at all.

Sometime later he tried to pull her round, caressing her, kissing her wide mouth. After a moment he heard her say:

'You mustn't let Sammy see you lying here when he comes. You'll be up, won't you?'

'Yes,' he said. 'I'll be up.'

It was over and they were equal now and she was just a girl who was coming along on an expedition to find diamonds in a swamp. Perfectly straightforward. Tonight was just a passing interlude. One night, a dead man under his bed; the next, a nice girl who missed her husband. Clay had said, take a sea trip — a change of air. He'd have a lugubrious laugh if he ever knew.

CHAPTER FIVE: THE MAN IN ROOM SIX

The brown emptiness of the plateau rolled past them, far out to where the darkness was breaking up at the edge of the sky, as the tires drummed along the concrete highway to the south.

The top of the Ford was down, the back seats piled above the level of the doors with the tent and sleeping bags strapped across the top, covering three rucksacks of clothing and cooking equipment, two Winchester repeater rifles and four ammunition cases with a hundred rounds in each. The trunk was stacked with the tinned food and water and kerosene cans which buried the maps, compass, binoculars and medicine chest. A crate of twelve bottles of White Horse whisky stood between the tent and the back seat, together with Mel's beautifying kit, two boxes of fifty 12-bore Number One shot and one box of fifty Henry Clay cigars. The well-worn double-barreled shotgun lay on the floor in the front between Ben's feet. It was loaded. If they were stopped by a police check, the plan was to make out they were tourists heading for a climbing jaunt in the Hiarra Mountains.

Mel was driving, her hair under a scarlet scarf, dressed in a white cotton shirt, dust-colored slacks and rope-soled sandals. Ben and Ryderbeit each wore sombreros of gray felt with stovepipe domes and broad brims that flopped down over their necks and most of their faces. Ryderbeit was already smoking a cigar which he did not remove, as he said: 'We should make Benisalem by late afternoon, in time to dump the car and find the mules and a guide.'

Mel said: 'I hope the car'll be safe down there. It's my last worldly asset!'

'It'll be safe. Well leave it at the hotel there and pay them fifty pesos to look after it. It's not the car I'm worried about.'

'What then?' said Ben.

'Just that we might not be the only visitors in Benisalem tonight.'

'And if not?'

Ryderbeit grinned: 'If not, we leave them to call the game. They killed Stopes, and they got the map, but Benisalem's not a good place to start a shooting match.'

Ben saw Mel throw him a quick glance. He thought: *If it was Ryderbeit who had killed Stopes there wouldn't be anybody in Benisalem — unless he was one of the gang, in which case they'd be waiting there for him to join them. Then what would happen?* It was not a happy thought; but then he still had no proof. He said: 'Where do we sleep tonight?'

'In the hotel in Benisalem. We leave tomorrow when the sun's up.'

'Will it be safe for me to stop in a hotel?'

'They won't have heard of you out there. Most of them can't even read.'

Ben sat back and thought: *It'll be a joke if they have heard of me!* — as he watched the road sweeping up towards them, straight as an airstrip, running out into the parched wastes where all life and movement seemed to have stopped as in a painting: the arms of the giant cacti signaling to each other; the static groups of mules and men marooned to scratch a living out of this wilderness that stretched from Parataxín in the north to the volcanoes of the Cordillera Hiarra in the south. And as he watched, something of the loneliness and hopelessness of these people was communicated to him. He remembered that his own situation was scarcely better than theirs: he had no job, and not even any money now, except five pounds in pesos — all that was left after buying the supplies — and he was still wanted by the police. On the other hand, somewhere out there ahead lay the Cordillera that cut off the desert and the unmapped swamps where there might be a fortune waiting for him. He could not believe it though: Ryderbeit was crazy and Mel was just doing it for kicks. And yet the one man who had really known about those diamonds had been murdered less that thirty-six hours earlier. It was the worst possible evidence to rely on: but it was evidence all the same. The diamonds might be there.

Ryderbeit was asleep with the charred cigar butt still between his teeth. The road hummed on. Mel's face behind the dark glasses held a quiet contentment: she might have been motoring on holiday in the south of France. Ben wondered again: childhood in Kent; ballet school in London; nice marriage in a registry office. Now running off after diamonds with two strangers? Did it make sense?

The sun was high and burning now, and the only vehicle they had passed since leaving Parataxín two hours ago was a ramshackle truck with two Indians asleep in the back. Slowly the landscape was showing forlorn signs of vegetation: blotched patches of scrubland sprawling into the haze where there was the occasional strip of white walls belonging to a hacienda. Then suddenly, perhaps two miles ahead, a dark blob began to form at the point where the road touched the horizon. It swelled and fluctuated like something seen through water, then broke up and became two blobs, growing larger until, about half a mile away, they saw it was two men astride what looked like a couple of squat animals.

Mel only began to brake when one of them moved into the road, waving a stick with a disk which flashed in the sun. They were two black-uniformed motorcycle police wearing white helmets and white gloves. For a moment Ben thought of the police on the road to Bordeaux. He felt slightly sick. These two had skeleton-handled machine pistols slung on their backs.

The Ford slowed down as the policeman with the disk signaled Mel to pull over to the side. His companion was sitting on his cycle a few yards on, waiting. Ben noticed that both machines were fitted with radios. He began to sweat.

The first man came round to Mel's side and touched a white glove to his helmet. He was a young mulatto with large black-luster eyes. He said in Spanish: 'Where are you going, Señora?'

'Benisalem.' She gave him a bright smile.

'May I see the papers for the car, Señora?' She had them ready in her hand, in a pigskin folder. He took it and looked at the logbook issued in Mexico City and her international driving license and insurance card, while Ben sat as far down in the seat as he could. It seemed a long time, out there in the silent emptiness, alone with two armed men only a few feet away. He thought of the shotgun between his legs. Ryderbeit was awake now, not moving, saying nothing.

The policeman handed back the folder and saluted: '*Bueno viaje, Señora.*' Mel switched on the ignition.

Ryderbeit sighed: 'Polite boy. Actually called you Señora!' He looked at Ben: 'You're sweating, soldier.'

'It's hot.'

'You're damned right it's hot!' Ryderbeit cried, as they drew away. 'Just a routine police check. What's the matter with you? If you're going to wet your pants every time you see a cop, what are you going to be like when you see a Xatu?'

'Go to hell,' said Ben; he reached into the back and lifted a bottle of White Horse out of the crate.

'For your information,' Ryderbeit went on, 'if either of those boys had made a false move I'd have that shotgun on them before they had time to make the sign of the Cross. Those machine pistols would have come in handy.'

Mel said sharply: 'You leave the police to me, Sammy. A nice smile's all they need.'

Ryderbeit grunted: 'I liked the look of those machine pistols!'

Ben slipped the whisky down by his foot next to the shotgun then lay back and closed his eyes. He felt vaguely ashamed of having shown his fear. Mel hadn't seemed to notice though; she seemed to notice nothing except the strip of shimmering gray that raced toward them out of the horizon where the volcanoes lay.

Toward the middle of the afternoon the horizon ahead began to thicken into a smoky darkness. At first, they thought they were driving into a storm; then slowly the darkness grew into the long high wall of the Cordillera Hiarra. The sun began to slant down behind them and they caught their first glimpse of Benisalem — a blur at the foot of the mountains — and far above they could now see the snow line.

It was a small dark town built out of lava bricks, with a black cathedral and a plaza where the hotel stood behind a row of palm trees drooping like broken parasols. The town seemed deserted except for a few Indians who squatted in the dust, watching the car pull up in front of the hotel.

The proprietor was a glossy *mestizo* in a white suit and black bow tie; he came skipping out, telling them they would have his best rooms overlooking the plaza. Each room had a basin, he said, and the car would be as safe as if it were his own. He bowed almost double when Ryderbeit gave him a fifty-pesos note.

They drove the car round to a yard at the back and parked it in a stable, unloading only what they needed for the night — which included the guns, in case of trouble. The rest of the equipment would have to stay in the car until they had hired the mules. There were two mules already in the yard.

Back in the hotel the *mestizo* gave them the police forms to fill out. He took no notice of the guns, and was too busy fussing and bowing around them to ask for their passports. Ben filled out his name as Tom Clay, businessman.

By the sound of the hotel they seemed to be the only guests. There was a silent unsettling atmosphere about the place — a sense of anticipation hanging in the warm twilight, as Ben sat up in his flyblown room, drinking whisky and studying the cloth-backed map of the route through the Hiarra. Mel was in her own room washing, and Ryderbeit had gone somewhere nearby where the proprietor said he could hire good mules and a guide for tomorrow. He had gone alone, telling Ben to stay in the hotel: if there was anyone in town ready to make trouble, he said, the hotel would be the safest place. Yet the idea of Ryderbeit going out alone worried Ben. The only reassuring thing was knowing that all three guns were still in the hotel.

Then it occurred to him that this in itself was sinister. If Ryderbeit had gone out unarmed, did it not mean that he wasn't expecting trouble? — that instead of going to hire mules, he might have gone to meet some friends who had already arrived? But then why leave the guns? Ben had looked into Ryderbeit's room just after he had left and seen the Winchester on top of his rucksack; the door had not even been locked. The second rifle was here in his own room, and Mel had taken the shotgun in with her.

He drank another whisky, then took the bottle and went along to Mel's room. She was putting up her hair in front of a slab of mirror over the basin. 'Like a drink?' he said.

'Love one!' She turned and let her hair drop onto her shoulders. 'Did Sammy have any luck with the mules?'

'He hasn't come back yet.' He poured her a whisky in a tooth glass, which she took without adding water, then sat down on the bed and for a moment they sipped their drinks in silence, listening to the insects pinging against the wire mesh over the window. Outside it was already growing dark; a row of acetylene lamps flared on across the plaza. Ryderbeit had now been gone half an hour.

'You know,' said Ben at last, 'I've had a funny feeling since we arrived that we've been expected here. I can't explain it exactly — it's just that that little fellow downstairs seemed a little too pleased to see us.'

She shrugged: 'Well, why shouldn't he? He can't get many tourists out here — and we paid him enough to keep the car.'

'It's not just that. I think he knew we were coming.'

'But that's impossible! How could he?' She had put down her glass and for a moment Ben watched her long silhouette as she began to scoop up her hair in her fingers.

'Because somebody told him,' he said at last.

She swung round: 'Who?'

'Sammy, for instance.' His voice was quite steady. 'It's just an idea. It would fit if he was involved with a gang that killed Stopes and stole the map.'

'But that's ridiculous! If he was with a gang, why would he have come this far with us?'

'I've been wondering about that too. The only reason can be money — and the car. He's got more than a thousand dollars' worth of equipment out of us both. That's useful to any gang.'

She stood staring at him, her hands still behind her head. 'But how can you be sure?'

'I'm not sure.' She had turned back to the mirror and he could see the soft whiteness at the nape of her neck as she began putting in the pins again.

'Well, supposing you are right?' she said. 'What are we going to do?'

He glanced down at the floor where the shotgun lay beside her toilet case. 'There's nothing we can do,' he said, 'except wait and see what happens.' He stood up to turn the light on, then paused and moved over to her. She finished putting the pins in, and when she turned her face looked even wider than before, with a bold exciting beauty that made him swallow hard. He stood in front of her, only a few inches away and said: 'Perhaps I was imagining it.'

She smiled and patted his arm: 'I think so. Sammy's all right really. Your trouble is you're overanxious — like today with those police. You don't want to worry so much.'

He felt a jab of anger and sat down again on the bed. 'If I'm being overanxious, Mel, you're being a bit too damned sanguine. We're in a dangerous situation — don't fool yourself! A man got murdered yesterday, and the murderer's still at large, and it's more than likely that he — or they — are going to turn up here.'

'Yes, I know that.' She stepped round him and turned on the light. 'But there's nothing we can do about it till whoever they are show up. And don't go on saying Sammy did it because it'll only lead to trouble.' She smiled suddenly, holding out her empty glass: 'This is going to be our last evening in civilization, so let's enjoy it!' She came forward and he gave her another whisky without standing up. They touched glasses and drank, then looked up suddenly. There was a quick tread in the passage outside, then a rap on the door. Ryderbeit's voice called: 'Mel — are you there?'

'Yes, come in,' she said, without moving.

Ryderbeit came in, shut the door and locked it. When he turned, Ben could see at once that something was wrong. The greenish pallor had crept back into his face and he was breathing quickly, high in his lungs with an asthmatic hunching of the shoulders. 'You haven't seen anybody?'

'No. Should we?' said Ben.

Ryderbeit didn't answer; he took Ben's glass and poured it full of whisky, emptying it in two gulps. His eyes widened and he blinked. 'That's better!' His breathing became slower.

'Did you get the mules?' said Mel.

He nodded: 'Six of 'em — they're down in the yard with the car. The guide'll be here in the morning.' He leaned over and gave himself another whisky.

'What's the matter, Sammy?' said Ben. 'You look as though you've seen a ghost.'

Ryderbeit looked up and began to smile: 'Yes, funny you should say that.' His voice was very soft. 'Down the corridor — in Room 6. I haven't actually seen it,' he added, sipping his second whisky, 'just what the proprietor told me downstairs. Very helpful he was — even showed me the entry in the register. Thought it might have been a friend of ours. Checked in this morning and hired a couple of mules — the ones we saw down in the yard.'

'What the hell are you talking about?' said Ben.

'Our fellow guest. We're not the only ones here, you know.'

'Who is it?'

Ryderbeit grinned over his glass: 'A Kraut called Hitzi Leiter.'

He went on grinning at them and for a moment neither of them said anything. A pack of dogs began yelping distantly.

'But Hitzi Leiter's dead!' Mel cried at last.

Ryderbeit nodded.

'Have you seen him?' said Ben.

'I told you — just the name in the book downstairs. H. Leiter, German nationality, Room 6. Almost like an invitation to step up and have a drink with him. Which is perhaps exactly what he wants me to do. Only I thought I'd better warn you both first — as well as take a few precautions.' He stepped round the bed and picked up the shotgun. His color had improved with the whisky. 'It gave me quite a turn, I can tell you!' he added. 'I've seen men die — I've even killed a few — but I never saw one rise yet.'

'Then who the hell is in Room 6?' said Ben.

Ryderbeit held the gun in both hands and nodded at the door: 'Shall we go along and find out?'

Suddenly Ben was scared. Something of the spooky terror of reading ghost stories in his childhood came back to him. He calmed himself, saying half aloud: 'Either there are two people in this country called Leiter with the initial H., or somebody's playing a peculiar joke.'

Mel looked at them both: 'Can I come too?'

'You want to?' said Ben.

'Why not?'

He shrugged. 'Why not?' — that was the key to her whole life: Why not marry a sadist, run away to South America, stake all her savings in a treasure hunt for diamonds, hop into bed with a stranger, go ghost-catching down hotel corridors? 'Come on,' he said.

Ryderbeit unlocked the door.

There was a single light in the passage, just strong enough to read the numbers on the doors. Ryderbeit led the way with the shotgun. Ben and Mel followed almost on tiptoe. They reached the room marked 6. 'Is he in there?' Ben whispered.

Ryderbeit put his head close to the door and knocked. There was a pause; a voice called: '*Quién es?*'

'Hitzi Leiter?' Ryderbeit had raised his voice, and there was a threatening confidence in it now. Ben was very glad to have him there.

For a moment nothing happened. Then the voice said again, much closer this time: '*Quién es?*'

'We want to talk to you,' said Ryderbeit, in English.

The lock turned immediately and the door opened: 'O.K., come inside!'

Ben stood looking at the young white-haired man he had seen two nights ago in the Casa Sphinx. This time he was wearing drill trousers, an immaculate khaki shirt and boots of polished calf leather. Against one leg he held a rifle equipped with a telescopic lens.

He could not have been much older than twenty-five; his smooth round face had a sharp nose whittled to a point and his white hair grew evenly over his head like fur. For a moment Ben had an urge to walk up and stroke it: there was something luxuriantly obscene about it.

The man's blue arrow-shaped eyes flickered over each of them, pausing for a moment on Mel, then he stepped back and closed the door. 'Put your gun down please.' He spoke with a slightly shrill American accent that had no trace of German in it.

Ryderbeit advanced into the room, looking solemnly at the rifle in his hand. 'That's a very handsome weapon you have there,' he said slowly.

The man swung the rifle up under his arm till it was pointing at Ryderbeit's knees. 'Put your gun down!' he snapped, and his voice was almost as high as a girl's.

Ryderbeit glared dangerously for a moment as the two of them faced each other, fingering their guns. 'I'm an awfully good shot,' he murmured; then shrugged and put the shotgun on the table. The young man smiled: 'O.K., make yourselves at home.'

On the floor was an aluminium-frame rucksack with ropes and cooking equipment tied to the flaps, and a rolled-up lightweight tent and two canvas kit bags. Ryderbeit looked them over and nodded: 'All right, who are you?'

The young man sat down at the table and laid his rifle beside the shotgun, pointing them both away at the wall. 'You know who I am. The name's Leiter. You just called me outside.'

'Like hell! Then how is it that Hitzi Leiter blew his brains out a few weeks ago?'

The young man grinned — a winning, boyish grin that became a giggle: 'So that was the story that crazy old man told you about me, huh?' He sat shaking his head, still grinning. 'So you must be the photographer, Sammy Ryderbeit — Stopes' pal?' He turned to Ben and Mel: 'And who are you?'

'Never mind about them,' said Ryderbeit. 'Just talk about yourself first. What are you doing here?'

'Exactly what you're doing, Ryderbeit. Please don't be stupid.'

'When did you get here? Are you alone?'

'Oh sure. I got here this morning on the bus — twelve hours from Parataxín. I must have missed hearing you arrive. I've been sleeping all day.' He paused, his hand resting on his varnished rifle. 'But I'm sure glad you showed up! I think it makes everything much easier, doesn't it?' His round face lit up with an expression of childish innocence, spoiled only by the sly, arrow-shaped eyes.

'Show me your passport,' said Ryderbeit.

The young man put his hand to his hip pocket and drew out the slim gray Reispass of the Bundesrepublik. Ryderbeit studied it, then showed it to the others. It gave the name of Heinrich Wilhelm Leiter, born on the 28th August 1935 in Konigsberg — in what was then East Prussia and now the Soviet Union. Profession, engineer. Color of eyes, blue; color of hair, blond.

Ben looked up at that round white crop. The description noted against 'special peculiarities,' None, and the photograph made him look about twelve years old. The rest of the passport was full of South American and United States visas.

Ben handed it back to him. 'You speak very good English, Mr. Leiter.'

'I lived a lot in the States,' the German said, and put the passport away.

'All right, Hitzi,' said Ryderbeit. 'Now tell us what happened out in that volcano with Stopes.'

The German gave him a thoughtful stare, his eyes growing crafty. 'First you tell me what Stopes told you,' he said at last.

Ryderbeit gave him Stopes' version of how, covered with mosquito bites, Leiter had apparently returned to the volcano and had shot himself.

Hitzi Leiter began to giggle: 'Oh that's great! That's crazy! Sure I got bitten by a few mosquitoes, and the old bastard gave me almost enough medicine to kill me. That's just what he wanted to do! I don't remember what he gave me — I don't remember anything. I was out for two days. And when I came round again, I was lying in that cave in the volcano with not even a blanket over me. Stopes had gone and taken every darned thing with him! Just left me up there to die like an animal!'

'How did you get back?'

'I was lucky — one chance in a million. A party of Indians from a pueblo just south of here had gone up over the Hiarra and round the desert. I never knew what they were doing there. Stopes told me sometimes the Indians go up to find the Eldorado over the mountains. There's a lot of superstition in these parts.'

Ryderbeit nodded: 'So they got you back here to Benisalem?'

'No, to their pueblo. I came here later, then five days ago I got back to Parataxín. It took me about two weeks to get fit again.'

'You look pretty fit to me, Hitzi. You're a lucky boy! One chance in a million, hey?' He grinned at the German: 'As I said, that's a very handsome gun you got there. Looks to me like a .416. What's sometimes called an elephant-gun, isn't it?'

Hitzi Leiter's only movement was a tightening of the fingers round the stock of his telescopic rifle. Ryderbeit stood poised forward on his toes, watching him with fixed intensity, and for a moment Ben thought he was going to leap at him. 'I don't blame you at all, Hitzi. It's a beautiful gun. And after all, it's yours, isn't it? It never belonged to Stopes.'

Hitzi Leiter's wrist flicked upward and swung the rifle round on the edge of the table, pointing it at the middle of Ryderbeit's body. 'Don't move! This is a big gun — it'll blow a hole straight through you and the wall behind.'

'I bet it will!' Ryderbeit breathed. The rifle was absolutely steady; Hitzi Leiter's movement had been so sudden that it gave the impression not only of agility but great strength, although the rest of him looked quite frail. 'The gun's yours,

Hitzi,' Ryderbeit added: 'and the map, too. You drew it, didn't you? Where is the map, Hitzi?'

The German glanced at the rucksack on the floor: 'In there.'

Ben heard Mel give a little gasp beside him: she opened her mouth to speak, but he gripped her arm and motioned her to say nothing, while Ryderbeit went on: 'So you got back to Parataxín and looked up Stopes, and he told you everything you needed to know — all about us planning to go back after the diamonds — then you got him to show you where the map and the gun were, and then you killed him.'

Neither Hitzi Leiter nor his gun moved. Ryderbeit sank back onto his heels and nodded: 'We found him yesterday, Hitzi — under the bed where you put him. I don't mind — he wasn't all that good a friend. But why wait till the night before last? You'd been back in Parataxín at least a couple of weeks.'

'I wanted to see what the old man was playing at,' Hitzi Leiter said. 'I went up to the club a couple o' times and watched him — seeing if he was making contacts. I was going to kill him anyway. He deserved it.'

Ryderbeit shrugged: 'Perhaps he did. But why the other night?'

'Because I knew he was planning something, and I didn't want to waste any more time.'

'That was the only reason?' said Ryderbeit.

'Sure — that, and to get back at him. I followed him from the club to his flat. He was pretty scared when he saw me — and I think he'd been hitting the bottle a bit. Anyway, I got him to tell me everything, then I knifed him.' He gave a nervous giggle, looking round the room.

'Why did he let you in?' said Ryderbeit.

'Oh well, first I knocked, you see, and he said, "Is that you, Mr. Morris?" — so I said "Yes," just like that. It was easy.' He giggled again, and as Ben watched him he felt a surge of revulsion that made him want to jump out and smash that round, cool, delinquent face. It was a cross between a cunning old man and a child that likes pulling wings off butterflies.

Ryderbeit said: 'All right, Hitzi. So Stopes is dead and now we know who did it. Where do we go from here?'

'Back to the river!' the German cried, his face lighting up again with its boyish grin. 'Things will be just the same, only now there are four of us and we have a lot of extra equipment, so it should be all just fine! Only one thing,' and he gripped the rifle again, looking slowly round the room: 'I'm the boss! This is my show and I give the orders. There'll be equal shares for all of us, but if I say something goes, it goes!' He paused for effect, then turned to Ben: 'Aren't you the guy I saw up in the club the other night with Stopes?'

Ben nodded.

'What's your name?'

Ben told him and the German gave a shrill whine: 'So, you're Mr. Morris! Thanks, Morris! If it hadn't been for you, I mightn't have got in the other night.'

Ben clenched his fists and said nothing. Hitzi Leiter was now talking to Mel: 'You're maybe Mrs. Morris, huh?'

'I am not.' Ben could not tell whether it was the question which offended her, or just the presence of Hitzi Leiter. She was looking at him with total contempt and the German seemed to feel it and moved his eyes away from her, simpering slightly: 'I don't want to be rude, Miss—?'

'MacDougall. And you can be as rude as you like.'

'O.K., O.K., but how come a girl gets into the setup?'

'Just that she's paying for it,' said Ben. 'Both of us are — and don't forget it!'

Hitzi Leiter frowned: 'But it's no darned setup for a girl. I know, for Chrissake, I've done the trip before. I don't think she should come.'

Mel stood and looked him up and down, slowly, as though he were something very disagreeable. 'I don't give a damn what you think, Mr. Leiter,' she said finally. 'By the look of you, I'd say that if you can get through to that river, so can I.'

Hitzi Leiter frowned. 'I'm still not crazy about going with a girl.'

'And I'm not crazy about going with you, Mr. Leiter.' She gave him an icy smile: 'I can think of a lot nicer people to spend a month with than a cheap little psychopathic murderer.'

Her voice was quite level as she spoke and for a moment they were all too startled to react. Ben remembered thinking afterward, *I never thought she had it in her.*

Hitzi Leiter had gone very white. At first he just sat and stared at her, his eyes bulging like blue marbles. Then he stood up very quickly and came toward her. At the same moment Ryderbeit jumped at the table and grabbed up the shotgun.

Hitzi Leiter slapped Mel twice, a back and front slap across both cheeks, as Ryderbeit lifted the gun till both barrels were aimed at the German's back.

Ben leaped forward and felt all the tensions of the last three days suddenly released within him. He had a split image of Mel with the crimson finger marks swelling up on both cheeks, and Hitzi Leiter's face with its pointed nose and ball of white fur, and when he hit it, it sounded as though he were striking a hollow pumpkin, and he could hear Ryderbeit yelling: 'Hold it!' and Mel began to shout something, and he went on hitting at the round white head until it had fallen down somewhere near the floor.

He stopped and blinked, his fists numb. Mel was behind him, sitting on the bed. Ryderbeit came round the table, still holding the shotgun, and nudged Hitzi Leiter with his foot. 'Come on, get up. You're not that badly hurt.'

The German cowered against the wall, whimpering behind his clasped hands. Ryderbeit took hold of his arm and hauled him up; there was blood on his khaki shirt. 'My eye! My eye!' he moaned.

'What's the matter with your eye? Take your hands away! How can I see if you don't take your hands away?'

Ben sat down next to Mel and put an arm round her shoulder: 'Are you all right?'

'Of course I am.' She put her fingers up to the edges of her eyes and sniffed: 'It was my fault — I shouldn't have said that. I think I'll go now. I'm tired.'

Ben went with her to the door: 'Don't you want anything to eat?'

'No, I'm not hungry. Good night.' She went out and closed the door.

Hitzi Leiter was sitting at the table, one hand over his eye, the other holding a handkerchief across his nose and mouth. Ryderbeit stood over him with the shotgun. He said to Ben: 'It's all right, you'd better clear out.' He winked at him over the German's white hair. 'Not to worry — I'll smooth it out.'

Ben glared down at Hitzi Leiter; he was still very angry: 'I thought you were going to use the shotgun on him just now — blow a hole right through him, as the little bastard put it earlier.'

'No, no, soldier! We can't do a thing like that — we need him. He's got the map — and remember, he's the only one who's been to that river.' He prodded the German with the butt of the shotgun: 'Only from now Hitzi's not the boss any more. When Hitzi says something goes, it doesn't go. We discuss it. And if we disagree over it, we think of something else. We all take equal shares and have equal duties and work together in the common interest, for the common good of each and every one of us.' He looked up and grinned: 'Sounds beautiful, doesn't it? Pure democracy! We may not be able to get along as the best of friends in the next few weeks, but at least we can try not to finish up shooting each other.'

Ben looked down at Hitzi and nodded. 'I hope you're right.'

'Sleep well, soldier!'

Hitzi Leiter sat holding his face and said nothing.

Mel had the rifle in her hand when she opened her door to Ben a moment later. She was fully dressed, her cheeks still flushed and her eyes bright, but not with tears. She looked excited and nervous as she let the butt down to the floor, standing in the doorway without moving. 'Oh, it's you! Is anything wrong?'

'What do you think? You were in there too. We've got a murderer on our hands — as you so tactfully told him.'

She nodded: 'Yes, I'm afraid that was rather silly of me, but he did deserve it, didn't he? He's a horrid little fellow!'

'He's dangerous, Mel, and it looks as though we're stuck with him for the next few weeks.'

'Sammy wants to take him along, does he?'

'I'm afraid so. Sammy seems to think he's going to be a great help as he's the only one who knows exactly how to get to the river.'

She shrugged: 'Well, that's quite true. He'll be very useful.'

Ben looked hard at her, suddenly exasperated by her coolness; after all, she had been the one who had precipitated this whole ugly situation by insulting Hitzi Leiter in the first place. She still hadn't moved; from behind her the dim yellow light from the room shone on the edges of her hair. There was no sound at all in the hotel. She suddenly yawned. 'God I'm sleepy!'

He nodded sourly. Either it was the oldest excuse in the world, or she didn't have the stamina. If she was as tired as this every night in civilization, what would she be like after a few days in a swamp?

'Do you want anything to eat?' he asked.

'No. Just sleep, that's all.'

He took a step forward, close to her, but she moved quickly back behind the door. 'No, not tonight. Please, not while we're on the trip. I don't know if you understand, Ben, but…'

'I don't.'

She gave him her hard dead stare. 'What's the use? We don't really want each other. Last night was special, you know.'

'Yes, I know,' he said. She was leaning against the door, closing it gently but deliberately. 'I do understand,' she said, 'about your wife and everything.'

He nodded again, and thought, *I'm sure you understand everything!* The silence in the hotel began to worry him. He wondered what Ryderbeit and Hitzi Leiter were doing.

'It's much better not to get involved, Ben.'

He looked away from her, down the deserted corridor, and said: 'Perhaps later, when we get back? If we ever get back.'

'Yes, perhaps.' She smiled: 'Goodnight, Ben.'

He turned and heard her close the door and lock it. *Sensible girl*, he thought, *considering her fellow guests. Nice and sympathetic too. One night spent in her bed, the next getting the door politely closed in his face. Every night a surprise*, he thought. *Better than Clay's flat in London.*

He went downstairs to the lobby where a bald dog was loping about near the door to the kitchen. The proprietor came up smiling and rubbing his hands, bowing him into an empty dining room where an Indian waiter with a pigtail smoothed out a grubby tablecloth. No one else came into the dining room. The food was so foul as to curb all hunger: black soup and lumps of black fruit stuffed with what looked like sawdust, a piece of dark stringy meat and some shriveled maize. He drank some tequila afterward to burn out the taste, then went up to his room. He thought of dropping in on Ryderbeit, but something told him it would be better to leave him. Ryderbeit was probably still in with Hitzi Leiter: as organizer of the expedition he would have a lot to discuss with Hitzi. And Hitzi might not be in the mood to see Ben again so soon.

That night, as he lay alone in bed and thought about the evening, he decided there was nothing about it he liked. Mel was the first girl to arouse his interest since Laura had died, and now even the sudden excitement of finding her had been quenched almost before it had begun. But now she held another, more positive interest for him. He needed her. In the next few weeks he might need her very much indeed. He was remembering again her outburst against Hitzi Leiter. She had called him a psychopath: and she had probably been right.

So that made two of them — Hitzi Leiter and Sammy Ryderbeit. Half the party: both used to guns, both self-confessed killers, both slightly unbalanced — Hitzi Leiter in a sly vicious way, giggling about having stabbed an old man in the back; Ryderbeit with an unreasoning savagery, whether it was mutilating his wife, butchering a pig, or up in his cockpit over an African village, cackling at the terror he was spreading below. Ben had not heard all Ryderbeit's exploits; there were no doubt others, perhaps even more grisly. And although he had been wrong suspecting him of Stopes' murder, he knew he would never really trust the man. But Hitzi Leiter was even more disturbing.

And as he lay in bed he wondered if there would be some unholy alliance between the two of them. They were the experts, after all: Hitzi knew how to get back to the river, Ryderbeit knew how to recognize raw diamonds when he saw them. All Ben and Mel had done was supply the cash. They were expendable now. And that evening they had also made a dangerous enemy. Hitzi Leiter had not looked the type who would easily forgive and forget.

CHAPTER SIX: HIGH RIDE

They were up before sunrise, loading the mules down in the yard while it was still dark. No one was awake to see them, and they worked fast and silently by the light of torches. Hitzi Leiter loaded his own mules by himself in the corner. He was wearing dark glasses and his face was puffed and purple. The only words spoken in the half-hour they worked were occasional instructions from Ryderbeit. Three of the six mules he had hired were fitted with stirrup saddles. All the equipment was strapped onto the other three, except the guns — all of them loaded — and an emergency supply of food and water, which was shared between the three riders in case any of the pack mules broke loose. The guns were slung through straps fitted under the stirrups. Ryderbeit took charge of the maps, compass and binoculars, as well as providing himself with the bottle of whisky they'd opened the day before and a pocketful of ammunition for his Winchester.

The guide arrived while they were working. He was a small neat Indian dressed in white, holding his sombrero in one hand and his mule by the other. Ryderbeit grunted at him, and he went over and stood beside the wall waiting.

It was just getting light when they started. Each pack mule had been leashed to a rider, and the column moved out in pairs, the guide leading, with Ryderbeit behind him. Hitzi Leiter took up the rear.

The town was cool and still, and the mules plodded through it with a slow rhythm, heading for the mountains ahead. The saddles had been deformed by heat and wear, and Ben found the stirrups too short for him; after a couple of hundred yards he got down and walked. Mel did the same a few minutes later. She pulled her animal up alongside him and said: 'We're going to get very sore up there after a few days of this.'

'I expect that'll be the least of our troubles,' he said, and threw a quick glance over his shoulder. Hitzi Leiter was riding about twenty yards behind them; he had a big straw sombrero pulled down over his face and he was looking at the ground.

'Did you talk to our German friend again after I saw you last night?' she asked.

'No. Sammy dealt with him — I don't know how successfully. But I noticed this morning he'd got his damned great gun back.'

'Is that very bad?'

'It's not good, that's for sure,' said Ben. 'Between us we created a nice little situation last night. I'm afraid he may try to get back at us.'

'You think so?' She sounded remarkably calm.

'I think it's in the cards.' He walked on, beginning to feel uneasy, with an itching at the back of his neck, knowing that Hitzi Leiter was only those few yards behind, up on the mule with the telescopic rifle slung under his stirrup. Ben wondered how long it would take him to draw it: not long, if his performance the evening before was anything to go by.

After a moment Mel said: 'Perhaps we ought to try and make it up to Hitzi. We don't want him hating our guts for the whole trip.'

'He can apologize to you first. Anyway, he'll hate us whatever we do — he's that sort of person.'

The track was beginning to rise now and the first slopes of the mountains were less than a mile away. Ryderbeit was studying one of the maps, with the compass strapped to the saddle beside him. Soon afterward he jumped down and raised his arm. 'All right, hold it! Well stop here and make coffee.' He turned and began to consult with the Indian over the map.

Ben and Mel made the coffee between them — a couple of pints — handing the metal cups round and pouring the rest into a thermos flask. Ben gave a cup to Hitzi Leiter and said: '*Prosit!*'

The German took it and said nothing.

Ryderbeit had laced his with a dose of whisky; he looked cheerful but quiet, with the same professional efficiency that Ben had seen while they bought the supplies in Parataxín. He and Hitzi hadn't spoken since they had left the town.

From now on they began to climb steeply, out of the scrubland of the plateau into banks of sandstone and pumice rock where the track had been cut in a terraced formation, looping above them in an almost vertical zigzag for several thousand feet.

It was light now, and growing hot, and there were no clouds in the mountains. The peaks were a shining white in the early sun, but some of the highest were blurred with a dark fuzz from the volcanoes.

Ben and Mel had remounted, leaning forward in the saddles against the incline, the pace of the mules dragging in the loose lava pebbles. The track had narrowed so that they were now riding in a single file, each leading his pack mule. The animals had pulled out from the side of the mountain until they were now treading the very edge of the drop. Ben kept his eyes averted, feeling his spine burning each time his mule made its awkward, lurching turn. He wondered what the statistics were of mules falling to their deaths. The track here was fairly easy, but later on it would get much worse. He looked down at his own animal, wondering about his health and age. What he saw was not particularly encouraging. It was a small bony beast, its tufty fur caked with dirt like a very old rug. He thought of Hitzi Leiter's luxuriant white hair and shuddered: the German was still behind, now between him and the pack mule, but less than ten feet away.

Ben's mule made another turn, halting for a moment, then swinging out, and he caught a glimpse of the plateau far below — a hazy emptiness with Benisalem laid out like pieces on a chessboard. He looked up at Mel who was riding just in front of him; her figure was well outlined, straight-backed and firmly rounded in her sand-colored slacks. The sight distracted him from the drop below. She had a beautiful body, he thought: taller, with longer legs than his wife. He tried not to think about Laura.

His mule did another swinging turn and he closed his eyes. His fear of heights was beginning to worry him.

The sun crossed the whole sky, away from the mountains, and there was to be no shade all day.

After a couple of hours they stopped and ate some bread and cheese which Mel had bought at the hotel. From now on their diet would consist mainly of soup, beans, beef, salami, tinned vegetables and whatever fruit they might find.

Before leaving again they passed the whisky bottle around and the little Indian guide bowed and drank deeply, smiling like a child. Hitzi Leiter had eaten from his own supplies, a little away from the others, and refused the whisky. Nobody spoke to him. Ben noticed that his face was more badly bruised than he had thought: there was an open cut on his lip, and his sharp little nose was now swollen up like a cork and looked broken. Ben decided that before nightfall he would say something to him. Already, as the day wore on, he could feel the tension between them both and knew that instead of getting less it was increasing, like the heat. Sometimes, perhaps before night, it would break.

And as they rode on, still higher toward the snow line, he realized he was frightened.

Toward noon, after they had been riding for nearly five hours, the mountain sloped back on to a dome of rock like a sugarloaf. Beyond they saw the first of the volcanoes directly ahead — a gigantic flat-topped cone, its rib-like lava flanks rising dark purple to become suddenly and symmetrically white, disappearing into the smoke that drifted out into the brilliant blue.

The track had finished and a raw wind swept down, stinging their eyes with lava dust. The rock ahead was strewn with clumps of strange, evil-looking cacti with stout bodies like lead piping, covered in needle-sharp spines that swung in the wind, smacking together and making each other bleed a milky juice down their stems.

Ryderbeit had called a stop to consult again with the guide; he seemed to take no advice from Hitzi Leiter. Ben got down and walked a little to work out the cramp in his legs and ease the soreness from the saddle. He looked round for Mel. She had disappeared behind some rocks. Hitzi Leiter was up on his mule, motionless against the sky.

Ryderbeit called Ben across and pointed up the dome of rock. 'We go straight over and down. By tonight we should be past the worst, and with an early start tomorrow we can be down to the Devil's Spoon by nightfall.'

'It seems easy enough so far,' said Ben.

'So far — but we've been following a mule track. On the way down it may not be so sweet.' He looked over at Hitzi Leiter. 'We go straight over! O.K.?' he shouted.

The German raised a hand in acknowledgment.

'How did you get on with him last night?' Ben asked.

'Not so bad. We talked mostly about the river. It sounds pretty hopeful. Hitzi seems to know his stuff — says the blue clay runs along the bed for several miles, and the lava shelf from the old volcano seems to be pretty consistent right up to the river.'

Ben frowned: 'But Stopes told me Hitzi didn't know much about diamonds. That's one of the reasons he only found three.'

Ryderbeit shrugged: 'Ah, Hitzi's no man's fool. He knows a bit about 'em.'

'And how does he feel about what happened last night?'

'Oh that!' Ryderbeit grinned. 'He says he wants to kill you.'

'I see. And when's he thinking of doing it?'

'Dunno. Whenever an opportunity arises, I suppose — and he's going to have plenty.'

Ben looked closely at Ryderbeit: his hooked, dark face was concentrating on the map. 'You're serious, aren't you?' he said.

'Me? I'm serious about one thing, soldier — getting those diamonds.'

'So am I. And I don't want to get shot in the back first.'

Ryderbeit shrugged: 'That's your lookout. You hit him.'

Ben grabbed his arm and spun him round, violently. 'To hell with that! We're in this together, Sammy — you said so yourself. He hit Mel and I hit him. You'd have done the same.'

'No I wouldn't. I was there — I didn't hit him. I don't believe in striking blows in the cause of chivalry. I only hit out if somebody hits me, then I wait till he's turned his back and hit him twice as hard.' The wind howled at them again and they put their heads down against the dust. Ryderbeit laughed:

'Don't worry! Hitzi's just a nervous boy. Oversensitive. He'll get over it, but just leave him alone.'

'I'm going to! But is he going to leave me alone? He's got a gun remember — the one you so kindly allowed him to keep after last night.'

'Well, it belongs to him, doesn't it? Can't go round stealing valuable property. It's immoral!' He grinned again, screwing up his eyes into the sun. Mel was coming down the slope toward them. 'What a shape!' he murmured. 'She could be trouble, that one.'

'She could be, but don't start it. You'd be wasting your time.'

'Hey, soldier!' He turned with his cunning leer: 'You're not holding out on me, are you? I mean, I don't detect a slight note of rancor in your voice? — or is it the whisper of repressed Celtic passion?'

'Neither, Sammy. Just common sense. Leave Mel alone. She's a serious girl.'

'Serious and deep — I know it! Too deep for me. I can't be bothered any more. Samuel David Ryderbeit is grown weary of women — he'll settle for a pair of nice shiny whores up in Mexico City when we're through and rich. Mrs. MacDougall is all yours.'

She came up to them, shading her face against the wind. 'Shall we push on?'

Ryderbeit nodded and pulled the whisky out of his pocket; he took a gulp, wiped the neck on his sleeve and passed the bottle to Mel. 'Go easy on it, darling — we're high up here — more than nine thousand feet. It goes to your head fast.'

She drank and gave it to Ben. 'How's Hitzi?' she asked.

'He's in a sulk,' said Ryderbeit. 'Isn't happy about our friend Morris here.'

She looked at Ben: 'You really ought to say something to him you know. His face looks awful.'

'I'll think about it,' he said, and walked back to his mule. In fact, he was thinking that perhaps there was nothing to worry about after all. There was a lot of difference between leaving a sick man to die alone in a remote cave and giving him a well-deserved black eye. In any case, Ryderbeit didn't seem worried; or perhaps he just didn't care.

Whichever was the case, Ben had already decided what to do. Only it would have to wait till nightfall.

The ride over the dome of rock was more difficult than it had looked. There was no track now for the mule to follow, and the clumps of cacti distracted them, heading them off in opposite directions, while the guide ran between them with a stick, trying to beat them back into line.

The horizon from below had been deceptive: the dome was only one of a series of rolling rock formations, building up like the folds of a fat chin. Each time one horizon was reached, another would rise perhaps a mile ahead, and the volcanoes seemed to come no nearer. They rode on upward like this for two hours, covering less than five miles. The wind grew steadily harsher until they could feel the gritty dust in their noses and throats, working under their hats and sunglasses into their hair and eyes, even between the seams of their clothing. They reached the summit of another long hump of rock, and suddenly the wind came up over the edge and hit them like something solid. The mules backed downward, their pointed ears flattened back against their necks.

Ben just had time to see the edge of the precipice: the horizon around and below made him feel as though he were lying on his back looking at the sky. His head reeled for a moment, the wind screaming in his ears, as his mule moved down into the shelter of the dome. His pack mule was dragging hard at the rope, and the other animals were stumbling around in a circle, bumping into each other. They retreated about twenty feet down the slope, then Ryderbeit hauled in his pack mule and yelled, pointing up at the ridge: 'The wind's too much! It could blow us right off the mules. We'll have to follow along below the edge till we get into the lee of that volcano over there.' He unstrapped one of the rucksacks and dragged out windbreakers, oiled sweaters, woolen caps and snow goggles, while Mel began spreading a layer of cold cream on to her face and lips. She looked up and grinned through the white mask: 'We're going to have a lovely tan when we get back!'

'If we have any skin left to tan,' said Ben. His face and hands were already beginning to feel chapped and burned.

They began to head out to the left, with the guide leading, now on foot, and the others riding in a circle around the four pack mules. Suddenly Ben realized that Hitzi Leiter was right beside him, riding within arm's length. He was wearing yellow snow goggles, a leather helmet with earflaps tied down under his chin, and a zipped-up field-gray jacket. The cut on his mouth was swollen and raw, glistening under a layer of protective grease.

Ben had to shout to make himself heard above the wind: 'Hitzi! — I'd like to apologize for what happened last night! I hope I didn't hurt you badly.' At first he thought the German hadn't heard: he rode on without turning his head. Ben leaned sideways and tried again: 'I'm sorry about last night, Hitzi! We all got a bit overheated.'

For a moment the wind seemed to drop a little. Hitzi Leiter still did not turn his head, but his wounded mouth began to move: 'You don't have to make up to me, Mr. Morris. I've got your number already.'

Ben stared at him: 'What does that mean?'

Hitzi Leiter said nothing.

'What the hell do you mean?' Ben cried, and felt a rush of panic. 'Listen, Hitzi, I'm only trying to be friendly. Let's forget about what happened last night, shall we? Just *forget it!*'

The wind had risen again and he was shouting with all his force. Mel had turned in her saddle ahead and was looking at him. Still Hitzi Leiter said nothing; he kicked his heels into his mule, trying to pull away a little. But the animal did not respond.

Ben shouted: 'Oh, to hell with you, Hitzi Leiter!' — and this time the German turned and looked at him and grinned. It was a stiff, lopsided grin, with the corner of his mouth gummed up with grease. Suddenly Ben felt sick. He looked down and saw the telescopic .416 elephant-gun lying in the leather sling under the German's stirrup.

He thought wildly: *Bombing raid when a child — white hair — teased about it at school. He was like a schoolboy — spiteful. Never forgot a wrong done him, whether it was being left to die in a cave, or punched a couple of times in the face. Hitzi Leiter would always wait to get even — several times over.* Ben remembered those school feuds — somebody you rubbed the wrong way. The hatred and malice, the ganging up behind your back, the bullies and their hangers-on. They'd get you when you weren't looking: hide your clothes, pour ink over your books, put a dead rat in your bed. Only with Hitzi it didn't have to be ink or rats. Stopes should have known that.

I'll still have to wait till nightfall, he thought.

An hour later they were in the shelter of the first of the volcanoes, still keeping just below the ridge. The wind had dropped and they could feel the sun again, burning with a hard alpine brilliance. They finished what was left of the bread and cheese, and had coffee washed down with Scotch. Ryderbeit then walked with the guide to the top of the ridge and stood looking out toward the volcano. Ben followed them up.

He looked over the edge, and stepped quickly back. The drop was about six hundred feet into a gully of rope lava, which ran down from the side of the volcano like a black glacier, flowing far out to the left between more volcanoes — some smoking, others charred husks in the folds of the mountains — down to a distant haze that would be the beginning of the Devil's Spoon. Without even looking at the map Ben could see that the only possible route lay along the edge of the precipice to the south.

Ryderbeit came back looking solemn. 'It's going to be rough riding, soldier. We've got about six hours' light left, so we ought to get down to within half a day's march into the desert. I just hope to hell the mules make it!'

'Aren't they likely to?'

Ryderbeit shrugged: 'I don't know much about mules — except these look a pretty seedy bunch. Then I suppose if I had to make do on a diet of cacti and bits o' weed and mud and old shit I'd look pretty seedy too.' He looked up and saw Hitzi Leiter, only a few yards away, sitting on his mule watching them. 'By the way, how goes it with Sunny Boy?'

Ben hesitated: 'Hitzi, you mean? I tried to apologize to him about last night, but he wouldn't have it. It's like some damned lovers' quarrel.'

'Except that Hitzi doesn't love you, soldier! Not one little bit, he doesn't!'

For a moment Ben thought of telling him what he planned to do, then decided against it. Perhaps he would tell Mel — later, when they made camp. He started back toward his mule and heard Ryderbeit say to Hitzi Leiter: 'That's a nasty cut you got there, Hitzi. You ought to put something on it.'

Mel called out: 'There's some antiseptic cream in the medicine case!'

'I already got something on it,' Hitzi Leiter said.

Ben climbed up onto his mule and adjusted his goggles.

It was probably the goggles that saved him. They had begun to steam up and all he could see were vague blotches of darkness against the blue. Somehow it was better like this — better than closing his eyes altogether, for then he had nothing to focus on at all and grew giddy with vertigo.

They were going down now, and this was far worse than the climb up. Not only that just a few inches to his left was a sheer drop of several hundred feet, but the slow lurching motion of the mule was throwing him forward in the narrow saddle where he had nothing firm to hold on. The top of the saddle was a ridge of twisted leather that kept slipping from his grip. There were no handles or proper harness; and as the path grew steeper and more uneven, he found the safest position was leaning right forward across the mule's head, his arms round its neck, being swung around in the saddle whenever the animal had to negotiate a particularly treacherous ledge above the precipice.

His one comfort lay in knowing that Hitzi Leiter was riding at the very end of the line, three mules behind. Mel was following Ben's pack mule, leading her own in front of Hitzi Leiter's. It would be impossible to try anything here.

They had moved out of the shelter of the volcano again, with the wind howling into them, shaking the mules as though they were on wire stilts. Ben crouched forward, his head down against the icy blast, his cheek pressed between the mule's long furry ears. Once he looked down and saw the beast's hooves against the edge. They looked incredibly small and unstable, like the frayed ends of chair legs.

He tried to think about something else: about Hitzi Leiter again: that the danger was all in his imagination. With Stopes there had been a reason — several reasons. But a fist fight was not a reason, for God's sake! He'd been in fist fights before, like the time he'd hit the drunk who'd insulted Laura in that Soho club. It was all right in Soho; but punching people in this country seemed to lead to complications.

His mule had stopped. He tried looking round, but his goggles had misted over completely now. He started to lift them and something jolted into him and the mule moved off again. *Hitzi won't try anything*, he thought: *he's too busy getting those diamonds*. Yet his instinct told him otherwise; and he remembered that the last couple of times his instinct had warned him — first, on that evening in Stopes' flat, then last night in the hotel in Benisalem — both times had been about Hitzi Leiter, and both times it had been right.

To hell with instinct! he thought. It had to be either this, or moping around the bars of Guadaigil, drinking Merrybeer and missing his wife. He had wanted an antidote — something to purge him finally of his grief — and this was it. And there might even be a fortune waiting for him at the end of it.

And then he was pushed. He thought for a moment that his mule had stumbled into a rock: he felt a quick nudge just above the small of the back, then a violent thrust outward, and he lost his balance.

Perhaps if he had been able to see everything clearly — the path narrowing against a wall of rock, then the black chasm swinging up toward him — he would have lost all control. But in that split second of falling he was blind, his body reacting without his brain. The track had become level a little way back and he had been sitting almost upright, holding only loosely to the buckled edge of the saddle. He now felt it torn from his fingers and slide round under him, and he went over sideways, his arms flying out, striking something — fur, a trouser leg, a boot. His hands smacked against rock, the breath knocked out of his lungs. He pressed himself flat, with one foot and one elbow hanging over nothing. He pushed his goggles up, just in time to see the Winchester and a water can spinning down into the gully. The gun struck with a faint click and broke in two and the plastic can burst and bounced away across the rope lava.

His face was a couple of inches from the edge. He could see the hooves of another mule — not his own — about two feet away, kicking nervously. He looked up and saw Hitzi Leiter. The other mules, strung out in single file along the track ahead, had stopped. He and Hitzi Leiter had been at the end of the train.

He scrambled up on all fours and flung himself against the rock wall away from the chasm. It had been all over in less than three seconds, with perhaps another three before the rifle and water can hit the bottom. Now he had time to think: somehow his mule had got to the end of the line — probably when it had stopped about ten minutes earlier. He had been left riding just in front of Hitzi Leiter, then when the trail had begun to level out, and he had not been holding on so hard, the German must have pulled up close, put his boot into his back and kicked.

Hitzi Leiter was looking at him; it was difficult to distinguish any expression beneath the goggles and leather helmet. Mel and Ryderbeit had climbed down and were coming down the track toward them.

'What happened?' Ryderbeit shouted, looking over the edge.

'He pushed me,' Ben said feebly, still pressing himself against the rock: 'Pushed me — tried to kick me over.'

'What are you talking about?' Ryderbeit cried furiously, and Mel said: 'The rifle went over!'

'I know the rifle went over!' Ryderbeit snarled, grabbing Ben's arm: 'For Chrissake, what happened?'

Ben pointed up at Hitzi Leiter: 'The little bastard tried to kick me over.'

Ryderbeit looked at Hitzi Leiter. 'What's all this?'

'I didn't see a thing,' said Hitzi Leiter. 'I guess the mule stumbled. I don't know.'

'You little liar!' Ben said, knowing that whatever happened he must hold his temper. This was no place to blow his top. He looked up and said: 'All right, Hitzi, you want trouble, you're going to get it! I've never killed anyone so far, but if I ever do, you're the…'

'Oh shit!' Ryderbeit screeched suddenly, smacking his forehead. 'Flaming giraffe shit! We're trying to find diamonds — do yer know that, both o' you? D'yer know it, Hitzi? You, Morris! Have yer forgotten?'

Ben drew in his breath; he was still too shaken to be angry. 'He tried to kill me just now, Sammy. You'd better believe it.'

Ryderbeit swung round, first toward Hitzi Leiter, then back to Ben, his eyes glaring red. Ben said again, quietly: 'You've got to believe me, Sammy. He's insane.'

'Ah screw it, both of you!' Ryderbeit was blinking with rage like a confused animal. 'We lost a good, expensive gun down there, you know that!' His voice caught as though he were going to sob. 'Come on, let's get moving!' he cried.

Hitzi Leiter was already riding on up toward the front of the mule train. Ben turned toward his own mule and was violently sick. The path reeled up in front of him and he thought he was going to fall again. Someone held him under the arm and distantly he heard Mel calling: 'All right, I've got him!' He peered at her. Ryderbeit was beside her, thrusting the bottle of Scotch at him. 'Easy now — take your time.'

He took a mouthful and choked, spitting it out, and for a moment thought he was going to be sick again. He took another, slower this time, and handed the bottle back.

'Better?' said Ryderbeit. 'You look bloody horrible.'

'Thanks. It's just that I don't like heights — especially when people try to push me off them.'

Mel said to him: 'What really happened?'

'I just told you — he tried to kick me over. I'm not crazy, you know. I didn't make it up.'

She stared at him with parted lips: 'But he couldn't do a thing like that!'

'He damned well could — and did!'

Ryderbeit came up beside him and said: 'All right, Morris, up on your mule.' He sounded calmer now, and a little worried as he added: 'You really think he pushed you?'

'I know he pushed me.'

'Could have been a rock hit you perhaps? Or the mule stumbled.'

'It wasn't a rock, and the mule was all right.'

Ryderbeit nodded and didn't say any more, and Ben thought, *the odds have lengthened badly: Hitzi's definitely out to kill me, and doesn't mind if it's in broad daylight in front of the others. As for*

Ryderbeit, he doesn't want to know. And on top of it all, I don't even have a gun now.

Mel was riding ahead, just behind Hitzi Leiter. Ben thought for a moment: *the little bastards' crazy enough to try to push her off too.*

Just over four hours left till dark.

Three hours later they came down off the precipice and began to follow the solid lava flow, winding down a long black canyon that shut out the sun behind walls of rock nearly a thousand feet high. It was a cold, lifeless place with a wind blowing down it in an unbroken moan.

The mules moved slowly; the rope lava was smooth and treacherous, congealed like huge streaks of licorice. The twilight came suddenly, passing into night scarcely before they had time to unload the pack mules and pitch the tents.

The darkness brought an eerie chill that communicated itself dismally as they worked, hardly exchanging a word. Hitzi Leiter put up his tent a little away from the others, unloading his own equipment into a separate pile. Again, as in the morning, no one spoke to him. Mel arranged the cooking equipment, pumped up the Tilley lamp and the stove in the shelter of the tent, and opened tins of beef and soup.

'Christ, what a place!' Ryderbeit cried shivering. 'Not even a cactus in sight. Like the beginning of the world all over again.'

Hitzi Leiter and the Indian guide joined them for the meal, which they ate almost in silence. Ryderbeit passed the whisky around, and again the Indian gulped it down, grinning and bowing. Hitzi Leiter refused it. Mel made two more pints of coffee and refilled the thermos. It was not yet eight o'clock, but pitch dark, with only a narrow strip of stars above them. It was very cold.

Ryderbeit yawned: 'Let's clear up and go to bed.'

Without a word Hitzi Leiter stood up, collected his mug and plate and carried them over to his mule. Ben and Ryderbeit turned to watch him. He reached the mule, paused for a moment, then laid his cup and plate down with the rest of his equipment next to his tent.

Ryderbeit had bent down to pack up the cooking gear. It was now too dark to see more than a few yards. Ben glanced back at the dim figure of Hitzi Leiter, and his heart began to race. The German had taken his telescopic rifle from the sling under his saddle and was carrying it into his tent.

Ryderbeit noticed it at almost the same moment. He straightened up and yelled at Hitzi Leiter: 'You always sleep with a gun Hitzi?'

The German stared at him.

'Put it back!' Ryderbeit called. 'Put it back on your mule. Nobody needs a gun out here.'

Ben, who had been watching tensely, looked away. He knew he must do nothing at this late point to arouse Hitzi Leiter's suspicions. For a moment the German went on staring at Ryderbeit; then suddenly he shrugged, stepped back and returned the gun to the stirrup sling.

Ryderbeit was grinning to himself as he went over to the large tent.

It was seven feet square, just enough to lay the three sleeping bags together. There was no argument about places: Ryderbeit accepted the outside, with Ben in the middle. It was too cold to take anything off except their boots and woolen caps. Before he lay down, Ben went behind the mules to urinate, and on his way back collected the flashlight and the shotgun, unnoticed by the others. He also checked that Hitzi Leiter's telescopic rifle was still in its place under the stirrup, and noticed the flaps of his tent were closed. The guide had settled down to sleep in the open, rolled up in a single blanket between the two tents.

Ben went back into the big tent and slipped the shotgun and flashlight down beside his sleeping bag, between himself and Mel. It was too dark for her to see him. Above the wind he could just hear Ryderbeit's steady breathing. He touched Mel on the shoulder. 'Are you asleep?' he whispered.

She murmured something, her face was turned away from him. Her presence began to worry him; for a moment he again considered telling her his plan. But she was nearly asleep; and Ryderbeit might always wake up and hear them. He thought angrily: *Why the hell can't I trust Ryderbeit? He's in it as much as I am. And he can't be too happy having a pathological killer among us.*

But then perhaps Ryderbeit wasn't averse to pathological killers — being something of one himself. *Pathological Killers Anonymous*, he thought. He gripped the torch beside him, knowing he must keep awake for at least half an hour. The darkness and warmth of the sleeping bag were hard to resist. He shook himself every few minutes, forcing his eyes wide open.

He waited exactly half an hour by his watch, then leaned out first over Mel, then Ryderbeit, and listened above the wind to make sure they were both asleep. Then very slowly, pausing after each movement, he drew up his legs, crept out of the bag and carefully opened the tent flaps. The wind tore at them with a sudden freezing gust and he closed them, standing dead still. Neither Ryderbeit nor Mel stirred. He wondered for a moment, *Does it matter so much if they know? I should be able to trust them, dammit!* He opened the flaps again and slipped out.

His eyes were now accustomed enough to the darkness to distinguish the line of mules and the guide lying rolled up between them and Hitzi Leiter's tent, which was about ten yards away.

He walked round the Indian, almost up to the mules, before he turned the torch on, shielding the beam with his hand so that it gave only a prick of light. The Indian did not move. His instinct for danger would probably be acute, Ben thought. He wondered what he'd do if he awoke. Probably nothing. There was no danger of strangers down here; he'd mind his own business.

Ben now wondered about Hitzi. How did he sleep at night? Alone, with that twisted little mind working away at his hatreds? Supposing Hitzi did awaken? Then another course of action would be open to him.

Ben moved quickly. Hitzi Leiter's two mules were tethered at the end of the line. He released a little more light from the torch, working with his left hand which was already growing numb with the cold. First he pulled the telescopic rifle out from the stirrups sling and examined it under the torch. It was a heavy Belgian weapon with an automatic, rapid-firing mechanism supplied from a magazine under the breech. He found the safety catch, slipped it on and off a couple of times, then broke open the breech. There was a shell in the chamber; he pulled it out and knew that Hitzi Leiter had not been boasting when he told Ryderbeit he could blow a hole through him and the wall behind. This was a high-velocity hunter's gun with a stopping power of well over a mile. He weighed the soft-nosed .416 shell in one hand and the rifle in the other, and looked back towards Hitzi Leiter's tent. The wind moaned monotonously.

The temptation was very great: to return the shell to the chamber, shoot the bolt, walk over to the tent and empty the whole magazine through the flaps.

The noise would be terrible. He tried to imagine the reactions of Mel and Ryderbeit. Mel would probably be shocked and speechless, or weep — or perhaps not react at all. With Ryderbeit it was also impossible to predict.

He went on weighing the gun in his hand and thought: *It would be in the dark, but an easy target in the small tent, and the noise would be too great for any screaming. Hitzi would be asleep — he'd never know anything. Like putting down a mad dog.*

He snapped off the magazine, shaking out seven more shells, put them all in his pocket, clipped the magazine back on, and returned the gun to its sling.

He moved now on to the pack mule. He had already seen where Hitzi kept his ammunition, in the strapped-down pockets at the back of his rucksack: two unopened oil-proofed cardboard boxes with stenciled lettering. He slit the sealed edged of brown paper at the bottom with his thumbnail, as cleanly as he could, and opened them. Each box contained forty-eight rounds. He thought: *Hitzi Leiter, the little man with the big gun. Without the gun he's going to be nobody.*

He was putting the boxes under his arm when he heard something move behind him. He swung round, stepping backward, and the torch flared into Mel's face. She stopped with her hand over her eyes: 'Ben? Is that you Ben?'

He didn't say anything for a moment. His heart was leaping irregularly against his ribs like a terrified animal.

'Ben? What are you doing?'

'All right, keep your voice down! I'm taking the sting out of our friend Hitzi Leiter. Here.' He thrust one of the boxes at her. We're going to hold these in safekeeping.'

She nodded and shivered slightly; in the torchlight her expression was flat and impersonal, shining under her face cream like a mask. 'And the gun?'

'I've unloaded it and put it back. With luck the only way he'll find out is if he tries to use it. And if it's for a legitimate reason — like an attack by Xatu Indians — we'll let him have the stuff.'

She stood watching him, expressionless. 'Ben, are you certain he tried to kill you today?'

'Absolutely.'

'Then why don't you shoot him?' She said it as though it was a perfectly innocent suggestion and she was surprised he hadn't thought of it already.

'Firstly,' he said, drawing in his breath, 'because as Sammy said, we need him — he's the only one who's been to the river and knows exactly how to get there. Secondly, I can't just kill somebody in cold blood while he's asleep.'

'He would.'

'I'm not Hitzi Leiter, Mel. I'm sorry.' He started over toward the other pack mules. 'We'll put it in your stuff,' he whispered.

She began unstrapping her rucksack. 'Have you told Sammy what you're doing?'

He hesitated. 'No.' He handed her the two ammunition boxes. 'I don't think Sammy gives a damn whether I get killed or not, provided he gets those diamonds. At the moment young Hitzi happens to be a good deal more useful to Sammy than I am — or you, for that matter.'

He looked at her carefully but his words seemed to have made no impression on her at all. She gave a little shrug, then shivered again and said: 'Sammy would shoot Hitzi if he was in your shoes.' She began emptying the shells into her rucksack, handing the boxes back to Ben.

'Sammy doesn't mind killing people,' Ben said, filling the boxes with pieces of lava. 'Without the gun I'm on equal terms with Hitzi. I'll just have to watch him the whole time — and you will too. His real big advantage was surprise, and he's lost that now. There are only a limited number of ways he can try to kill me, like braining me in my sleep or pushing me off a cliff, and I'm going to be ready for him. If he tries anything else, then I will kill him!'

'I must say, you're being very moral and fair minded.' She spoke in little more than a whisper, but he caught the note of contempt. He put the lids on the boxes — the broken seals were not easily visible from the top — and walked over and stuffed them back into the rucksack. He realized then that it was a feeble ruse. It might buy him a little time, but sooner or later Hitzi Leiter would check the gun.

It was hard to guess exactly what he would do. He'd most likely complain straight to Ryderbeit, and the chances were that Ryderbeit would take his side. Ben was still not sure whether Ryderbeit believed that Hitzi had tried to murder him that afternoon — or whether he even cared. Mel was right, of course: he should go over and shoot Hitzi Leiter now.

She was standing where he had left her, beside her pack mule, and suddenly he was angry, almost hating her. 'You talk about being moral!' he cried, not bothering to whisper anymore: 'Stay faithful to a husband you left over a year ago. Shoot a man in cold blood while he's asleep. That's all O.K. But making love — that's wrong, I suppose? Not at all nice, is it?'

She shrugged again: 'Well, back in civilization it's different. You can't kill people there. But in a place like this we've got to make our own laws — to protect ourselves. Surely?'

'Oh yes, surely,' he said. 'And suppose we make our own morals too? You just get down into my sleeping bag and we'll try again. It can't always be as bad. Perhaps the night air will help.' He wasn't talking quite seriously; it was almost as though he wasn't talking to her at all.

She gave a tiny laugh: 'What, with that dirty-minded Rhodesian in there! I've got some sense of decency left!'

He nodded: 'Perhaps I ought to go and shoot Sammy too. Then we'd have the whole Hiarra to ourselves.' He was no longer angry; he remembered he could relax a little now — Hitzi Leiter had been neutralized.

There was no movement from inside either of the tents.

They awoke at five, had breakfast and packed up the tents while it was just growing light. Ben had a bad moment while Hitzi Leiter was loading his mule, but the German noticed nothing wrong. As Ben climbed on to his own mule, Mel gave him a quick wink and smiled. He thought with relief: *Whatever else is wrong with her, she's at least on my side.*

They set off again through the black canyon, winding slowly downward, with the rock walls growing higher, closing out all view of what lay ahead. Then suddenly, after more than five hours, it ended. The wind dropped and they walked out again into sunlight onto the top of a vast slope of cinders that plunged down to the desert.

At first the glare was so strong that all they could make out below was a diffuse yellow fog stretching away on all sides to meet the sun; and Ben understood now what had stopped the Conquistadores here — those bold men, who still believed the earth was flat, coming out on to this high platform and looking down into the void. To them it must have been the edge of the world, as endless and empty as the sky.

The mules started down the slope, their hooves slithering dangerously on the cinders; they had only gone a few feet when the heat hit them from below — a dry blast like that from an oven — and Ryderbeit yelled over his shoulder: 'Get back! Back, Mel! It's no good — we'd roast down there!' The guide had already leaped down and was dragging his mule up into the shelter of the canyon. 'We'll have to wait till sundown,' Ryderbeit called, looking over at Hitzi Leiter: 'That right, Hitzi?'

The German nodded. 'It's very hot down there,' he said woodenly, and Ben noticed that his face was still very bruised and swollen, a greenish mauve now that gave him a grotesque look behind the yellow snow goggles.

'We'll stop in the shade and rest a few hours,' said Ryderbeit, already wheezing with the heat. He took the whisky bottle from his pocket and passed around the little that was left in it, offering it to Hitzi Leiter, who again refused. 'What's the matter, Hitzi — don't you drink? I thought all Krauts drank?'

'I don't like it,' Hitzi said, and Ben had another nasty moment as the German began unloading his rucksack from the pack mule. He didn't touch the ammunition pockets. Ryderbeit swallowed the last of the Scotch and hurled the bottle far out over the slope, listening to the clink and purr of cinders, then went over and fetched another from the crate, together with a cigar, and lay down against the rock with the felt sombrero over his eyes.

Above the slope the wind had fallen to a steady tepid breeze. They had stripped off their heavy clothing, tied the mules up in a circle, and while Mel prepared the meal, Ben boiled a mug of water and shaved. Hitzi Leiter and the guide were squatting down beside Ryderbeit, who was sprawled out with the bottle of White Horse at his elbow, a Henry Clay in his mouth and a sheet of paper across his lap. Hitzi Leiter was pointing at the paper, talking rapidly, and now and again Ryderbeit would interrupt, rolling the cigar between his teeth and muttering something in translation to the guide.

Ben realized that this must be Hitzi's famous map of the swamp. He strolled over to them, still scraping his jaw with the safety razor, and looked down over Hitzi's furry white head.

The map was drawn in neat ballpoint on a sheet of foolscap that had been folded and creased many times. Most of it consisted of wavy lines, like the markings on a weather chart. Ben guessed they represented the desert and the massif beyond, traced or copied from available maps of the area. The course they were following was marked in a dotted line that meandered down about half the page; then the map became complicated. There was a shaded border marking the edge of the mangroves, and in the middle of it the contours contracted suddenly like the knot of a tree trunk.

Hitzi was explaining that this was the extinct volcano where he and Stopes had taken refuge. Against several of the contour lines were compass bearings, taken at points where the course skirted round the volcano from northeast to southwest, then turned due south into the swamp. In the left-hand corner was the serpentine line of the river, about thirty miles inside the swamp.

Ryderbeit poked his finger at the dotted line south of the volcano. 'So this is the course of the lava flow, is it?'

Below Ben the white ball of hair nodded. Ryderbeit took another drink and said, 'I hope to hell these markings are right, Hitzi. Will you be able to read 'em again?'

The white head nodded again: 'Sure I can read 'em!' Hitzi's voice was slightly thickened by his swollen lips.

'They look a bit crude to me,' Ryderbeit said, drawing on his cigar. 'We got about fourteen liters of water left, O.K.? What's the water situation up on the other side?'

'From the top of the Chinluca Wall,' Hitzi Leiter said, 'we got about fifty miles to the swamp.'

'And is there any water before the swamp?'

'I didn't find any.'

'Hell!' Ryderbeit took a drink and looked up at Ben: 'We go easy on the water from now on, soldier. No washing, no shaving, and we take our whisky neat. And tell Mel — for the next few days we go ugly and dirty.'

Ben went back to Mel and finished his shave. He said: 'We may be running short of water. Sammy says no more washing or shaving — we keep it for drinking only.'

She pulled a glum face: 'That's going to be charming! I'm feeling filthy enough as it is.'

'You look all right,' he said. *She'd look all right anywhere*, he thought; she had a smooth, clean tan the color of brown eggshell and she moved beautifully, with the training of a dancer.

She said casually: 'Is everything all right over there?'

'They're looking at Hitzi's map.'

She nodded, stirring a saucepan of bean soup. 'And how is dear Hitzi?'

'As lovely as ever. He hasn't noticed anything yet. Maybe he won't.'

'Perhaps he's got over it by now. He tried once — maybe that's enough for him.'

'I just hope you're right.'

They carried the food over to the others and ate it under the rock, then lay down in the shade and slept.

They woke with the sun hanging like a fireball in the corner of the sky. The glare had gone and they could now see the great hollow of the Devil's Spoon below. From here it looked less like a spoon than a frying pan full of steam. The rim ran the length of the horizon in a dark line that was the cliff called the Chinluca Wall. The sky above was the color of asphalt; below there was not a single landmark — not a drop of water or blade of grass or cactus or weed or insect; not the smallest living thing.

Before leaving they tied all the mules together with the guideline, in case one should slip on the steep cinder slope; then they set off in the familiar formation: the guide in front, followed by Ryderbeit and Ben, with Mel and Hitzi Leiter in the rear.

The slope dropped away at an angle of nearly forty-five degrees, and they were having to move with extreme care, the mules picking their way along an almost horizontal path, their hooves sinking into the cinders with an ugly slithering sound, each step raising dust as heavy as smoke. There was no wind.

Ben looked back and saw Mel riding with a scarf over her mouth, her eyes streaming. He said to Ryderbeit: 'Let her go on ahead — the dust won't be so bad in front.' It was small comfort to think that Hitzi was having the worst of it at the end of the line.

'We'll have to spread out a little,' Ryderbeit said, in a tight wheeze, beginning to play out the guideline. Ben could see nothing through the dust but the blurred shape of Mel in front and the grimy orange ball of the sun out on his left. But as they gradually got used to the dust, they became aware of the heat. It was no normal heat — neither humid nor burning, but a suffocating dryness that choked the pores even before they had time to sweat, shrinking up their mouths and throats till they tasted like chalk.

Ben tried to imagine what would happen if one of the mules slipped. Would it roll the whole way — more than a mile to the bottom, starting a landslide that would bury it under a mountain of cinders? He remembered now that his generosity in letting Mel go on ahead had left Hitzi Leiter once again riding behind him.

He looked around and could just see the German about five yards away, slightly above him. His mule had been tethered to Mel's, and now that she was riding ahead of them both Ben realized that the guideline, which she had played out behind her, was dragging along the ground a few feet above him, about level with his knee. Occasionally it pulled closer and he knew that if he leaned out he could reach it.

Hitzi Leiter was riding just near enough to give Ben a chance. All he had to do was get hold of that rope, pass it over his head so that it was hanging down the slope away from him, and give it one swift pull.

What would happen? A mule was a tough climbing animal; it might stumble a few feet, as Ben's had done on the precipice, but would probably recover its balance almost immediately. But Hitzi Leiter might not. If Ben pulled hard enough, the German might be jerked right off the mule's back, and down. If he didn't roll right to the bottom he'd never have the strength to climb up again in this heat, and in the dark they'd never find him. If he wasn't buried and was still alive by morning, the sun would kill him.

But then, of course, it was possible the mule would fall more than a few feet — and if it did, it would drag Mel's down after it, and then he and Ryderbeit would go, and the Indian guide and the three pack mules with them, all rolling down the cinder heap like a jolly old romp in a slapstick comedy.

He sat and watched the guideline sliding like a long snake through the cinders beside him.

CHAPTER SEVEN: THE DEVIL'S SPOON

They rode all night, with the moon high over the bone-white desert and the dust rising around them like river mist. The heat had gone with the sun and the air now had a stagnant chill as though exhausted of oxygen, making their lungs ache and their heads giddy.

Ryderbeit sat hunched forward, breathing in gasps, his only movement being to take a gulp of whisky every ten minutes or so. Mel was still out in front, just behind the guide, leaning slightly sideways with her head down, her hand trailing round the guideline at her side. Hitzi Leiter was in the rear, keeping a distance of about twenty feet. No one spoke. The only sound in the dead stillness was the rhythmic crunch of cinders, broken by the occasional braying of a mule.

Ben had forgotten about trying to pull Hitzi down to his death. As the night dragged on he began to lose all sense of time and reality. *We'll never get out of this place*, he thought, *the mules can't make it. Scrawny little beasts, they'll never get back up. We're going to die. Down to a river where there are trees and diamonds in the shade, where we can drink water and sleep under the trees.*

The mules had gone and he was alone with Mel on the grass and he could hear the river moving between the trees, and she was cool under him, and him feeling the stirring smoothness of flesh, the flakiness of his mouth, eyes stinging, his groin scraping painfully against the saddle.

He lifted his head and heard Ryderbeit laughing. Mel had turned and ridden back level with them. Ryderbeit took a deep drink, still laughing, and shouted over his shoulder at Ben: 'We're down! Y'hear soldier! We're down! We're off it!' His laugh burst into a cough that bent him double across the mule's back. Ben looked round and realized that he was no longer breathing dust. The cinders had finished; the slope was now far shallower, made of smooth boulders like enormous cobblestones shelving down into the bowl of the desert. The moon was full, giving the landscape a lunar quality etched out in black against the wastes of white.

Ryderbeit lifted his head and uttered a noise that was half choking, half cackling: 'Hah! Hah, soldier! We made it, eh? We made it off the shit heap!' He lifted the whisky from his pocket and Ben saw it was more than three-quarters empty.

'How about some water instead?' said Ben gently.

'Drink your own bleeding water!' he shrieked, drinking noisily. Ben knew he was already very drunk — and by the look in his eyes, perhaps dangerously drunk. Short of outright calamity, this was one of the worst things that could have happened — and curiously enough, one Ben had least expected. For although he no more trusted Ryderbeit now than on the first meeting with him, he had come to have confidence in the man's capacities as organizer and leader. Now the illusion was gone: Ryderbeit was back in his savage private world where he attacked his wives and stabbed pigs.

Ben got down and drank some water and sat with his head between his knees. When he looked up he saw Mel sitting a few feet from him, her face gray with dust, eyes closed. Ryderbeit was leaning down from his saddle, shouting at her in his wheezy croak: 'Have a drink, my darling!'

She shook her head, her eyes still closed. Ben murmured to her: 'Are you feeling all right?'

She opened her eyes and her mouth cracked into a smile: 'Tired. Just very tired!'

'Have a drink, my beauty!' Ryderbeit yelled, waving the bottle at her like a club.

'Sammy, put it away,' she said wearily.

'Hah, put it away!' he mimicked, lifting it to his mouth again.

'Come on, Sammy,' said Ben, standing up, 'we've got to get going. The sun'll be up in just over an hour. Do we know the way?'

'Hitzi knows the way! Hitzi knows everything!' He broke into another fit of coughing, and was still bent double with the breath hissing through his teeth, when Ben removed the bottle of whisky from his hand and gave it to Mel, who put it in her rucksack.

'He's a chronic asthmatic,' he said quietly. 'The dust must have damn nearly killed him.'

'That and the whisky,' she said, getting back onto her mule. 'He must be crazy — like my damned husband. God, people get boring when they're drunk!'

Not only boring, Ben thought, as he climbed up behind Ryderbeit. Hitzi Leiter had ridden round them and was now about fifty yards ahead. 'Let's go,' said Ben.

'Where's the bottle?' Ryderbeit croaked.

'That's O.K.,' said Ben, 'you get the bottle back when you've taken a few deep breaths. In — out — slowly. There's no dust now.'

'You're a bloody doctor, aren't you?'

'That's right. Just breathe in and don't talk. You'll get your whisky later.'

'Hah! Hah!' Ryderbeit's shoulders were hunched high again, and for a moment Ben thought he was sobbing; then he heard his painful breathing and suddenly realized he felt sorry for

Ryderbeit — there was something at that moment so broken and helpless about him.

They rode on over the giant cobbles towards a far point in the moonlight where the bowl of the desert narrowed into a chimney of rock choked with boulders. Ben looked at his watch: it was nearly five o'clock. It would be light in about twenty minutes. The moon was going down. About half a mile on they came to a place where the cliffs had been worn away into huge grooves of rock rising above them like the buttresses of a cathedral. They rode right under them where it was dark and cool. Ryderbeit slid off his mule and spat on the stones. 'Where's the whisky for Chrissake?'

Ben glanced at Mel and shrugged. 'Give it to him,' he said, beginning to unload the tent. He had it unrolled on the ground and was reaching for the pegs, when he glanced up and saw the one thing he had been dreading all day.

Hitzi Leiter had taken his elephant-gun from its sling. He had a rag and cleaning rod in his hand, and was standing with his back to Ben, about to break the gun open.

Ben turned and reached Mel's mule in three strides. She was busy unloading her sleeping bag and toilet case from her pack mule beside him. Behind her, Ryderbeit lay sprawled out on the rock with his eyes closed, the empty whisky bottle next to his leg. Ben realized there might after all be a certain advantage in Ryderbeit's drunkenness. He reached down for the shotgun under the stirrup and Mel said: 'Anything wrong?'

'Yes.' He pulled the gun out and swung it round; it was much heavier than he'd expected, almost as heavy as Hitzi Leiter's .416. The German had put his elephant-gun back in its sling and had gone over to his pack mule; he was now unstrapping the side pockets of his rucksack. His movements were quick but strangely unhurried. Ben walked toward him until he was less than two yards away, pointing the twin barrels of the shotgun at the German's head. Still Hitzi Leiter did not turn round or even look at Ben. He pulled out both ammunition boxes and emptied them on the ground in front of him.

'Mr. Morris, you're a big fool.' His voice was soft, without anger, his round bruised face regaining some of its childlike innocence.

'All right, Hitzi. Just walk over here and don't touch your gun.'

Hitzi Leiter smiled sadly: 'My gun's empty, Mr. Morris. You know that — you emptied it yourself didn't you?'

'Yes, I emptied it,' said Ben. 'Now just start walking.'

They had come almost full circle now, and he knew they were near the end. First it had been Hitzi holding a gun on Ryderbeit in the hotel in Benisalem, then Ryderbeit holding one on Hitzi — and now it was Ben's turn. He had Ryderbeit's Winchester beside him, and Ryderbeit was drunk and out of it, and there wouldn't be another time like this. It had to happen sooner or later: today, tomorrow, while Ben was asleep, looking the other way, had his back turned, Hitzi Leiter would kill him. The elephant-gun wasn't the only way.

Hitzi Leiter had taken a couple of steps forward. Ben motioned with the shotgun out toward the desert. 'Go on, keep walking.' Without moving his head he whispered to Mel: 'Get Sammy's rifle. Watch us both.'

'What are you going to do?'

He didn't answer. He began to walk away from her, following Hitzi Leiter into the desert. The German's boots rang solemnly on the rock floor; Ben noticed it was growing light. Then he became aware that Ryderbeit was awake, still lying on his back with an idiot leer on his face.

Hitzi Leiter stopped. 'Ryderbeit! Hey, Ryderbeit, get over here! This guy's crazy!'

Ryderbeit just cackled.

'He's drunk,' Ben said, and Hitzi Leiter did not move. 'What do you want?' he whined.

'Keep walking!' Ben had come so close that he could almost touch him with the shotgun. 'Go on!'

Suddenly Hitzi Leiter began to tremble. Ben knew it would have to be now. He tried to work himself into a rage, to hate Hitzi Leiter with a murderous passion, only to realize that he was trembling too. He said: 'Hitzi, you tried to kick me off that cliff, didn't you? You're a little bastard, Hitzi! A little murdering cold-blooded bastard.'

He was still saying it as he pointed the two barrels at Hitzi Leiter's face and pulled both triggers.

He closed his eyes and heard the two simultaneous snaps of the hammers. There was a moment of total silence. He and Hitzi Leiter just stared at each other. Then from behind them came a shriek of laughter.

'Hah, you stupid sods! Had you there, eh!' The empty whisky bottle came spinning through the air and shattered on a rock a few feet from them. 'Come on over here, you yellow-livered cowards!' Ryderbeit roared. He was struggling to his feet now, still laughing, moving over to where Mel stood with Ryderbeit's Winchester rifle held loosely in her hands.

'Give it to me, darling!' He reached her and she gave him the rifle without protest. The light was coming up quickly now. He stood crouched over his Winchester, grinning. 'You stupid sods!' he yelled, the words carrying up into the vault of rocks above.

Ben broke open the shotgun, thinking perhaps the cartridges were dead. Both chambers were empty. Ryderbeit laughed again. Ben dropped the butt to the ground, dragged the gun over to Mel's mule and slid it back under the stirrup. 'Give me some water,' he said to her.

'You're a sod, Ben Morris!' Ryderbeit cried.

'So you said already.' Ben was too tired to argue.

'You thought you could just walk the little fellow out there and shoot him, huh?' Ryderbeit wagged his head playfully, but there was nothing playful about the look in his eyes. 'But Sammy Ryderbeit was expecting it, see! He knew. You and Mel were bleating away outside the tent last night like a couple of characters at a cocktail party! I'm surprised Hitzi didn't hear you too. I saw you taking the little sod's bullets and I thought to myself, we can all play that game, soldier! So while you were out there jabbering, I found the shotgun in the tent, and just took out the cartridges and sat tight.'

'And supposing I'd decided to kill him with your Winchester?' said Ben.

'Ah, well then it might have got a bit rough. But a Winchester's not an easy gun, even at short range. I reckoned on the shotgun.' He smiled: 'But since we don't seem to be able to behave ourselves, from now on I take charge of all the guns and the ammunition.' He looked at Mel and shook his head: 'I'm ashamed of you, my darling! Being an accessory to a silly man like Morris.'

Ben noticed that the guide had been sitting all the while on his rug watching them. Ben wondered what he must make of it all. Ryderbeit was drunk, but a good deal less than Ben had thought. He said, 'O.K. Sammy, let's go to bed.' He began to walk toward the unrolled tent and heard Ryderbeit saying to Mel: 'Come on, get all that ammunition out of your rucksack and hand it over to Sammy. You're a naughty bitch, you know — I ought to smack your pretty bottom for this!'

Hitzi Leiter had begun to put up his own tent; he looked at none of them as he worked, and Ben noticed he had a high color in his cheeks, and he thought, *I should have killed him last night. I'll never get another chance now.*

Ryderbeit and Mel came over and helped him pitch the tent next to Hitzi's, against the rock wall that would get the least sun. The guide still sat on his rug without moving. 'What do we do about him?' said Ben: 'He can't sleep in the open, can he?'

'He goes in with Hitzi,' said Ryderbeit, and yelled something at the Indian who stood up quickly and bowed, holding his hat in both hands. 'Hitzi, the Indian's going to sleep with you!'

Hitzi Leiter shook his head: 'No, he sleeps outside with the mules. That's his job.'

'You do as you're told, Hitzi!' Ryderbeit was grinning to himself as he went over to the pack mules and collected Hitzi Leiter's elephant-gun and the two canvas bags they had brought to carry the diamonds, which he now stuffed full of the entire stock of ammunition.

No one else had moved. Ryderbeit put the bags and gun inside the big tent, then nodded at the Indian: 'Go on, Hitzi! Where's the German hospitality?'

Hitzi Leiter stood with his tight little face flushed red. 'On our last expedition,' he said, 'the guide slept outside under his rug.'

Ryderbeit leered: 'I bet he did! At the command of you and old Stopes, eh? The big white bosses, old British bwana and little Hitzi Hitler! Now get into that tent and take that guide in with you! We're democratic here.'

He cackled with pleasure, waving the guide towards Hitzi's tent. The Indian bowed again, picked up his rug and darted in under the flaps.

Hitzi stood looking at Ryderbeit, a little muscle twitching near his mouth. 'Why doesn't he sleep in your tent, huh? It's bigger.'

'Don't be silly, Hitzi. We got a lady in our tent.'

Ben and Mel were standing aside, watching carefully. Ryderbeit seemed to be enjoying himself hugely: 'Go on, Hitzi, get in there and snuggle down. Never bunked with an Indian before?'

The German lowered his head in a funny nodding movement, almost a bow, and stood for a moment with his fingers stretched down at his sides, his face very red, then swung round and disappeared into the tent.

Ryderbeit began to cackle again: 'Good little Hitzi! Break him in yet!' He fetched a new bottle of whisky from his mule, and still chuckling to himself, went into the big tent, pulled off his shirt and boots and socks and flopped down on the edge of the ground sheet, leaving the flaps open for ventilation. Ben followed him in and lay down beside him, but shared none of his good humor. 'That was unwise, Sammy.'

'Ah wisdom, soldier! Give me wisdom!' He took a gulp of whisky and settled his head down with a groan. 'An eventful evening, I think. Uncommonly eventful.'

'Why did you make the Indian go in with him?' Ben asked drowsily. 'Not for the Indian's sake?'

'No — for little Hitzi's sake. Teach him a lesson — assert my authority, soldier. Show who's boss.'

'Fun and games,' Ben murmured. 'You shouldn't do it that way, Sammy. Not with Hitzi Leiter. He doesn't react normally.'

'He's a Kraut. Respects the iron hand — iron hand of the Jew. Fist o' Moses. God, I hate Krauts!' He began to chuckle quietly in the darkness. A few moments later Mel slipped in through the flaps and Ben felt her lie down beside him and could smell the warm saltiness of her body, thinking: *We've gone past the full circle now, starting again with Ryderbeit on top. But for how long? Game and set to Ryderbeit. Good last volley there, but rash in the long run. In the long run it'll lead to trouble.*

He woke suddenly, sometime in the afternoon. There was a burning spear of light between the tent flaps and the air full of the hot stench of sweat and whisky. When he moved, he felt his clothes clinging wet to his skin. He looked at his watch: just 4:15. He moved his tongue and his lips made a crackling sound. It was the thirst that had woken him. He groped for the water can at the back of the tent. Mel was lying on her stomach with her face turned away. She had stripped down to her brassiere and pants, both soaked dark with sweat, her hair lying wet across her shoulders and the sweat glittering on the tiny blond hairs in the small of her back and in the hollows behind her knees.

He swallowed drily, still tasting the dust, and took a deep gulp of water; it was warm enough to shave in. His throat suddenly contracted with cramp, and the atmosphere in the tent was too much for him. He pushed his way out through the flaps, his eyes half closed against the white-hot glare.

At first he thought he had come out on the wrong side. The rock behind the tent was bare: there was no sign of the second tent or the mules. He took a couple of steps out of the shade, and then he saw the Indian. He was lying on his face, almost hidden by the buttress of rock where Hitzi Leiter's tent had been. There was blood on the top of his white clothes. Ben did not look closely; the back of his head was a clotted mass, glistening darkly.

He ran back into the tent gasping, 'Sammy, quick! Mel!'

'What's up!' Ryderbeit was out of the tent with the Winchester in both hands. Mel followed sleepily.

'Hitzi's gone. Taken all nine mules and murdered the guide.'

Ryderbeit was already bending over the Indian's body; he put a hand down and touched the blood at the back of his head. Ben flinched. Mel was standing beside him, still half naked, crying: 'Oh God, how awful! Why did he do it?'

'Get dressed,' said Ben. Ryderbeit came back, wiping his fingers on his trousers. 'Get the tent down!' he shouted. 'The blood's nearly dry. That means the little bastard could have got as much as an hour's lead.' He was already dragging their clothes out of the tent, then the guns and ammunition bags, pulling on his trousers, loading the guns. Ben began to speak and Ryderbeit almost spat at him: 'The tent! Get on with it!'

Mel finished dressing outside, while Ben worked frantically, scorching his fingers on the steel pegs, the sweat stinging his eyes, his head burning as though a band of iron was being screwed tight round his scalp.

Ryderbeit said breathlessly: 'He must have reckoned he'd get at least two hours' start on us before we woke. Perhaps more. What made you wake, soldier?'

'Thirst.'

'God bless your thirst! We're going to get that little bastard. We're goin' to get him and I'm goin' to chop off his family jewels and pickle 'em in whisky!' He was tying the two ammunition bags together in a crude halter, which he wrapped inside the ground sheet. 'We'll take turns with these and the tent and water can. We'll have to leave the sleeping bags.' He now lifted Hitzi Leiter's .416 and began to scan the horizon through the telescopic lens. Then he shook his head, slinging the gun over his shoulder: 'Nothing — too much haze.'

'How much water have we got?' said Ben.

'Just what was left in the tent — about two or three liters I'd say.' He shook his head savagely: 'If we don't get the little bastard by tomorrow, we're in trouble.'

'But do we know which way he's gone?'

'There's only one way he can go — unless he's gone back, which he won't have done. I've seen enough of the maps to know them almost by heart. He's gone on round the desert under the Chinluca Wall. Most of it's practically sheer, and there's only one place he can get the mules over — about fifteen miles from here. It's a big climb, he told me — about six or seven hours. And that's where we're going to get him — if we get him at all.' He hoisted the two ammunition bags over his shoulder along with the water can, rolled tent and telescopic rifle, handing the Winchester to Ben and the shotgun to Mel, who was staring bleakly round her. 'But why?' she cried. 'Why did he do it?'

'Because he's a vicious little nut,' said Ryderbeit. 'Didn't fancy us — thought he could make it on his own.'

'But why kill the poor Indian?' said Mel.

'Maybe he smelled — or perhaps he just didn't approve too highly of what Hitzi was doing. After all, we hired him.' He paused, looking sourly at Ben: 'All right, don't tell me! I should have let you kill him last night. I made a mistake.'

'We both did,' said Ben. 'I should have killed him two nights ago.'

'We'll both get another chance. Let's go.'

'What about the Indian?' Mel cried. 'Aren't we going to bury him?'

'Bury him — hell!' Ryderbeit was already striding out under the rock, stooped forward under the tent and ammunition bags, his tall felt sombrero making him look for a moment like the Pied Piper of Hamelin. 'What do you want?' he yelled over his shoulder: 'Dress up in black; a decent period o' mourning? Every half hour wasted, Hitzi gains a mile on us. Anyway, the condors'll finish him by tomorrow night.' He turned to Ben: 'We'll do it in half-hour stretches, with five-minute rests. Unless he stops himself I don't think we can hope to catch him before the pass in the Chinluca Wall. We ought to make that in about nine hours — say, between one and two in the morning. Then we'll track him down before sunrise.' He grinned wryly: 'Ever done any hunting?'

'No.'

'Well, this is going to be the old days on the velt, tracking lion. Only maybe easier, huh! Because Hitzi may o' taken everything else except one damned way of defending himself. We got the guns, soldier.'

'He's got a knife,' said Ben, 'the one he used on Stopes.'

Ryderbeit laughed: 'Just let him come close enough to use it!'

They were walking along the edge of the rock, heads bowed against the thumping wall of heat, their eyes narrowed behind the sunglasses, watching the air shudder off the glowing rocks. After a few minutes Ben dropped back and took Mel's arm: 'How are you doing?'

'A bit shaken. I'm not very good at the sight of blood. That poor Indian.'

He lifted the shotgun from round her neck and slung it over his shoulder next to the Winchester. 'Thanks,' she murmured. 'I always thought I liked the sun. When I was in London I used to dream of just spending the rest of my life lying on a beach in a bikini.'

173

'It's only about a hundred up here,' he said. 'You should try it further down.' He nodded out toward the desert, and even behind the dark lenses his eyes ached as though the sand and sun and sky had all been joined into a dome of burning glass. *And there are three tiny insects crawling round the edge of the glass,* he thought: *heads swelling with pain, throats closing up, lips black and cracked, and only enough water for twelve hours. Unless we find Hitzi Leiter. One man and nine mules somewhere in this bleached wilderness, and twelve hours to find them in, getting less every minute that passes.* He was holding Mel's arm, taking her weight, his eyes cast down, following Ryderbeit's shadow as it rippled over the rock, his boots smoking dust.

The first half hour was over and they slumped down panting in a patch of shade, passing the water round. Mel put her hands over her eyes. Ryderbeit had taken off the tent and ammunition bags and pushed them over to Ben, who in turn gave him the water can and Mel's shotgun. Mel lifted her head and said: 'I'm sorry — I don't seem to be doing my share.'

'You're doing all right,' said Ben. He looked at Ryderbeit: 'So what do you think, Sammy?'

'What do I think what?' he growled.

'Can we make it?'

'We damn well better!' He leant out and spat on the rock in front of him; the gob bubbled fiercely for a few seconds and was gone. He sat for a moment in silence, his face dark and cruel.

'Let's look at it this way,' he said at last. 'The boy Hitzi may be a nut, but he's no fool. He wants those diamonds as badly as we do. First rule of hunting is, if you've got a cunning prey, work out what it'll do. So let's work out what Hitzi does. He wants us dead, but we got all the guns, and he can't risk taking us on all together, even asleep. So he does the next best thing.

He waits till the worst of the heat's over, giving himself what he hopes is a few hours' start and leaves us stranded out here. Like that he can be pretty certain we've had it. And I'd guess that at the moment young Hitzi Leiter's not too worried — not on our account, at any rate.'

Mel had lifted her head and was listening. Her face, shaded under her wide-brimmed hat, had a parched sunken look that gave her mouth a strangely sensuous expression.

Ryderbeit went on: 'Only there are two things in Hitzi's calculations that have gone wrong for him. First, we happened to have a little more water in the tent than he probably bargained for — in fact, he may have thought we didn't have any water at all. And secondly, we've cut his start on us by as much as three-quarters.

'Now, if we look at things in the best possible light, it goes like this. Hitzi's heading for the diamonds and there's one way out of the Devil's Spoon, about fifteen miles away. It's going to take him several hours to get over the Chinluca Wall, and there — as I told you — is where we get him.

'On the other hand,' he said, standing up and taking another sight through the telescopic rifle, 'it's possible Sunny Boy's taking no chances. Perhaps he's already calculated that we might have got after him in rather less time than he hoped, and that we might have reserves of water.' He slung the rifle back on and began leading the way out again along the foot of the cliffs. Ben followed, still holding Mel by the arm, hearing Ryderbeit's voice grinding on, beginning to grow muffled now: 'Supposing you were Hitzi Leiter, what would you be doing now?'

'I'd make for the river as fast as I could.'

'You might — but you might not. Supposing you thought we could get after you first — catch you before you could get up the Chinluca Wall? I'll tell you what I'd do — use the trick of the Rhodesian ridgebacks, the lion dogs. Let their prey run on till it's exhausted, then move in for the kill. And if we're unlucky that's what Hitzi'll do. He'll hide up there on the Chinluca Wall and stalk us till our water runs out. We may have the range of the guns, but he's got his U-boat day-and-night glasses he took back from Stopes' flat. He'll be able to pick us out with those pinpoint lenses even in the dark. And all we've got is his telescopic rifle.

'What'll he do with the mules?' said Ben.

'I dunno yet. But the mules are our big hope. Because if he can't get them up the Chinluca Wall in time, he's going to be in trouble. Once we get hold of those mules, we've got food and water, and can start hunting him down in our own time.'

'And if we don't get them?'

'Then we provide a good square meal for the condors tomorrow evening. If we haven't found either Hitzi or the mules by daylight, I'm afraid we've had it.'

Ben shielded his sunglasses and peered ahead, and all he could see were the hot naked cliffs above the haze that rose less than a hundred yards away.

'The sun'll begin to go down in about an hour,' Ryderbeit said.

Ben looked at his watch: five o'clock. Nearly an hour gone, and beginning to get cooler. Just over eleven hours left; and as he trudged on he could hear the water clonking about inside the plastic can on Ryderbeit's back.

The sun went down and they walked on into the second night, round the edge of the Devil's Spoon — cruel and monotonous and dry as a bone. The moon was almost full. After sunset they took turns searching the horizon through the telescopic rifle; but the round two-dimensional frame with its cross-sights was like a blurred photograph. Twice — just after dark, and again about midnight — they thought they saw something: a vague grouping of objects that appeared to be moving along the foot of the cliff. Then it disappeared and they could not find it again.

They walked almost in silence, the dead air weighing them down with a depressing lassitude. They had now extended the marches to an hour between the five-minute rests, rationing the water to a single mouthful every half-hour. But soon after midnight Mel's strength began to fail. She was leaning on Ben's arm, forcing him to pause every few minutes while he supported her round the waist, shaking her gently to keep her awake. He tried talking to her, but she answered only in murmurs, her head sunk sideways till her hair brushed against his neck. He looked at his watch: nearly one o'clock. Four hours till sunrise. And water for about as long — perhaps less.

'Shouldn't we be getting near the break in the Chinluca Wall?' he asked.

'Yeah but where is it?' Ryderbeit said, staring out along the unbroken cliff that rose from the desert like a gray curtain in the moonlight. It would be a challenge to an experienced mountaineer; for a mule train it was plainly impossible.

A little later Ben felt Mel go limp on his arm; her legs stumbled and dragged like someone drunk. He stopped and turned her face upward: it was streaked with dust and sweat, and felt cold. Her eyes were closed and there were bubbles of spittle at the corners of her mouth. He let her down gently, propping her head against his arm and putting the water can to her lips. She coughed and half-opened her eyes.

'Come on, drink — careful.'

She swallowed, dribbling a little, then closed her eyes again. 'I'm sorry — I can't. I can't go on.'

He felt a wave of tenderness for her, then despair, taking her hand and speaking with soft urgency: 'Mel, can you hear me? You must try to keep going. Do you understand? You must get up!'

'Let me sleep,' she whispered. 'Just for a few minutes. Please.'

Ryderbeit stood over them both, scowling: 'Come on, get up, Mel!' She opened her eyes and peered at him with a heavy glazed look. He bent down and grabbed her arm: 'What's the matter with you?'

'You can see what's the matter,' said Ben. 'She's completely beat.'

'Of course she is! So am I — so are you. Now up on your feet, girl, or I'll drag you up!'

'Shut up,' said Ben quietly. He began squeezing her hand, beginning to pull her up by the arm. 'Try, Mel — you must try.' She had closed her eyes again and did not move.

'O.K.,' said Ryderbeit, 'if she's sick we'll have to leave her.'

Ben dropped her hand and leaped to his feet. 'Now look, Sammy, we're not having any talk like that! If the girl's sick, we stay with her.'

Ryderbeit was clenching and unclenching his fists: 'Sure — stay with her and die with her! All nice and honorable. And in the meantime that little Kraut walks off and collects the diamonds and returns a millionaire. And why? Because old Ben Morris has gone sweet on some sick girl. Don't be so bloody stupid!'

Ben felt his hands shaking as he looked at Ryderbeit, nodding as he spoke: 'Yes, Sammy, I really think you would. I think you'd be quite willing to walk off and leave her to die, and not miss a wink of sleep over it. Well, you walk off. I'm staying.'

Ryderbeit leered grimly: 'O.K., soldier, I'll go. I'll get Hitzi and I'll get those diamonds. But don't expect me to share 'em with you. You stay here and die with your girlfriend.'

He made a move to reach for one of the rolled ground sheets under Mel's head; but before he could reach it or Ben could stop him, there came a sound far out along the cliff ahead.

They both turned, straining to catch it again. It had been very faint — scarcely more than a scratch of sound, gone almost at once. For several seconds the silence was total, then it came again — perhaps a little louder this time — a tiny metallic bloop, all on one note. 'You hear it?' said Ben.

'I heard something,' Ryderbeit said. They stood with hands cupped behind their ears, waiting.

'What do you think it was?' said Ben.

'Sounded like some sort of siren or hunting horn. Xatus perhaps.'

Ben felt a cold tightening in his stomach. 'I didn't think they came down as far as this.'

Ryderbeit lifted the telescopic rifle and began scanning the horizon. 'I'm no expert on Xatus,' he said slowly, moving the sights along the cliff face. 'In fact, I'm not too worried about Xatus. They don't have guns, for a start.'

He paused, lowering the rifle. 'It occurs to me, soldier, that it might be somebody else who's out there. Somebody young Hitzi was anxious to meet — without us. You see how it figures?'

Ben nodded: he was not quite sure, but he could guess. 'You mean, somebody else who's after the diamonds? That gang Stopes mentioned, for instance?'

'For instance,' said Ryderbeit, lifting the rifle again. He covered the whole horizon, then shook his head: 'Not a thing. If only I had those U-boat glasses!'

'You still want to walk out there alone?' said Ben.

Ryderbeit glared at him, then let his breath out in a hiss: 'O.K., you call the game. What do we do?'

'Stay here and rest for a quarter of an hour. Then move on. And if she's not strong enough, we'll carry her.'

Ryderbeit groaned and sat down. 'Bloody women — I've been carrying them around my whole bloody life. Why the hell did we have to bring her?'

'You know damn well why we brought her. It was your idea.' He looked down at her. She seemed to be asleep. 'Anyway, it's too late to think about that now. We've brought her here, and we've got to look after her.'

'And die doing it,' Ryderbeit growled, stretching himself out flat.

'Nobody's going to die,' Ben said, with no conviction. He knew that when the sun came up, and there was no water left, the end would come fast. 'How long can we live without water?' he asked.

'In normal conditions three days — which is longer than I can do without hard liquor. Down here I'd say about half a day.'

Ben closed his eyes. He felt sad — but an oddly detached sadness as though he were missing something that couldn't be helped. He was surprised that he felt none of the acute terror he had expected. Just over three hours till dawn, and by the time the day was over they would all be dead.

There was a long pause. Mel's breathing was quick and heavy.

Then they heard the sound again — louder, in two distinct blasts with a slightly agonized note, almost a cry of pain. They sat up. 'Whatever it is,' said Ben, 'it's getting closer. If it's really Xatus, we might be better off dying of thirst.'

Ryderbeit was on his feet. 'We don't know it's Xatus. We don't know it's anything.'

'Supposing it is a gang?' said Ben. 'Do we have a chance?'

Ryderbeit looked at him and laughed: 'You yellow?'

Ben felt himself flush. Ryderbeit shook his head and looked down at Mel: 'Let's go. Whoever it is, we've certainly got a chance.'

Ben leaned over her and put the water can to her lips again. She was now asleep, but the touch of water woke her at once. He lifted her into a sitting position and said, 'Do you think you're strong enough to stand?'

Her eyes were half open, but her blackened lips scarcely moved as she murmured: 'I'm so tired — I feel sick.'

'She feels sick!' Ryderbeit mimicked.

'Oh belt up,' said Ben wearily. 'You weren't feeling so damned good yourself yesterday morning with your bloody asthma.'

Ryderbeit took a step forward: 'Asthma's been the bane o' my life since I was a kid, so leave off it, will you!'

'Then try to have more sympathy,' Ben said, turning back to Mel. The sweat was rising in big gray beads on her forehead.

Ryderbeit said: 'Is she really sick? Something bad?'

'Anything's bad down here. It may be heat stroke or plain exhaustion.' He raised her limp cold hands, clasped them together round his neck and lifted her round the waist. She began to sway, her knees buckling. 'Get hold of her!' he cried. Ryderbeit grabbed her ungracefully under the arms. She murmured: 'I'm sorry, I can't help it.'

'You're doing fine,' said Ben.

'Yes, fine,' said Ryderbeit morosely. 'We'll all be doing fine in a few hours.'

Mel's body felt extraordinarily heavy; there were moments when Ben thought he was going to collapse under her, his limbs growing rubbery without feeling, his head swelling and exploding like a great puffball scattering its dust into the desert.

They were moving very slowly. It was past two o'clock. Hitzi Leiter must have gained a long head on them by now. But then there was always the climb over the Chinluca Wall. Perhaps he was near the top already.

Ryderbeit had stopped. He had the telescopic rifle trained again on the cliff face ahead. 'Hey, soldier!' He thrust the gun at Ben, taking all Mel's weight himself. 'Have a look — about a mile down.'

Ben sighted the crossed frame slowly along the cliff face. It was some time before he saw it. At first it looked in the moonlight as though the sheer rock was made of layer cake, broken up into undulating lines that ran far out into the horizon. At the foot of the cliff were a number of rockfalls that did not look too difficult to climb.

He moved the telescopic sight a little higher, and about fifty feet up he saw something move: a dark blob like a fly crawling along one of the lines on the rock face. Then his eyes misted over; he shifted the rifle and the next moment the focus had gone. He turned to Ryderbeit: 'There's something moving halfway up the cliff.'

'I know. And that's the break in the Chinluca Wall.' He grinned: 'Soldier, we've got him.'

'But what about the Xatus?' It had been more than a mile ahead — one figure on the rock wall, a sentry perhaps who had given the signal to the rest of the tribe beyond the Wall. He was about to repeat his thoughts to Ryderbeit, when they heard the sound again — much clearer this time, in short rasping honks like metal scraping on metal.

Suddenly Ryderbeit began to laugh. He folded up with his head near his knees, tipping Mel almost on to the ground. 'Soldier, we're crazy! We're all bloody crazy!' He lifted his head, waving toward the blob on the cliff and began laughing again: 'Xatus! We thought they were Xatus!'

'What do you mean?'

He straightened up and wiped his mouth: 'That was no Xatu, soldier! That was a bloody mule!' He let out another shriek of laughter, while Ben stared ahead along the cliff. It made sense: the echoes could have distorted the braying of a mule just enough to confuse the sound with a siren or horn.

Ryderbeit had the telescope trained again on the rock face. 'It's on a ledge halfway up. Seems to have stopped. Can't be sure if it's a man or a mule, or both.' He lowered the rifle and took hold of Mel's other arm; her head had sunk down on Ben's shoulder and she seemed only half conscious.

'We can make it out there in less than an hour,' Ryderbeit urged. 'And if Hitzi hasn't got those mules up yet, we may be able to blow him off the cliff before he gets to the top.'

They began to plod forward, dragging Mel's legs after her, spurred on with a fresh dash of hope. There was now a chance — a big chance. Ben only wondered whether Mel could last till morning. The possibility of having to watch her die out here, helpless to save her, then having to bury her, filled him with a painful gloom. He began to think of her with a kind of abstract fondness, with a deep, inescapable sense of responsibility, rather than with lust. Ryderbeit would let her die without a second thought. Whatever happened, Ben would have to protect her — if necessary, to a bitter end.

He plodded on, holding her up, feeling her hair against his neck, savoring the thought of how he would perhaps claim her again when it was all over. He deserved it, after all. When they were back with the diamonds, it would be different; he would enjoy her somewhere where there were air-conditioned cocktail lounges and fresh sheets and showers and floor waiters to bring them iced drinks and dinner on the balcony. Now there was just the chance that they might get away with it.

They had been going for more than a quarter of an hour since sighting the blob on the cliff face when Ryderbeit stopped again and swung up the telescope. 'Sweet Jesus!' he gasped. 'It's coming this way!'

Ben grabbed the rifle, trying to focus the sights along the uncertain line between the cliff and boulders. Then suddenly and soundlessly, like something seen in an old jerky film, a mule stepped into the frame. He held it for a moment, noticing it wore a saddle with a water can strapped to the girths. There was no rider.

Ryderbeit flung an arm round him: 'See it, soldier! It's one of 'em — and it's got water!'

Ben frowned, still looking through the telescope. Hanging behind the water can was a round leather case; he recognized it as Hitzi Leiter's compass.

'It's Hitzi's own mule,' he said, lowering the rifle. 'What's it doing out here? And where's Hitzi?'

They reached the mule ten minutes later. When it was still about fifty yards away Ryderbeit ran out to greet it, shouting across the stillness: 'God bless yer, yer lovely sexless beauty!' — kissing it between its floppy ears while it plodded relentlessly forward, kicking and trying to shake its head free of his embraces.

Ben watched them approach and said a prayer to a God he did not recognize, thanking Him that he had been spared — that this fantastic gift of water had come to them at the

184

eleventh hour, without explanation. He remembered there had been no thanks after Laura died.

Ryderbeit was leading the mule up to them, drinking from the water can and laughing. Ben laid Mel down on the sand and poured what was left of their own water between her lips; she gulped and spewed most of it down her chin, reviving only partially, her eyes still glazed, her breathing like a snore.

'It's all right,' he whispered, 'we've found one of the mules.'

Ryderbeit reached them and shouted, still laughing: 'We got him cold, soldier! He must be up there on the cliff just waiting for it!'

Ben nodded: 'And just tell me why.' He stood up and took the water can from him, drinking deeply, almost dizzily. Ryderbeit had dragged the mule to a halt, and between them they seized its neck and poured water between its drooling jaws; then Ryderbeit began to laugh again.

Ben looked at him. 'I don't like it, Sammy. Where are the other mules, for a start?'

Ryderbeit had the telescopic rifle focused again on the rocks. 'There's one up there — that thing we saw before. It's a mule all right. Standing dead still on a ledge.' He gave the rifle to Ben: 'A bit weird, isn't it?'

'It certainly is.'

Through the telescope Ben could now see that the horizontal lines along the cliff face were a series of low escarpments, almost in the form of steps rising above the boulders. The second mule was about a third of the way up. Ben could make out the hump on its back that would be its pack. He moved the cross-sights along the ledge as far as the focus reached, then back along the ledges above and below, and up to the very top of the escarpment. There was no sign of Hitzi Leiter.

He lowered the gun. 'I don't understand it. He must have got the mules that far up, and then something happened — something to make this one climb down again and start back.'

Ryderbeit stood pulling down his lower lip, staring at the mule, then at the escarped cliff ahead. 'Must be a trick,' he said at last. 'He's up there all right — must have seen us coming from miles away.' He winced: 'He's probably got those U-boat glasses on us right now. Makes you feel bloody naked!'

'But what the hell's he after?'

Ryderbeit grabbed the telescopic rifle out of Ben's hands: 'This! A little guy like Hitzi Leiter doesn't feel a complete man without his gun. He's been planning this all along — the old lion-dog technique, like I said. Let the prey get up close and keep it running.'

'Then why the devil does he let us take this mule, with the water and compass thrown in? It doesn't make sense.'

'To give us a better chance — he wants to make sure we go after him. He can't tackle us down here.'

'Then why didn't he leave us the mule and water in the first place?'

'We'd have been suspicious.'

Ben shook his head: 'Not anything like as suspicious as I am now. No, Sammy, it doesn't wash. Something damned odd's going on up there.'

Ryderbeit nodded, raising the telescopic rifle again: 'Take a look — at the bottom of the cliff to your left.'

Ben again moved the sights along the foot of the rocks, holding it on a gray shape that at first looked like another boulder. There was a dark object on top of it, which he could not make out. He swung the sights farther to the left and saw two more shapes; attached to one of them was what he now recognized as a harness and stirrups. 'They're mules!' he cried.

But Ryderbeit had already started out towards them. Ben followed, almost at a run, leaving Mel lying on the sand.

The first mule was about three hundred yards away. Its eyes were open and its head lay in a pool of thick brown blood that had not yet soaked away. There was a long white gash across its throat. On its back was the pack containing their rucksack of clothes, half the food supplies and two plastic water cans which were unopened.

There were seven of them altogether, spread out at intervals of about fifty feet under the cliff. Each one had had its throat cut. All the equipment was intact, including the whisky, maps, medicine case and food.

Ryderbeit began to hurry back towards Mel, talking almost to himself: 'So that's his game. Steal the mules — kill the mules — leave everything else to rot. Does it mean he wasn't even worried about us getting here? What's the little bastard up to?'

They reached Mel. 'Give me the Winchester,' he said to Ben.

Ryderbeit took the rifle and swung it twice round him in a wide arc; then he walked over to Mel, who was asleep now, and placed it across her lap, arranging her hands along the stock. She did not move. He opened one of the sacks they had left near her head and took out three boxes of ammunition: one for the shotgun, one for the .416, one for the Winchester. The first two he stuffed into his jacket pocket; the one for the Winchester he placed beside her. Then he looked up at Ben and grinned: 'Don't look so worried! With any luck, Hitzi's watching every move.' He leaned down and shook Mel awake. She looked at him from under heavy lids. 'What's happened?' she murmured.

'Now listen, Mel! We're going ahead after Hitzi — he's up there on the cliff. We're leaving you with this gun. Hitzi may try to come down after it. Ben and I are going to keep you covered every minute. But if Hitzi does try to come down…'

Ben broke in angrily: 'You can't do this, Sammy! You're just using her as bait!'

'That's right. It's the only way to get him down off the cliff.' He was squatting down beside her, speaking in a soft coaxing voice: 'But if Hitzi does try to come after you, you know what to do?'

She looked up at Ben: 'I've got to shoot him?'

Ryderbeit nodded: 'But that's only a long chance. We'll have you covered all the way.'

She gave a small nod. 'Can I have the shotgun instead?' she whispered.

'No.' Ryderbeit stood up and turned to Ben: 'He's more likely to be tempted down by the rifle. In any case, the shotgun's better for stalking him at close range. Any long-range shooting's going to be done with this' — he shook the telescopic .416.

He took a last deep drink from the water can, then put it down beside Mel. The mule was standing motionless a few feet away, still shaking its head.

'All right, soldier — let's move!'

Ben took a last look at Mel. She was lying with her face turned from the moon, her hands clasped across the rifle like a stone saint lying with her sword on a tomb. He said: 'Sammy, this is crazy! She can't defend herself.'

'She won't have to. The little bastard won't get within a hundred yards of her!' He was striding out under the cliff, crouched forward like a hunter with the telescopic rifle in both hands; then after a moment he turned and leered at Ben, his eyes bright yellow in the moon, and Ben realized that Ryderbeit was idyllically happy: all exhaustion gone, he was now the hunter going in for the kill, and nothing else in the world mattered.

Ben followed submissively. Now that he was no longer carrying Mel, his body had a weightlessness as though his feet were not touching the ground. After a few steps he found he was beginning to reel about, and once he nearly fell.

It took them a quarter of an hour to reach the foot of the boulders where the cliff began to break up. Each of the rock steps was between about three and six feet high, and under the moon they gave the effect of a huge marble staircase climbing into the night sky.

They halted a hundred yards from the spot below where the mule was still standing motionless on the ledge. Ryderbeit was examining it again through the telescope.

'It's got a guideline round its neck leading up the rock,' he said; but Ben was looking back to where they had left Mel. The sheer rock rose massively above her, and as he looked an ugly idea came to him.

'Supposing Hitzi's got climbing ropes?' he said. 'He could swing down and get the gun that way.'

'Very smart, soldier! That's exactly what I'm waiting for him to do. Only he'll be waiting too — waiting for us to get up the cliff after him. That's why he's left the mule up there, just as we've left the gun with Mel,' — he bared his white teeth — 'for bait!'

Ben felt very uneasy. The whole theory was either too simple or far too elaborate; he couldn't decide which. He said slowly: 'So you think that without any idea of what we're going to do, he risks sending one mule down with water, just to encourage us, and leave the other one on the cliff to tempt us up there? — all the time knowing we've got three guns against his bare hands. It doesn't make sense, Sammy. He's not going after Mel.'

Ryderbeit sneered: 'So what is he after? You tell me!'

'I can't. I don't know.'

Suddenly the mule above them let out a panting bellow, its echoes shuddering off the cliff as though the rock was crying out in pain, ending in a last, awful honk; then the silence closed back, deep and frightening. Ryderbeit said: 'That mule's bloody scared o' something!'

'So do we go up?' said Ben.

'We do. You start farther on and go straight up toward the mule. I'll go up here and wait for Hitzi to show himself. '

'And what if he doesn't show himself? Supposing he's up there with the mule?'

'Blow his head off — sharpish, before he throws a knife into you.'

Ben glanced again at where Mel lay, and at the cliff above her, and nothing moved. He broke open the shotgun, checked that the two Number One cartridges were in place, the firing pin clear of dust, the safety catch off. He cracked it shut and Ryderbeit said: 'Good hunting, soldier!'

Ben began to walk away past the rock falls under the cliff. After only a few paces he felt very alone. He looked back and saw Ryderbeit moving like a spider up over the smooth white boulders.

Ben reached the spot below where the mule was standing and walked on another fifty yards, so that while he climbed he could keep both Mel and Ryderbeit in sight. He looked at his watch. Nearly three o'clock. He could just make out the mule on the ledge above. Ryderbeit had disappeared for the moment into the confusion of rock and shadow, and Mel was now only a tiny speck, scarcely distinguishable from the mule beside her.

Ben slung the shotgun over his shoulder and began to climb. The moon was hard in his eyes, and his bones and muscles ached as he heaved himself up over the boulders on hands and knees, pausing every few minutes to rest and study the landscape. Still nothing moved.

It took him five minutes to reach the top of the boulders and clamber onto the first ledge. He had to move more carefully here; it was not easy to see above him and each time he pulled himself higher he had to shoulder the gun again. He remembered that Hitzi Leiter had a knife — and could also, of course, stone him from above. He might be up there watching him through the night glasses at this very moment.

He began to feel giddy; the moon distorted height even more than distance, and each time he reached a new ledge he took care not to look down; he even began to shun looking upward, except for quick glances to make sure of his bearings. The mule was still about thirty feet above him; and now the ledges were becoming steeper, narrower, in places shrunk or broken away to give no foothold at all. He began to feel the clutch of panic. He was shuffling along a ridge about six inches wide, the shotgun back over his shoulder, feeling his way with both hands on the rock face in front of him. Another few feet and the ledge began to widen. If Hitzi tried to rush him here, he might just have time to get the gun off and fire both barrels together. But no more. He'd have no chance to reload.

He edged his way round a shoulder of rock and looked up. The mule was on a ledge about ten feet above. He waited. There was no sound. He took off the shotgun and began using it as a lever to haul himself up, feeling the scree crunch under his weight, trying to keep his eyes on the rock above, and at the same time control his growing vertigo.

A guideline was tied under the mule's belly and reached back up the rock to another ledge about fifteen feet above. Ben tried to calculate what had happened. Hitzi Leiter must have been riding the other mule, slowly working his way up the ledges, leading the second animal by the rope, when something had happened to separate them. The pack mule had managed to climb down, while its companion had stopped. Ben now saw why: the ledge in front of it had broken away as though someone had taken a great bite out of it. Below was a drop of more than fifteen feet. The animal would have to move backward, and would only do so if led by someone. Hitzi Leiter had not come down to do it.

Ben thought: *Is this part of his plan? Or has something else happened? — something that even Hitzi hadn't been expecting?*

He began to move with sudden, frantic determination, knowing that whatever was going to happen, was going to happen in the next few moments. He edged his way along below the mule, to a point where he could climb up behind it, and now saw the rope disappearing almost directly above him. He knew then, with a deep visceral instinct, that Hitzi Leiter was up there.

He clambered up behind the mule and found the pack and water cans all in place. He had the shotgun in both hands, using it again as a lever to work his way up the last few yards to the end of the rope. He was gasping, his body strained and cold with sweat when he reached the ledge just below where the rope disappeared. He held the gun in his right hand, two fingers round the trigger, and with his left hand he took hold of the rope and tugged. It gave a couple of feet then sprang taut, as though pulling on some heavy object. Still holding the gun in one hand, he sank his whole weight on the rope and dragged downward.

There was a slither and a long white shape rolled up over the edge of rock above him, thumped down at his feet, rolled over again and dropped onto the ledge below. The rope was pulled down with it, gripped by something that came over in a swinging movement — a swollen black hand, its wrist puffed up round the sleeve of the khaki shirt, the fingernails shining in the moonlight like a row of teeth.

For a moment Ben stood utterly still. Then slowly he lowered himself onto the ledge below. Hitzi Leiter lay with his round head lolling over the edge, his face bloated the color of red wine. Against the sheen of white hair he had the appearance of a photographic negative; the eyes were closed, but the mouth was wide open, locked in a grin.

Ben stared and could not understand. There was no sign of blood on him, except the dried flecks on his shirt and trousers from the fight back in Benisalem. He leant out to touch his arm, but at the last moment the thought of making contact with this obscene metamorphosis made him shrink away. He began to yell Ryderbeit's name. The call was returned in a shattering echo. He cried again: 'He's dead! Dead! Dead!'

Five minutes later Ryderbeit came springing up the shelved rock face. 'I didn't hear any shooting!'

'There wasn't any.' Ben nodded at the bloated face.

'Holy Moses!' Ryderbeit murmured, then jumped back, his hands tightening round the telescopic rifle. 'You hear something?'

In the silence Ben now caught a faint rustling sound from above, like leaves being stirred in a breeze. Ryderbeit crouched down and hissed: 'Let's get away from here.' He crept along the ledge for about twenty feet, then began to climb. Ben came up behind and whispered: 'What is it?'

Ryderbeit turned, his long eyes glaring: 'Up there!' He was now climbing back across the rock to where the sound had been coming, reaching a ledge just level with the top of his head.

'Keep down!' he cried. Very slowly he raised his head and looked over; then his whole body stiffened, and he let out a low whistle. Ben crept closer and looked too. For perhaps a second he was confused by the contrast of moonlight and shadow, and did not at once realize what he was looking at.

About ten feet away along the ledge there appeared to be a mass of shiny ropes being rapidly uncoiled and rippled across the sand and scree. He glanced up to see if someone was manipulating them from above, for something was wrong with them: they were moving wrong. Then suddenly he knew what they were. He was looking at a nest of snakes. There were at least a dozen of them — long and dark, with pale bellies, looping with astonishing speed, their scales making the same rustling sound he and Ryderbeit had heard from below. About half of them were moving flat on the ledge in rapid figure-eight patterns, the others crawling in and out of holes in the rock, streaking upward, their diamond heads flashing like the points of spears, then plunging back into the sand to reappear a few feet away, always in the perfect arabesque movements of a meticulous ritual.

Ryderbeit let out another whistle. 'Moon snakes!' he murmured, 'doing their dance in the full moon. I've heard about this, but very few people have ever seen it. God, if only I had a camera! Isn't it beautiful?'

Ben shuddered. 'How long did Hitzi take to die?'

'About three minutes — perhaps less. Give me the shotgun. This isn't going to be pretty, but it's got to be done.'

He took the gun and a pocketful of cartridges and climbed carefully up onto the ledge, lay down on his stomach facing the snakes, then began to crawl toward them. Ben kept behind him on the lower ledge. 'Keep absolutely still!' Ryderbeit called: 'they'll strike only if they see us move or feel vibration. Snakes can't hear.'

Ben stood holding his breath, watching with horrid icy fascination. When Ryderbeit was less than six feet away from them he fired. The two explosions were simultaneous — a long crash that went on ringing off the cliffs, while he reloaded and fired again, the twin barrels close to the rock, throwing up a blast of dust and splinters and bright shredded skin, as the snakes whirled and whipped round and smacked against the rock wall, striking feebly out with their fangs as they slithered back onto the ledge. Then suddenly one of them darted up out of a hole, coiled back like a spring and came running at Ryderbeit on its tail.

He fired in the same second and the snake snapped in two, its upper half flying into the air like an elastic band. He fired six more shots, then climbed down beside Ben. He was grinning: 'Nice shooting, eh?'

'Lovely.' Ben began to retch. 'Did you get them all?'

'I don't miss. Not when I'm serious.' He turned and began to climb down towards the body. On the ledge just above the body they found the U-boat binoculars; Hitzi Leiter must have been carrying them when he was bitten. They were still in their case, undamaged. Ryderbeit knelt down beside the body and began to tear open the buttons of the jacket.

'God, what a way to die!' said Ben. 'Do you think he suffered much?'

'Not as much as he would if I'd taken him alive!' He began to search Hitzi Leiter's body, stripping back his jacket, turning out his pockets, rolling the body over and back, pulling out a black leather wallet, a gold-topped Shaeffer pen, an ivory-handled switch-blade knife with a serrated edge, and the buff envelope which Stopes had shown Ben in the Casa Sphinx. He peeled it open, shook the brown pebble into his hand and grinned: 'Nice to have it back!'

The map was folded up inside the wallet next to about two hundred pesos in small notes and five American twenty-dollar bills. Ryderbeit stuffed them away inside his own jacket, along with the pen, switchblade and the diamond, throwing what was left in the man's pockets — his German passport, identity card and some insurance vouchers — back on the body.

'Isn't it all just beautiful, soldier! We got everything, haven't we? The map, a hundred bucks — another tent and rifle and night glasses, extra food and water — and this little bastard off our backs for evermore!'

He stood there grinning, yellow-eyed and happy; but Ben felt none of his confidence — only a dull fear that he could not fully define, knowing that death had probably been only postponed.

Ryderbeit said: 'Start getting that mule down.'

'What about Hitzi?'

He answered with a savage cackle and walked up to the body, tipped it over the edge with the toe of his boot and leaped down after it, laughing, kicking it over again, following it down as though it were some hideous game.

Ben turned away, sickened, and went over to the mule. He pulled at the rope which had now been wrenched out of Hitzi's dead hand, and began leading the animal backward along the ledge. He managed to turn it after about ten yards, and looked down. Ryderbeit and his plaything had reached the foot of the cliff. He was resting on a boulder with the corpse at his feet. Ben and the mule reached him about five minutes later.

They buried Hitzi Leiter without ceremony, in a shallow grave scraped out with their hands under the boulders. It was nearly four o'clock when Ryderbeit rolled the body in. It lay on its belly with the ball of white hair shining in the moonlight like a dandelion fur.

'May you roast in Hell, Hitzi Leiter,' he said, and began kicking the sand and rocks back over him. The body disappeared in the dust, and Ben stood there for a moment with his head bowed, feeling no pity or sorrow for Hitzi Leiter, only a gloom that was close to terror. This was the second man to die in just four days, and all for a sackful of diamonds. The odds are still long, even without Hitzi Leiter.

They pushed the last of the sand over him, picked up the two guns and the night glasses, and began to lead the mule back to where they had left Mel.

She was sleeping with the Winchester still across her lap; she had slept even through the shooting. They woke her with water and salt tablets from the medicine chest, and Ben wiped her face down with surgical spirit while Ryderbeit told her what had happened. She listened calmly, and when he had finished she just nodded and said: 'So he's dead?'

'Dead and buried, my darling! But you should have seen the snakes: Ah, the snakes were beautiful!' He crouched down beside her, smiling, stretching out his hand till it rested across her stomach close to the Winchester. 'The rest is going to be all downhill, my darling! We're goin' to be rich.' He showed her the diamond. 'We got the map now. We got everything — including Hitzi Leiter's share.' He pressed his hand harder against her stomach, his yellow eyes widening with that glare that was both mad and dangerous. Ben did not like the look of it at all. He began putting up Hitzi Leiter's tent. The sky was beginning to grow light above the mountains.

Ryderbeit was purring in Mel's ear, and Ben heard her say: 'I feel better now. I'll be all right after I've slept properly.'

Ben went over and collected their own tent from the dead mule. He moved laboriously, bringing back all the rest of the equipment, piling it close to where Mel had been lying. Ryderbeit had taken her round the waist and pulled her to her feet, his dark hooked face bent over her, his hands moving confidently, one holding her under the breast, the other squeezing her buttocks. Ben felt a confusion of fury and dismay, as he watched Ryderbeit unbutton her shirt, saying, 'Come on, you're goin' to have a lovely sleep. He held her hard against him, unstrapping her belt, peeling her trousers down her thighs. He helped her step feebly out of them, then sank his hand down under her cotton pants. She made an attempt to struggle and cried out something, and Ben shouted: 'For Chrissake, leave off, Sammy! We've no time for that sort of monkeying around.'

'We've got all the time in the world, soldier,' Ryderbeit said pleasantly; but he removed his hand, still smiling, and laid Mel down inside Hitzi Leiter's tent. 'An arse made by the Gods,' he murmured, straightening up and reaching for the water can.

Ben looked at him angrily. 'Let's not have any more of that.'

'Take it easy, soldier. Not jealous are you?' He passed him the water can, grinning: 'We'll leave her to sleep all day. She'll be a nice strong girl when she wakes up!' He spoke with a fierce gaiety which Ben found even more alarming than his outbursts of rage and drunkenness. This was the first time he had witnessed the lecher in Ryderbeit, and the spectacle was not encouraging.

'Help me put up the big tent,' he said.

Ryderbeit leered at him: 'Sleeping together, are we? Mustn't crowd the lady out, old boy!'

They stripped and each took a long drink before climbing inside, lying naked on the ground sheets. Ben closed his eyes and the world sank away round him and in the darkness he thought of Mel's body, full and tender and washed cool with surgical spirit.

The ground under the sheet felt hard and dead.

He awoke with someone shaking him by the shoulder. It was Mel.

He had been alone in the tent and the flaps were now pulled back. Ryderbeit was not there. She stood above him, holding the shotgun. 'Ben! Please get up!'

He sat up slowly, embarrassed by his nakedness. 'What! What's going on?' He began groping for his trousers, and she cried: 'Please quickly!'

He pulled on his trousers and stumbled into the sunlight which was dying across the bronze bowl of the desert. Ryderbeit was sitting outside with a bottle of whisky in one hand and the elephant-gun in the other.

'What the hell's going on?' said Ben.

Mel stood beside him, still gripping the shotgun, and he saw she was beginning to tremble: 'Just keep him away from me, that's all!' She was very pale and her eyes were large with mushroom shadows under them. Ben looked at Ryderbeit again and noticed he was bleeding from a gash just below the ear.

'What's going on, Sammy?'

'You ask her — the dried-up bitch!'

'Oh do stop it!' she shrieked, with a note of hysteria. Ben wheeled round, feeling his anger rising: 'Come on, what happened?' He took a step toward her and she seemed to shrink into herself like a scared animal.

'Just keep him away from me!' she said again. 'He's horrible! Just because I've been sick he thinks he can do what he likes. He's a maniac!'

Ben turned. Ryderbeit still had one hand on the elephant gun and was drinking whisky with the other. He lowered the bottle and spat: 'She was never sick! She's not human enough to be sick!'

'Shut up!' said Ben. He turned back to her and saw there were red marks on her wrists. 'Tell me what happened, Mel.'

She lowered her eyes: 'I don't want to talk about it. I've hardly had any sleep at all — I've had to keep him away with this!' She lifted the shotgun.

'Did he rape you?'

'He did about everything else, the bastard! I've had plenty of people make passes at me, but not like this one. I thought he was going to kill me!'

Her voice had taken on an accent of well-bred peevishness, and for a moment the whole situation seemed so outrageously incongruous that Ben almost found it amusing. He nodded at her and said: 'You're all right now. Just get your things together.'

'Thank God you're here,' she murmured. He watched her bend down and disappear into Hitzi Leiter's tent, and realized he felt a grudging sympathy for Ryderbeit. 'O.K., Sammy, let's put the whisky away and get the tents packed up.'

Ryderbeit leered nastily and wiped his mouth. 'Trying to get you on her side, is she?'

'Get the tent up,' said Ben. He began pulling out the pegs.

'She lets us drag her all the way out here,' Ryderbeit went on, 'waving it right under our noses, and when one of us asks her what any normal man would ask, she goes bleeding berserk!'

Ben tossed him a handful of pegs. 'Get on with it.'

Ryderbeit took another drink. 'If she hadn't had a gun I'd have thrashed the arse off her!' He fingered the gash beside his ear and nodded: 'That's what she really needs, you know. She's not capable of any normal feeling — she's not bloody human! Just a lump of well-shaped mutton!'

Ben turned and looked at him. 'You're a louse, Sammy. A crazy hopeless louse! What is it? Unhappy childhood? What went wrong?'

'Stuff it, will you!'

'No I won't. I'm going to tell you a few things. You got pretty wild yourself when I started scrapping with young Hitzi back there — only I happened to be right. And now what do we have, but you starting a sordid little feud here with Mel, and all because she won't open her legs to you. Good God! Haven't we got enough troubles already?'

Ryderbeit spat: 'She wanted it all right! She wanted it but I'm not good enough for her. I'm just a bloody Jew — not good enough!' He paused, glaring at Ben with miserable defiance. 'That's it! She wanted it — she was wet for it!'

Ben seized the whisky bottle from his hand. 'Oh sure she was! The old excuse. She wanted it, but she didn't want it, so it was all her fault! And you're a Jew, of course, which makes me weep with sympathy. Oh, I feel sorry for you, Ryderbeit. Now get to work! If she doesn't want to sleep with you that's your problem — only I don't want it mine too. So just make one more bit of trouble with her and I'll take this shotgun and blow your head off — from behind, if necessary.'

Ryderbeit studied him, his eyes growing cautious. 'You don't understand, soldier. She led me on. You saw — this morning. I was giving her the feel right here in front of you. She wasn't clawing at me then like some bloody wildcat!' His face took on a look of pained rage, seeking some sign of consolation. 'I thought she was going to kill me just now! I've been scared of her.'

'Scared of a girl, Sammy? Oh, tough luck! Now get the mules ready.'

He was strapping up the large tent when Ryderbeit came slowly round behind him. 'Don't talk about using a gun on me, soldier. Like that one of us might not get back alive.'

Ben hauled up the tent and said nothing.

CHAPTER EIGHT: SNAKE WATER

As the sun went down, they began to climb the Chinluca Wall. They steered the mules clear of the ledge where the moon snakes lay, and at each new ledge paused and listened. They saw no more snakes, but long before dawn there was a sound above them like canvas in a wind and down through the moonlight came the condors. They circled slowly, settling in seven groups along the foot of the cliff where the dead mules lay, their wings closing in a huddle of umbrellas; and for some time, the silence was pierced with cries like squealing pigs.

A couple of hours before dawn the three of them reached the top of the Chinluca Wall and found themselves at the beginning of a gently rising massif of sandstone, broken up by huge towers of black rock. *A splendid, terrible landscape*, Ben thought: *a way up to the roof of the world*. Ryderbeit growled: 'Xatu country!' He had the U-boat night glasses and elephant-gun ready at his side. 'We keep our eyes peeled from now on,' he added.

They rested at the top and watered the mules; then Mel made soup and coffee, while they chewed the usual ration of tinned beef and drank several mugs of whisky without water. But the meal did nothing to relax the ill feeling between her and Ryderbeit, and Ben was reminded ominously of the tension that had built up between him and Hitzi Leiter on that first day. It was almost as though the ghost of the German were still with them, infecting them with his hatred, turning them against each other. Then he thought, Perhaps it's just exhaustion — and three is always a bad number. He decided to pretend nothing had happened, to concentrate on the only two things that really mattered now that Hitzi Leiter was dead: survival and finding the diamonds.

They marched on in silence for another two hours until the sun was burning hard and the Devil's Spoon now lay far below and out of sight. The atmosphere between them had deteriorated even further since Ben had agreed to let Mel ride one of the mules. Ryderbeit had cursed and jeered, refusing to share the pack with him; and Ben carried it alone and held his tongue, determined not to be provoked by Ryderbeit.

It was going to be a hard journey, and there would be worse to come.

They pitched camp toward midday. Mel slept again in the small tent while Ben and Ryderbeit kept alternate watches in case of an attack by Xatu Indians. There were hot blasts of wind blowing down on them when they started again at four o'clock in the afternoon. Ben helped Ryderbeit take their bearings from the cloth-backed maps, checking them against Hitzi Leiter's own map; and it occurred to Ben, as he again studied the neatly drawn sheet of foolscap, that for such a fragile document it was remarkably well preserved. It was hard to imagine that in these neat ballpoint markings lay the key to a potential fortune. The map reminded him of a schoolboy's tracing for a geography lesson — an hour's work, perhaps less. And yet this had been drawn in painful stages while its author picked his way through a mangrove swamp.

Ryderbeit still took charge of the maps and compass; but it was Ben now who led the way, walking just ahead of the mule that carried Mel. She had thanked him again — he was still carrying the pack — but her tone was casual and easy, adding, 'goodness, what I'd give for a bath!' She smiled: 'I just want to spend a whole day soaking up to my neck, then twelve hours in a clean bed and I'll feel fine!'

'You seem to have recovered pretty well,' he said, trudging wearily beside her. Ryderbeit was several yards behind, scanning the horizon every few minutes through the night glasses.

'I'm still pretty tired,' she said placidly; then glanced over her shoulder and added with sudden venom, 'I wish to God he'd get something wrong with him! It might keep him busy.'

'Forget him, Mel. Humor him — be nice. We're going to spend a long time together.'

'He's nothing more than an animal!'

If he was just that, Ben thought, *I wouldn't be worried.* He said: 'I warned you he was wild, Mel, back in Parataxín. You had time to make up your mind.'

'But I didn't think he'd try what he did when I was sick, then threaten to beat me up when I said no to him.'

Ben shook his head. *Terrible behavior*, he thought. Of all the lone wolves in South America, he had to be landed with these two — a mad Jewish outcast with a love of firearms and a nice English girl with good legs and scruples.

The sun was beginning to go down and the towers of rock were now expanding into black table-mountains divided by dry valleys. They began to see cacti again and the flitting movement of lizards among the rocks; but these were the only signs of life. Towards the north were the frail white teeth of a mountain range; but to the south, where the swamp lay, there was nothing but a stone-colored haze.

They pitched camp again at dusk, dividing the night again into watches. Mel slept by herself in the small tent and there were no incidents.

Ryderbeit had the last watch and woke the others at dawn. His eyes had a bleak hungry look and his mouth was slack, as he swallowed his coffee in silence. Ben guessed that he had been drinking during the last three hours.

After they had eaten, Mel sat outside her tent with an array of lotions and creams and used tissues spread round her, her hair combed tightly back and fastened at the nape of her neck. Her complexion had that shiny mask-like texture of an actress before she has put on the final grease paint. She reminded Ben of how filthy he felt himself: his hair matted like rope, the stubble itching under his chin, the sweat and dust now worked into his pores with the permanence of coal dust on a miner.

Ryderbeit finished his coffee, strolled over to Mel, stood over her and began to laugh. It was not his usual cackle but a slow gurgling sound without any movement of the lips, and quite mirthless. For a moment she took no notice, beginning to scoop off the grease with a tissue.

Ryderbeit leaned down and said loudly: 'You're lovely, aren't you? Aren't you a lovely little girl! All alone in the desert, dolling yourself up. Who are you doing it for? Ben here?'

'That'll do!' said Ben, stepping between them; he had the maps and compass in his hands. The .416 was lying by the large tent and the other two guns were slung on the mules. They were supposed to be having a quiet breakfast together. 'Let's take the bearings,' he said.

Ryderbeit gave his gurgling laugh again: 'Isn't she pretty, soldier?'

Ben began to lead him away. 'The map says we head south-southwest twelve degrees. Check it, will you?'

He gave him the compass and Ryderbeit's laugh stopped. He squinted at the map, swiveled the compass and watched the needle settle, then threw his arm round Ben's shoulders. 'Learning fast, aren't you!' Ben caught a vile whiff of his breath as he clutched Ben closer: 'You could almost do without me, eh? Just a little more practice!'

Ben pulled himself free and said, 'Let's get going, Sammy.'

He began packing up the breakfast things, fighting down a new fresh fear of a danger he had so far not considered. He had known all along that Ryderbeit could not be trusted: he was unstable and perverse, and in the last resort, if the diamonds were ever found, he might well try to double-cross them. What Ben had never bargained for was the possibility that Ryderbeit might not trust him — or rather, an alliance between him and Mel. From the start, Ryderbeit had been organizer and unspoken leader of the expedition; and while Hitzi Leiter had been with them, Ben and Mel had been the ones who were expendable.

But now, with the subtle shifting of initiative to Ben, it was Ryderbeit who was odd man out. Ben had mastered the technique of compass navigation; he had studied the map; he had seen the specimen diamond. Mel and he could probably get to that river, and back, and even then they didn't have to rely on Ryderbeit. Mel had been in Parataxín more than six months; she would know her way round. And if you had a few million dollars' worth of uncut diamonds, and you kept your head, eventually you'd find a buyer, as well as a way to get the stuff into a foreign bank account.

Somehow Ryderbeit would have to be reassured — or at least, made to feel that he was not expendable.

They plodded on all day, through a landscape of wild yellow rock and canyons full of cacti as tall as trees, with horny spires and spiked pods and giant furry fingers that the mules attacked with a furious appetite. The wind had dropped, and the glaring sky gradually dulled to the stone-gray of the haze ahead where the swamp stretched the length of the horizon. Toward evening they came to the first water they had seen since leaving the Hiarra: a trickle at the bottom of a dark valley where there were flies and insects and a sweet smell that might have been the first breath of stagnant vegetation.

They stopped and boiled enough water in saucepans to fill all the plastic cans; then Ben and Ryderbeit stripped and sluiced themselves down and shaved while Mel withdrew a hundred yards up the stream to wash carefully under a towel. They waited for her, sitting with their feet in the stream, drinking tepid whisky from the bottle. Ryderbeit murmured something about expecting mosquitoes by evening, but most of the time he was silent, gulping the Scotch noisily with his head back and eyes closed. When it was almost empty he lifted it and scowled. 'Which bloody bottle is this?' But before Ben could answer he was on his feet, stumbling over to the mule, where he rummaged in the White Horse crate for a moment, then returned, muttering to himself.

'The fifth,' he said, slumping down again beside Ben. 'Only seven to go. I got to make it last.'

'You go easy with it and you'll make it last,' Ben said, although he wondered which would be less tolerable, to have Ryderbeit always on the margin of another manic bout of drunkenness or running dry and perhaps cracking up altogether.

Ryderbeit emptied the bottle, tossed it away into the shallow water, and was lighting up a cigar when they saw Mel coming back down the edge of the stream. She had put on a change of shirt and trousers, and her face was clear-skinned, her hair wet and gleaming. She smiled at them both. 'Gosh, I feel better for that! Is there any Scotch?'

'Can't spare any,' Ryderbeit growled.

'But we brought a whole case full,' she said, looking at Ben.

'We're running short,' Ryderbeit repeated, watching her through the cigar smoke, his face narrow and cruel.

Ben stood up and said to her, 'I'll get another bottle out of the crate.'

'You sit down and leave the crate!' shouted Ryderbeit.

'You go to hell,' Ben said, starting over toward the mule.

Ryderbeit was on his feet in one deft leap. He still held the cigar, but his hands were tensed and rigid, and his eyes had a wild look that made Ben stop for a moment.

'What the hell's wrong with you?' he cried.

'I'm not having this bitch drinking my Scotch,' Ryderbeit said, in a tight gasping voice.

'Who said it was your Scotch? If it belongs to anyone, it belongs to me and Mel. We paid for it.'

Ryderbeit took a step forward. 'Morris, you leave that bleeding drink where it is! You're always the one who's trying to stop me having my swig, and now just when I feel like going easy on it, you and your girlfriend decide it's time to start hitting it. You know what that is, Morris? That's being perverse.'

Ben shook his head sadly, wondering how much longer he could put up with Ryderbeit, when Mel said, 'Leave him, Ben. I don't really want it. Let him have all the Scotch he wants, let him get as drunk as he wants, like a spoiled little child.'

Ryderbeit turned to her and laughed. 'Darling, you're beginning to overdo it. You really do want trouble, don't you?' For a moment the two of them faced each other, Ryderbeit with his crooked leer, she with her blank stare of contempt; and Ben thought, *There's going to be trouble*. And as he watched her standing there, lithe and clean and cold, he cursed her. Why couldn't she be a bouncy, jolly girl who cooked and giggled and jumped into bed with both of them whenever they wanted?

At last the three of them turned and packed their things back on the mule, and Ryderbeit finished his cigar and said no more as they started off again down the valley.

As darkness fell, the first of the mosquitoes came out of the damp twilight ahead, and that night the three of them slept under nets inside the two tents. During the three-hour watches they smeared every inch of exposed skin with insect repellent. Ben took the last watch. The moon was blurred with thin cloud, and by dawn the sky above the swamp was a livid mauve which darkened as the day drew on into the tortured patterns of a storm that never broke.

They marched all that day, down through the valleys between the table-mountains; and about an hour before sunset at last reached the end of the massif.

The clouds ahead had suddenly parted and the sun flashed down in long yellow shafts onto what at first might have been English countryside on a summer's evening: lime green and smooth as a lawn, rolling away with the curve of the earth. Far out to the west was a dark swelling that was the dead volcano where Stopes had taken refuge. The bearings on Hitzi Leiter's map were correct. Ryderbeit studied it all for a long time through the night glasses, then turned and grinned: 'It's all there. Just as the map says.'

'Can you see the river?' said Ben.

'Too far. But it'll be there.'

'It had better be,' said Ben.

They reached the beginnings of the swamp in the late afternoon of the next day. The last ten miles led through scrawny vegetation where the flies grew fat and the air dank and the sky the color of steel. The ground passed from rock to gravel, to a soggy soil sprinkled with flowers. Later came the salt pans shimmering with insects, then the first glimpses of bog water under trees that were full of movement and overripe smells of decay. They pressed on through the last hour of light and camped just before nightfall in a clearing between bamboo groves. They had just finished putting up the tents when the silence was broken by a deep whine. It came from no particular direction, but swelled out of every corner of the forest, growing louder and louder till it seemed to be coming from inside their own heads.

When the first shock was over Ryderbeit ducked across to the mules and dragged down the medicine case, yelling: 'Inside the tent quick — under the nets!' He was back only just in time. The first swarm of mosquitoes rose out of the trees ahead, moving across the clearing like some poisonous cloud, the whining now reaching a crescendo, as the three of them crouched down inside the large tent with the nets fastened across the flaps, smearing the repellent over their hands and faces, pulling woolen caps over their hair and necks.

It went on for nearly half an hour. When it finally died out, the night was alive with a thousand sounds — tickings and purrings and snufflings and hummings that went on till dawn. There was no moon. None of them knew what to expect or what to look out for — snakes, hyenas, scorpions, Xatus. Ben and Mel shared the first watch, outside the large tent, where Ryderbeit had shut himself away with his whisky. Mel hugged the shotgun to her breast, staring into the almost pitch-darkness, and for a long time neither of them spoke. The sounds of the jungle were growing familiar now, like traffic in a city. She was sitting only a few inches from him, but when she spoke her voice sounded far away, as though reaching him from the edge of sleep. 'Ben? Ben, are you awake?'

'Yes.' He blinked into the darkness; it seemed to be full of invisible movement.

'I want to talk to you.'

He waited, saying nothing; his heart began to beat fast.

'It's not going very well, is it?'

Still he said nothing. After a moment he felt her stir next to him and could smell the insect repellent on her skin, as she added, with growing urgency: 'Ben, listen to me! You know what's happening. It can't go on. Sooner or later he's going to do something. He's mad — you know that! He won't wait forever.'

He stared into the darkness, listening to the throb of the jungle as she went on: 'The swamp goes on for more than fifty miles, doesn't it? It'll give him plenty of opportunity — just like it was with you and Hitzi.'

'He won't do anything,' he said, without conviction.

'Why not?'

'Because he still needs us.'

'You perhaps. Not me.' She was silent for a moment, then pressed herself against him, breathing closely: 'Ben, we've got to do something! Before he gets another chance. Tonight — while he's asleep.'

'No. We'll do nothing tonight.' His tone was calm, but his mind was working frantically, in fear. When she next spoke he could hear the contempt in her voice, just as he had done that first night in the Hiarra when she had surprised him stealing Hitzi Leiter's ammunition: 'All right, you worry about your skin — I'll worry about mine. I'm finished with trekking along beside him, putting up with his insults, knowing he's just waiting for a good moment to do me in. I'm not that soft, I can tell you!'

'We'll do nothing,' he said quietly, 'until we get to the river.'

'Why the river?'

'Because we need him to help us get there.'

'We can get there without him. Hitzi did it — and he was alone.'

'He was lucky. And even then he damned nearly didn't make it. No, Mel, we wait until the river — then maybe we think again.'

'At the river it'll be worse. You know what he's like. He'll get his hands on those diamonds and nothing'll stop him. Listen, Ben! Please! I'm scared to death of him!'

He felt the drop of despair, knowing she was right; but he said again: 'We do nothing until the river.'

He swung round. Ryderbeit loomed above them, swinging something at his side. Although the leer was invisible in the dark, Ben knew it was there. Mel sat beside him absolutely still, the shotgun in both hands. Ryderbeit bent down and thrust the thing he had been swinging at his side in front of Ben's face. It was a bottle of White Horse. 'Have a drink soldier!'

Ben wiped the neck and drank. He offered it to Mel and she did the same. Ryderbeit did not move. 'All right, children!' His voice was thick but measured: 'My turn now. Give me the gun.'

'It's not time for your watch,' Ben said, and began to stand up. 'And you've got a gun of your own.'

'Don't argue, soldier.' Ryderbeit reached for the shotgun and lifted it easily out of Mel's hands. He turned to Ben who now stood facing him. 'You get some sleep.' Ben looked at him, then down at Mel. Slowly she got to her feet and, without a word, disappeared into the small tent. Ryderbeit put his free arm round Ben's shoulder and squeezed: 'Everything fine?' His breath was heavy with Scotch.

Ben slid out of his grip. 'Fine,' he said. 'Call me if anything happens.'

'Don't worry!' Ryderbeit had laid the bottle on the ground next to the .416 and now just stood there in front of him grinning. A bird started to shriek somewhere in the darkness with a sound like a dog that's been run over. Ben went into the big tent and lay down. The air reeked of kerosene and whisky, and his face began to sweat through the cloying insect repellent. He could not sleep.

He wondered: *How long had Ryderbeit been standing there? Had he heard everything, or nothing, or perhaps just enough to guess what had been said? And even if he hadn't heard anything, what about Mel? Would she really try something? What was she doing now? Asleep, or lying in her tent like him, worrying and planning?*

He looked at his watch. Ten to eleven. He had the last watch from two o'clock till dawn.

At six o'clock he woke them both and they boiled up coffee under a sky already hot and sluggish. In the last hour before dawn the jungle had become strangely quiet. It was now beginning to stir again, with a vast invisible life of its own that seemed to close them in, trapping them together with their private conflicts.

They ate breakfast in silence, keeping their guns within easy reach; and when they set off, Ryderbeit was careful to leave last. Ben had decided to keep up his pretense that nothing serious had happened between Ryderbeit and Mel. He was reasonably sure she would try nothing drastic without his sanction. Whatever happened, they would have to wait until the river. If Ryderbeit then tried something, Ben would just have to be ready for him.

As the morning drew on the heat became almost unbearable, reflected off the sweating cloud and sucked down into the mangroves ahead. They could not strip because of the flies and insects, and in the first six hours covered less than eight miles. To go by night would have been impossible because there was now no moon.

The volcano still lay about ten miles ahead; but already the ground was rising, the bog soil becoming firmer as they began to reach the lava crust, pushing their way through grass that came up to their shoulders, stretching ahead as far as the lower slopes of the volcano. They had to walk warily, beating the ground with bamboo sticks to warn off snakes. The air was full of the shrilling of crickets and the stench of pollen, which soon had Ryderbeit dragging behind, panting like a dog.

Late in the afternoon the volcano rose suddenly in front of them out of the steaming grass. It was far higher than any of them had expected; and as they plodded on round its dark slopes Ben began to feel a strange power emanating from it — a power that seemed to follow him until dusk, when they made camp at the foot of the mountain.

What was it about the volcano? Just an instinct warning him, as it had already warned him twice before? There seemed to be nothing wrong here: the bearings on Hitzi Leiter's map were correct, even to a tenth of a degree. He had been a painstaking little fellow, Hitzi Leiter.

Next morning it took them another four hours to reach the point south of the volcano where the course of the map changed radically. It had led them around the volcano from the northeast and now plunged due south, straight into the swamp. Ben and Ryderbeit spent some time rechecking bearings and distances. Although the directions on the map were exact and unambiguous, Ryderbeit said he didn't like it. He had already noticed over the last hour that the ground was beginning to grow spongy again like foam rubber. None of the official maps marked the lava shelf — according to them the whole area was swamp — so now they had only Hitzi's map to go on, and Hitzi said due south.

They set off again in low spirits, for although they were glad to be out of the snake-infested grass, the very presence of the volcano had given them a curious confidence. Those barren slopes could be seen from miles away and could hide nothing. Besides, they always knew that over the summit there was refuge in the caves and fresh water in the lake. The mangroves ahead gave no such confidence. Ben knew, for no rational reason, that they should not be leaving the volcano.

They tramped on until nightfall, out of the grass into a meaty vegetation full of huge flowers and fungi and creepers that wound round the branches like snakes. Soon after they made camp the mosquitoes came out of the swamp again with their thundering whine, but this time the assault was so massive that the three of them could feel the outer sheet of the tent vibrating under their weight. Some even managed to penetrate the nets and sewn-in ground sheets, and soon the three of them had several bad bites, some right under their clothing. They decided to stay together that night in the large tent, lying in the airless heat, scratching and rubbing themselves with anti-sting lotion, but finding little relief except in whisky, of which they all drank more than they needed.

The rhythm of watches was abandoned; there was again no moon, and they decided to conserve their energies in sleep. Even the conflict between Ryderbeit and Mel seemed to have been damped down by the sticking, itching misery of the swamp.

Ben was up first and had to kick Ryderbeit in the ribs to wake him. They all had headaches, and drank quinine with more than a pint of coffee each; then took their bearings against the various peaks of the volcano — all carefully marked on Hitzi Leiter's map — and set off again into the swamp.

By noon the jungle was high and heavy all around them, and their boots were sinking into mud that burst in evil-smelling bubbles at every step. At first sight the mangroves might have passed for trees in an English park — stout branches and sedate green leaves. But looking down, it was as though they had been caught in panic, their roots writhing out of the mud like the hands of drowned men, each joint a festering nest of lice and leeches; and in the dark hollows under the roots the mud was lit up with a phosphorescent glow to match the sky, which had turned a jaundiced color, like bad marble.

There was also a peculiar smell all around that did not belong to normal vegetation. It was a fleshy smell exuding from the fungi that grew sometimes taller than a man, or sprouted pink and succulent from the mangrove branches like uncooked sausages. The flowers also began to smell of flesh: great water lilies the size of bathtubs, floating on a carpet of swamp weed, or bright long-stemmed flowers that peered out of the undergrowth with little mouths and tongues wrapped in fat velvet petals.

The three of them were now testing the ground at every step with their bamboo poles; but already the mud was squelching up close to the top of their boots. The mangrove trees had grown as big as oaks, their roots silver and moving, completely covered now in a scaly bark of live insects.

They stopped again to check the compass, and knew that something had gone badly wrong. Ben looked up, wiping the sweat and slime from his eyes. The compass bearing pointed down a tunnel under the roots that narrowed into total darkness. They started to go around it, prodding the ground, noticing that in places the mud was turning into pools of khaki water lying stagnant under the trees — probably part of a complicated network of tributaries that spread out from the diamond river. The implication was obvious. The closer the river, the more impenetrable the swamp. It would probably have been impossible at this point even with a canoe; with a couple of pack-laden mules it was hopeless.

They paused and looked at each other. Insects whirled round them like a veil. The sun was almost completely shut out now, and the darkness was full of darting shadows. Ryderbeit picked something off the ground that looked like a brown stocking. It crackled in his fingers and part of it broke away and floated down into the mud. Ben recognized a pattern of scales. Ryderbeit grinned sadly: 'Looks like an anaconda — shedding its skin for the new season.' He plunged his pole in after it, and it sank down several feet. He looked up savagely: 'What does the bloody map say now?'

'Straight on,' said Ben.

'We can't go straight on!'

'I know we can't.' He tried to smile: 'So what would you do? Follow through this stuff?'

'No I wouldn't!' said Ryderbeit, 'and nor would that little bastard, Hitzi Leiter! The map's wrong.'

Mel looked at them both in horror: 'But the map's all we've got!'

'That's right, darling. And it's wrong. Hitzi couldn't have got through this. No one could.' He paused. From somewhere above the noise of the jungle came a whining sound, growing louder. Ben began to say: 'Perhaps we took the wrong bearings…'

'Shut up!' said Ryderbeit. They stood listening. The sound was coming closer. It was not the whine of insects this time, but the steady beat of an engine.

'A plane!' Ryderbeit cried, and they all stood staring up at the fragments of sky between the trees. The sound was beginning to move off now.

'What sort of plane would come out here?' Ben asked, realizing that he didn't much care: whoever it was would be well on their way by now; they didn't have to tramp knee-deep through lice-ridden mud.

'It couldn't have been an airliner,' said Ryderbeit. 'None of the civil companies fly this way.'

The engine droned away into the din of the jungle, and Mel said suddenly: 'It could have been a military plane.'

'Doing what?' Ryderbeit growled.

She looked at Ben: 'It could be Romolo dropping his prisoners over the swamp,' she began.

'Sure!' said Ryderbeit and gave a nasty laugh. 'Or it could have been a few nice people from Parataxín looking for a river full of diamonds.'

They both stared at him. The sound of the plane had died away entirely now. 'Do you think that's really likely?' said Ben.

'Well if it isn't, you just tell me something that is likely!' Ryderbeit cried.

Ben was staring into the mangroves, and for a moment he thought of that plane: of the dry antiseptic smell of the pressurized cabin, the crisp, smiling airline hostesses and the pencil beam of light above his seat in the humming darkness. It meant escape. And it had gone. And all around was the creeping poisonous swamp.

'What's likely?' he repeated: 'I'll tell you what's likely. In fact, what's damned certain! Hitzi Leiter's map is wrong. What's more, I think it's deliberately wrong. I think he drew it wrong, specially for us.'

He was already turning the mules around, but even the way back now looked a dismal prospect. It was past four o'clock: dark in three hours. 'Give me the map,' he said. He had the compass out and stood between the mules who were kicking, their skinny legs crawling with insects and leeches. 'We'll head back to the volcano,' he added, without looking at either of them. 'This way's hopeless.'

Then, under the mangroves about thirty feet away, he saw a movement. At first he thought it was a trick of the shadows: a broad undulating mass of copper-red helmets, each the size of a soup plate, moving slowly toward them like a battalion of surrealist troops without heads or bodies. There must have been more than fifty of them, stretching back under the trees, creeping round the roots in several streams; and along the front ranks, where the faces should have been, there were hundreds of thin white legs like macaroni, treading the mud in a steady rhythmic motion.

Ben looked round and saw more of them coming from just ahead. He seized Ryderbeit's arm and pointed, and Ryderbeit studied them for a moment, then frowned: 'We'd better get out o' here. Swamp crabs — can paralyze you in a few seconds. Get hold of the mules.'

Ben had grabbed both mules by their packs, when an explosion crashed behind him, almost throwing him flat in the mud. He jumped around, his ears ringing, and saw Ryderbeit crouched forward over the .416, firing into the mass of crabs.

Mel had her hands over her ears, and Ben watched the empty shells springing out still smoking into the mud. At the third shot the mules panicked. They began braying above the gunfire, charging straight into the mangroves. There was a crash and thrashing of hooves, and Ben saw the first mule's neck sticking up out of the khaki water, bubbles bursting all round it, then suddenly plunge down and disappear.

Ryderbeit stopped firing. Ben had leaped sideways and just managed to grab the guideline of the other animal, as it began to drag him under the sticky leaves. He tried to dig his heels in, yelling at Ryderbeit: 'Get hold of it!' Something hit him in the face; his legs and arms were scraped and bruised, and he was half on top of the mule now, hanging on to the pack with both legs off the ground, when it suddenly halted, quivering. He heard Ryderbeit shout: 'I got her!'

Ben climbed down and looked back. In the darkness under the roots he saw a slow churning of the helmets, several of them cracked open like eggs, bubbling with gray slime. Ryderbeit stood there wheezing, looking as though he were about to weep.

'Well done!' said Ben. 'And you who know such a hell of a lot about guns! Didn't you think at all before you used it?'

Ryderbeit slung the rifle back on his shoulder. 'It's a beautiful gun,' he murmured; 'haven't used anything as good for a long time.'

'Well, it's put us right in the shit now!'

Ryderbeit nodded: 'All up the spout, eh? Has the whisky gone?'

'Not only the whisky. The medicine case, cooking stuff, half the food, the shotgun. You've done well, Sammy!'

Ryderbeit nodded again. 'What have we got left?'

Ben looked at the pack. 'Both compasses and binoculars, three water cans, both rifles, maps, most of the ammunition.' He paused: 'We may still be all right — if we can only get back to the volcano.'

They both looked up quickly. The plane was returning, flying lower this time with a fast stuttering sound, like a loud motorcycle, coming very close until the whole jungle seemed to be full of the engine and the trees were answering back with the shriek of birds. It roared almost directly overhead and for a moment they saw a shape flicker through the leaves, then vanish.

'That was no ordinary plane!' Ryderbeit cried. 'I know that sound — it was a bloody helicopter!'

'You sure?' said Ben.

'I'm sure, soldier. I've flown enough of the things in Africa.'

'But what's it doing out here?' said Mel.

Ryderbeit smiled crookedly: 'You tell me, darling. Just give me one healthy reason why a helicopter comes out over a mangrove swamp?'

'Perhaps they're doing what we're doing?' she said.

He nodded: 'And that's no healthy reason, either!' He broke into a cough; the stench of the swamp had been sharpened with burnt cordite.

Ahead, under the mangrove roots, the crabs were beginning to creep forward again. Ben shuddered: 'Come on, let's get out of here!'

Ryderbeit watched them and shook his head: 'They make beautiful targets, those crabs! I wonder what they'd taste like fried? Or better boiled, d'yer think?'

'Save your ammunition, Sammy. Let's get going.'

Ryderbeit sighed: 'Save it for what, soldier?'

Now that they had their bearings they retreated fast. The mule floundered along with them, a twitching, pitiful creature now, its scrawny rump and legs bleeding from bites and burned leeches which Ryderbeit had painstakingly removed with his cigarette lighter.

By dusk they had managed to escape the worst of the swamp and were back on the edge of the lava shelf where they pitched the large tent, which had survived the loss of the other mule.

Before the mosquitoes came, all three of them were crouched under the nets inside, lying on their hands with their heads buried in sweaters, waiting for the terrible whine to pass by. They lay together, with Ben in the middle, just as they had lain on that first night up in the Hiarra. They were too tired to hate each other anymore. The despair of finding they were lost seemed to have brought them closer.

Ryderbeit shouted suddenly: 'Hitzi had it planned this way right from the beginning, didn't he? We must have been bloody slow not to realize! Christ, we were slow!' he began to cackle miserably in the dark. Ben and Mel lay in silence, listening to the mosquitoes humming against the cotton tent.

Yes, this was how Hitzi Leiter had wanted it: even the red crabs and the lost mule now seemed to have been part of his plan. Hitzi was dead and buried, yet his spirit was still with them, and it had won.

Ryderbeit went on: 'He needed us — needed a few extra guns, just like old Stopes did. Needed us right up to the swamp, and then he guessed he could do without us. After all, he'd managed to get through the swamp and back all by himself once before.'

'So he drew the map,' said Ben, 'and planned to send us into the swamp where it was impossible to get through. Is that what he did?'

'That's what he did,' said Ryderbeit: 'all for our benefit. Lead us into the swamp and let us die — just like he wanted back in the Devil's Spoon.'

'So why didn't he wait till the swamp?' said Ben, 'instead of trying to ditch us so early?'

'How do I know? Perhaps we upset him, or he got impatient or he just guessed that we had it in for him. How would I know what went on in his nasty little mind?'

You wouldn't, thought Ben. *None of us would. But we can still have a damned good guess.* It couldn't be quite as simple as Ryderbeit had made out. Or perhaps it was much more simple? If only they knew all the facts. There had been so much lying between Hitzi and Stopes; they were the only two who had known everything that had happened on that first expedition, and they were both dead.

However, there were a few facts about that expedition that were indisputable. *We'll take these first*, he thought. *Right from the beginning.* And for a long time, while the other two fell asleep on either side of him, Ben lay under the shroud of the mosquito net and went over in his mind the whole sequence of events since Stopes and Hitzi Leiter had set out to find the river nearly two months ago.

He divided the facts into two categories: in the first, those either proved or corroborated by both Hitzi and Stopes; and in the second, those that could be deduced from the first. Later there would be a third, made up of inconsistencies stemming from the other two. For Ben was certain that somewhere down the line something was missing — something, however small, that could have a vital bearing on the whole story of that river. Even now, with only one mule, and half their equipment lost, it still might not be too late.

He started on the first category. Captain Leonard Stopes had been a geologist who had deduced from survey maps that there might be diamonds in the swamp river. He had been in poor health and unable to reach the river, but had got as far as the extinct volcano where he had calculated from the formation of ancient lava flows that there was a possible way through the swamp. He had stayed behind inside the volcano, suffering from exhaustion, while Hitzi Leiter pressed on alone.

Hitzi had found the river, and brought back three diamonds to prove it. In the meantime he had been badly bitten by mosquitoes and had reached Stopes in a state of collapse and delirium.

Ben now moved on to the second category, deductions from the known facts. Since Stopes had lied about Hitzi shooting himself, Ben would have to consider Hitzi's version on its own merits. He was inclined to believe it. Stopes had fed Hitzi what he hoped was an overdose of medicine, and while the German lay in a coma, had divested him of most of his possessions, including the three diamonds, binoculars, telescopic rifle — and the map. For Ben knew that Hitzi must have drawn a map — and one that marked the true course to the volcano. Why else would Stopes have wanted him out of the way? And how else would Stopes have known how to reach the river if Hitzi were dead? Equally, how would Hitzi himself have known how to reach it? Unless he chanced his memory?

Stopes had had all the information he wanted. He knew the diamonds existed and he knew how to get to them. And above all, he didn't want Hitzi Leiter to share that information after they returned to Parataxín. Yet Stopes had not been a cold-blooded killer; instead, he had done the next best thing and left Hitzi Leiter in the wilderness to die by himself.

But Hitzi had not died; he had been rescued, made his way back to Parataxín, and avenged himself with an act of plain murder — but not before he had learned that Stopes had already recruited an expedition of his own to return to the river.

The rest followed as Ryderbeit had said: Hitzi had waited in the hotel in Benisalem where he had prepared a duplicate of the original map, correct in all details from the desert to the extinct volcano where he had rejoined Stopes. From then on, Hitzi had used his imagination, drawing the course down into a part of the swamp that was impenetrable.

At this point Ben could only guess what he had planned to do. Perhaps try to sabotage them, as he had done in the Devil's Spoon, by stealing their mules and equipment. It would have been easier in the swamp than in the desert; but the method was unimportant. What was important was that the map had been drawn wrong — and drawn wrong deliberately.

Here Ben struck the first inconsistency. If Hitzi Leiter had brought a false map with him, *where was the original?*

He was suddenly wide awake, hot with excitement. This might be the clue to what he'd been looking for. Calmly he went through all possible explanations. Firstly, the map might not be wrong after all; they might have simply misread it that morning. Ben dismissed this as very unlikely. They had taken great trouble with the bearings that morning; he was certain they had followed them correctly.

Then the compass might have been wrong. But they had checked the bearings that morning against two compasses — their own and Hitzi Leiter's. They could not both be wrong.

Or perhaps Hitzi had made a mistake in the first place when he drew the map? Again, highly unlikely. He might have been out by a few degrees, but the route due south was plainly many miles off course.

The most plausible explanation was that Hitzi had had the original map on his body when they buried him; yet Ryderbeit had gone through his clothes fairly thoroughly, as well as his pack, and had not found it. True, it might have been hidden somewhere like the lining of his jacket, but this Ben doubted. If Hitzi had been afraid of being robbed, why hadn't he hidden his money as well?

But there was another, even simpler explanation. What would it mean if Hitzi Leiter had only had *the one map* on him when he died? — that the original had been destroyed, or left behind in Parataxín?

Ben was shaking Ryderbeit by the shoulder: 'Sammy, I think I've got it!'

Ryderbeit woke noisily, grabbing at the elephant-gun: 'What's up?'

'Just listen. I may be onto something.'

'You'd better be. What is it?'

Mel was awake now, and Ben sat up between them in the darkness and began to explain the course of his thinking. He had to repeat much of it twice. Ryderbeit was impatient and skeptical, and at the end of it scowled: 'So you say he only had the one map? All right — so perhaps he knew the course by heart? He'd done it before without a map.'

'Certainly he had. Only if I'd found a river full of diamonds in the middle of a swamp, I'd at least draw a map to help me find it again.'

For a moment there was silence; it was Mel who spoke first: 'But why would he have only one map, if it doesn't lead through the swamp?'

Ben paused before replying: he suspected Ryderbeit had already guessed the answer.

'Because Hitzi Leiter never had any intention of going back through the swamp. The map's accurate only as far as the volcano — and that, if I'm right, is as far as Hitzi intended to go.'

Ryderbeit began to laugh: 'Oh you're a genius, Morris! A bloody wonderful genius! Only what the hell would Hitzi Leiter want in some crumby volcano?' His voice grew more level: 'You ever heard of people picking up diamonds in volcanoes?'

'Not unless somebody put them there.'

It became very quiet again inside the tent. For a moment even the mosquitoes seemed to grow still. Ryderbeit said: 'A good try, soldier. Only it won't work.'

'Tell me why not.'

'In one sentence I will. If Hitzi Leiter found a horde of diamonds and was trying to hold out on Stopes, he'd hardly have brought back three to show the old Captain, now would he?'

This time Ben took a long time before answering. It was something, he remembered, that had worried him before. If Hitzi Leiter had found the river, why had he not brought back a sackful of diamonds? Stopes had explained that Hitzi had been running short of food, was exhausted, and that he didn't know enough about geology to be able to select raw diamonds in the little time he had. And yet Ben now remembered that Ryderbeit had talked to Hitzi Leiter on that first evening in Benisalem, and had told Ben afterwards that according to Hitzi the prospects of finding a mass of diamonds on the river were 'very hopeful.' He tackled Ryderbeit again about this.

'Doesn't prove a thing,' Ryderbeit growled. 'Perhaps he knew a bit about diamonds — perhaps he didn't. The fact is he knew enough to bring back three and show them to Stopes.'

Ben thought again, and remembered something else. 'But he didn't show them to Stopes! Stopes found them on him while he was unconscious.'

Now it was Ryderbeit's turn to think. Ben continued slowly, trying to keep everything within logic. 'Sammy, if you were Hitzi Leiter and had really managed to pick up a fortune in diamonds, wouldn't it be perfectly natural for you to put a couple of them away in your pocket, just as nice little keepsakes, while you went on picking up the others?'

Mel broke in excitedly: 'I once saw a film about some jewel thieves who got caught because one of them did that.'

'All bloody make-believe!' Ryderbeit snarled. 'No, Morris, you'll have to do better than that.'

'I'm not even going to try to do better,' said Ben. 'If you've got another theory, you press on with it. I'm making for that volcano — not only because there's fresh water up there, but because I think we might find something very interesting in that crater.'

Ryderbeit was silent for a moment, then let out a long gasp: 'God, what I'd give for a drink!'

They reached the lower slopes of the volcano just before dusk the next day. The going had become very slow. They were all at the extremities of exhaustion, swollen with bites, filthy and hungry and dispirited. Ben tried to convince himself that his deductions the previous night had been logical — that the diamonds must be somewhere up in the volcano. But already the obstacles were obvious and enormous. Even if Hitzi had hidden them up there, how were they to know where to start looking? Food was short; they had no cooking equipment, no kerosene, no medicine. And even if they did find the diamonds, how were they to get them back to civilization? For worst of all, the mule was now showing signs of collapse. Over the last few hours it had been seized with spasms, shuddering and kicking, its eyes gummed up and jaws dripping foam. It seemed a wretched hope to expect it to carry their equipment back up the mile-high cinder mountain on the other side of the Devil's Spoon. Yet somehow that mountain had to be climbed, and this time the three of them would be on foot.

Then he remembered the helicopter. Long-range fuel tanks probably, but fatal if there was a mechanical failure. The swamp was no place to try a forced landing. And yet if there had been one plane, there might be others. It was perhaps a chance.

They pitched the tent that night in a lava field just above the high grass. The insects were less bad here and there was a breeze that moved around the side of the mountain. Ryderbeit had disappeared to relieve himself, and in the twilight Ben noticed that Mel was crying. The sight infuriated him; he was too weary to feel compassion, and even this feeble emotion on her part seemed unreasonable. He said: 'For God's sake, what's the matter now?'

'What do you think's the matter?'

'I don't think anything. Only that tomorrow we go up the volcano and hope for the best. Personally I don't hope for much. I think we've had it.'

'So do I. Especially if we find something up there. You know what that'll mean for us, don't you?'

He knew too well; yet while he knew she was right, he felt a dull rage rising against her. It was unjust to blame her, but he was also aware that if he had been alone with Ryderbeit none of this would have happened. He now told her: 'We haven't found any diamonds yet. We'll worry about it when we do.'

'I wish to God he was dead,' she said quietly.

He started towards the tent: 'You go and kill him, Mel. I'm too tired.' He remembered that both guns were still slung on the mule. He lay down and pulled the mosquito net over him. All he wanted now was sleep. He heard her come in a moment later. She stretched herself out very close, between him and the tent wall, and he could feel her breathing and thought, *She means nothing to me anymore: I don't even like her much.* He had thought once, not very long ago, that she would cure him of his grief for Laura. He had been cured all right. But not by Mel. Hitzi and the desert and the swamp had done that: perhaps a little too thoroughly.

Ryderbeit came in and said: 'So what about keeping a watch tonight? There's a bit of a moon and we're pretty exposed up here.'

'What do we keep watch for?' said Ben.

'There could be Xatus around.'

'What the hell!'

'O.K., what the hell,' said Ryderbeit tonelessly, and closed the flaps behind him. 'You'd better be right about those diamonds, Morris.' He lay down on the other side of Ben, away from Mel, cuddling the elephant-gun in both arms.

'I got a feeling,' he murmured, 'that tomorrow something's going to happen.' When no one spoke, he added: 'It had bloody well better happen!'

Ben was already asleep.

They had been climbing for nearly seven hours, up through the long lava fields into the higher slopes of wrinkled pumice stone, until they were now on the last stretch — the steep eruptive cone, rising above them to where the jagged line of the summit jutted into the sky like a jawbone full of broken black teeth.

Ben paused. They were very high and the air was fresh and cold, though the sweat was running warm under his shirt and trousers. Over the last few hundred feet they had been struggling upward almost on all fours, their palms and fingernails torn and chafed by the brittle lava pebbles. Ryderbeit was leading, about twenty feet above them, climbing beside the mule, giving its scrawny rump an occasional happy smack. Ben had noticed that as they went higher Ryderbeit seemed to like the mule more and more. He had good reason to like it, Ben thought. With one mule, and the rest of the food, and the water cans freshly filled from the crater lake, he might still make it back alive — and alone. Both guns were now under the mule's pack.

He looked down at the swamp far below and now saw something that none of them had been able to see from the ground: the shape of the prehistoric lava crust as it spread out from the volcano like a dark stain across the mangroves, curving toward the southwest where, perhaps thirty or forty miles away, it would reach the diamond river. Ben needed no compass or map now to tell him where they had gone wrong. This must have been the route which Stopes had calculated, and Hitzi Leiter then followed. It looked very simple now. Below, directly due south on the course marked on Hitzi's map, there was no lava — nothing but the dense carpet of mangroves.

He wondered whether Ryderbeit would see it too and realize its significance. But at that moment he saw something else. Far out over the swamp a speck was moving along the blurred horizon, heading vaguely in their direction. For a few seconds he thought it was some kind of bird; then he heard the throb of an engine. It was the sound they had heard in the swamp the day before.

It came toward them quite slowly — a giant dragonfly with it big belly and delicate tail and the rotor blades whirring like insect wings. For a moment he had difficulty believing his eyes. It was a marvelous thing that had nothing to do with reality. And yet it was real: there were men up there sitting behind the bubble-glass windows, comfortable and safe, feeling the engines throbbing round them, watching the swamp and jungle and lava slopes slipping away below.

Ryderbeit and Mel had seen it too. Mel was shouting and waving, but Ryderbeit just stood with the night glasses, watching the machine fly to within about three miles of them, then disappear around the far side of the volcano.

Mel gave a little wail that became a sob: 'Oh it's gone! It's gone! Oh please God, why's it gone?'

'Did they see us?' Ben yelled.

Ryderbeit lowered the glasses and stared down at them both. 'I don't know. I guess they didn't or they'd have come over.'

'They must have seen us!' Mel cried. 'What are they doing up there? They're a patrol, aren't they? It's their job to look out for us!'

'Sure it is,' said Ryderbeit. 'A nice convenient patrol looking out for three lost wanderers in the swamp.' His face grew savage. 'What do you think, you stupid bitch! You really think that was some left-footed patrol up there sent out by the government? Don't be daft!'

Mel looked bleakly at Ben, and he saw her eyes were red-rimmed, her lips beginning to quiver. 'That's enough, Sammy,' he said, without looking at Ryderbeit. He took her arm and began leading her on upward. 'They may be back — don't give up! If they come back they'll see us. We'll light a beacon for them on top of the volcano.'

Ryderbeit was studying the swamp again through the night glasses. 'That was a bloody big helicopter!' he muttered. 'Big enough for a crew o' four, I'd say. They'd need one like that to get over the mountains.'

'It was the same as we heard yesterday, wasn't it?' said Ben.

Ryderbeit nodded and turned back towards the summit. Ben was climbing just below him, beside Mel. 'What do you really think it was doing out here?' he said.

Ryderbeit smiled without turning. 'What do you think? It was flying back from the swamp — twice in two days.'

'Then they are the gang that Stopes talked about?' said Ben quietly.

'Well, it was no government job, I can tell you that! It didn't have any official markings, for a start. Romolo's boys would be blazing their credentials for every living thing in the swamp to see. Those boys up there were in a private job. And on a very private mission, I'd say.'

He paused, frowning. Ben stopped too, and was aware of an odd silence. Then he realized that the sound of the helicopter had gone. The volcano must have cut it off from the other side. He wondered for a moment how many flying hours it was across the Hiarra Mountains. Mel began talking in a quiet rapid voice close to hysteria: 'Do you think they'll come back! Do you think so?'

'How do I know?' Ryderbeit snarled, and began striding on up the last thirty feet to the summit. Mel stared up at him, then looked desperately at Ben: 'Do you think they'll come back?'

'I don't know, Mel. They've been over twice now. That means they may well come back. But it also means they may not be too pleased to see us when they do.'

She gave him a blank stare. 'You mean they really are a gang after the diamonds?'

'Perhaps. And if they are, well soon find out.' He turned again towards the summit. Mel looked up too, then cried bitterly: 'God, I don't care who they are, as long as they can get us out of here!'

CHAPTER NINE: THE LAST CHANCE

They reached the summit ten minutes later. Ben had been clambering, panting, half blinded with sweat and dust, and did not see it.

He stepped up and looked over, and although he was still sweating he suddenly felt cold. Mel came up beside him, and drew back with a shudder. For a moment Ben and Ryderbeit stared down in silence. The crater was about a mile wide — almost perfectly round, except at the far side, where the rim of the cone had decayed into a honeycomb of caves and crumbled shelves of rock. But from where they now stood it fell away almost sheer for several hundred feet, down into the black lake below, lying as smooth as a mirror that reflected no light, only the dead walls of the crater.

Ryderbeit pointed out to the far side where the caves led down almost to the level of the water. 'Out there! That's where the old Captain must have camped — and that's where I say we start looking.'

Ben and Mel had already climbed a few feet down below the precipice, and began picking their way round the edge of the cone. It was well past noon now, and the sun had already begun to sink behind them. They had about four hours' clear daylight left for the search. Ben tried to be hopeful: to reassure himself again that Hitzi would never have drawn the map correctly as far as this unless there had been something up here.

They reached the far side and began to climb down toward the lake. They came to the first of the caves, some of them just shallow holes under the rock; but they examined each one carefully, hunting for tunnels or fissures that might serve as a hiding place. There was nothing, and as the sun passed below the top of the crater, Ben began to feel a deep despair.

There was no sound at all now. Not a breath of wind: nothing but the cold silence above the water. Ryderbeit hurled a rock over the edge. It fell for several seconds and when the splash came it was like dropping a stone into a well, only a hundred times louder.

A little further down they found traces of excrement on the corner of a ledge. Ryderbeit cackled bitterly: 'So the old Captain left his visiting cards, eh?'

But at least they were on the right track, Ben thought. They found the cave a few feet below: a deep hollow in the lava wall with a pile of rusted tins and cigarette butts scattered at the back.

'This is where he was!' Ryderbeit shouted. 'Now where are the diamonds?'

'Hitzi wouldn't have left them here, right under Stopes' nose,' said Ben.

'All right, so he wouldn't! So where? Where, Morris!' he cried, his eyes glaring yellow in the twilight of the crater.

'Don't look at me,' said Ben, 'how should I know?'

'It was your idea!'

Ben nodded: 'Let's look lower down, shall we?' He led the way out of the cave, down more than a hundred feet to a ledge of rock just above the lake. The others followed, Mel coming last, leading the mule.

A bleak chill hung over the water with an almost physical presence of evil. Ben walked to the edge and looked over. Mel was waiting a few feet above, holding the mule. Ben heard Ryderbeit move up beside him and for a moment the two of them stood staring into the water.

'How deep do you think it is?' Ben murmured.

'Damned deep. Perhaps as deep again as the crater up there.'

Ben looked up at the circle of sky above. *As deep as a cathedral is high*, he thought. He looked down again. The black water now had a faint greenish hue and he began to see vague shadows far down. He was leaning right out over the edge when Ryderbeit clutched his arm. 'Holy Moses!' he muttered, and spun around, leaping back up the rocks, pushing past Mel, grabbing at the mule's pack.

Ben peered down again into the water, and through the green darkness he thought he saw something move — a pool of gray that stirred slightly, somewhere at an indeterminate depth; and as he looked, part of it floated outward, then back again, like something being slowly waved.

Ryderbeit was back with the coil of guideline.

'What is it?' said Ben.

Ryderbeit didn't answer. He crouched forward at the edge of the platform, watching the gray shape directly below, then swung the rope out over the water and cast it down in a loop. He let it go for about two yards, then gathered it round one wrist and pulled sharply upwards. The water lapped sluggishly, and for a moment the shape disappeared. Then very gently, with a rolling movement, it swelled up through the water, burst with a little splash on the surface, rolled again, then lay still, floating.

At first Ben could not see what it was. The cloth round it was a shiny gray, and there were other parts that were greenish black like the water. It was about the size of a fat sack of corn, yet it was not a sack. It had arms and legs, and what had once been a head, which now looked like half a coconut with strands of hair clinging to the sides and mushy gray slime inside. The teeth had gone, and what was left of the face was now flaking away in strips of fibrous flesh like cheesecloth. The hands were big and gray like gloves.

The smell reached them a moment later. Ben stepped back, tasting the bile in his mouth, and heard Mel shout from above: 'What is it?' She was already climbing down. Ryderbeit was still crouching forward holding the rope, examining the corpse undismayed.

Mel reached Ben and now caught the smell and shrank back. 'What is it?'

'Go back,' he said quietly.

'Is it a body?'

'Yes.'

'But who?'

'I don't know who. Go back.'

Ryderbeit stood up and began walking backward, playing out the rope with great care, then fastened it to a lump of rock. He grinned at them both: 'Pretty, isn't he?'

'Who is it?'

'Who do you think?' He shook his head and chuckled: 'I'm afraid we seem to be back with our old friend Hitzi Leiter!'

Ben stared at him. 'Hitzi Leiter?'

'Hitzi Leiter?' Mel repeated, and stepped up to the edge. Ryderbeit leered at her: 'That's what I said, darling. Take a good long look.'

She stumbled back, white faced, then began to run up the slope making a choking noise.

'Come on, let's get out o' here!' said Ben. 'It stinks!'

Ryderbeit shook his head: 'No proper respect for the dead! I'm surprised at you, Morris. Especially as we seem to have been rather unfair to poor Hitzi Leiter.'

Ben put his hand to his eyes. The stench was making him feel ill. 'This is crazy, Sammy! It can't be Hitzi Leiter. We've already buried him.'

'We buried a boy who had Hitzi's passport — who had stolen it from Stopes after murdering him. Do we have any other proof it was Hitzi? None of us had ever seen him before Benisalem.' He pointed into the water: 'But we got more proof who that was. By the look of it, it's been down there about the right time — seven or eight weeks. And look at the head! Top's been blown clean off just like the old Captain said — shot himself through the mouth.'

Ben nodded, keeping his eyes away from the water: 'O.K., so it's Hitzi, and Stopes was telling the truth after all. But then who the hell was the man we buried?'

Ryderbeit was staring out across the lake, and when he spoke his voice had a sleepy, far-off sound.

'Could have been anybody. Anybody who happened to find out the Captain's little secret and murdered him for it — stole the map and came out after us. He must have found out about us from the Captain. Perhaps he was a friend of his — old Stopes kept some pretty odd friends, you know.'

'And his white hair? Hitzi's passport says he was blond.'

Ryderbeit shrugged: 'Dyed perhaps — or perhaps it was real. Anyway, it was enough to pass himself off with us as Hitzi Leiter. He must have planned to stick around until the right moment came to do us all in.'

'Very neat,' said Ben, 'except for one thing. The map. Either that white-haired boy had two maps when he died, or just one — but either way, it doesn't make sense. If he stole the original from Stopes and made a copy of it to lead us astray in the swamp, then where is the original?

'And if he had only the one map — the false one — and if he really was an impostor, then how was he going to reach the river? He needed the original to get through the swamp. If he was Hitzi, of course, it makes sense: he'd hidden a horde of diamonds up here and was coming back to collect them. He wouldn't have needed the map. But then you say it wasn't Hitzi Leiter. Sammy, it just doesn't add up.'

'It has to add up!' Ryderbeit cried. 'We've seen a couple of corpses, haven't we? One of them had the map and the other's lying with its head blown off in the very lake where Stopes said Hitzi killed himself. That's enough for me. That thing down there just has to be Hitzi Leiter!' He turned: 'Soldier, I'm buying that theory of yours from last night. I'm betting there was only one map — the false one. And I'm betting, too, that that white-haired boy who impersonated Hitzi Leiter stole the original from Stopes and made a copy of it in order to get us lost in the swamp. And the reason he didn't bring that original map with him was because he didn't need it! Just as you said last night, he never intended to go into the swamp. He was heading for this volcano — and I'm going to find out why. How's your stomach?'

'What's that got to do with it?' Ben asked.

'Because we're going to start by pulling that thing out of the water and searching it.'

At that moment there came a cry from above. It was Mel. They had scarcely noticed her as she scrambled back up the rocks away from the body. She was now standing far up on the rim of the crater, waving frantically. Her voice carried down across the lake like a distant birdcall: 'Quick! Come up!' She began waving now down the side of the volcano, out of sight.

They were already running back up the rocks. Ryderbeit reached the mule, seized the two guns, the ammunition and both binoculars, and they clambered on, breathing the sudden fresh air above the stench of the lake. Mel had started down to meet them; she was very pale, but her eyes were wide and shining with excitement. 'Quickly! It's down there!'

They ran past her, up into sunlight above the crater where Ryderbeit stopped and slapped his thigh: 'Ah, beautiful! Just what I'd been waiting for!'

At first all Ben saw was the same lunar wasteland they had passed through on their climb from the swamp, only less steep on this side. Here the flanks of the volcano had flowed out in a great sea of lava, wave upon wave of once red-hot magma, now congealed cold and black between high banks of ash and cinders. Then in the middle of it, about a quarter of a mile away, and almost lost against the grim wilderness all round, he saw the helicopter. It was a big, gray machine, built to carry a crew of four, with a powerful engine and rotor blades that could lift them all away in that bubble-glass body, across the volcanoes and the desert, back to civilization.

In that moment they forgot the gang, the map, the corpse, the diamonds. Ben felt as though he had been struggling through a long dark tunnel that had been growing narrower, lower, till he could not even turn round to get out — and suddenly he had squeezed through the gap and was in the open again and free.

Mel came up behind them, almost weeping with excitement. There was a whole camp round the helicopter: two big khaki tents, what looked like a canvas privy, a barbecue and table and chairs and a stack of equipment half covered by a tarpaulin.

A man in a gray shirt was standing under the helicopter. A moment later two more men came out of one of the tents, and all three stood looking up toward the volcano. Ryderbeit went down behind a bulge of lava, laying the .416 down in front of him, getting out the night glasses.

Mel was coming up behind them, shouting: 'We're all right! We're saved!'

'Shut your mouth,' he said. 'Morris, get down!' He was moving the night glasses across the camp. Ben lay beside him and looked through the other binoculars.

A fourth man had now appeared. He was big and bald, stripped to the waist with a chest of black hair. He was talking excitedly; two of the men were listening, while the third — the one who had been under the helicopter — had his arms raised and was shouting. He began pointing up at the volcano, and they all began shouting, then the big man turned and went back into one of the tents.

Ben moved the glasses over to the helicopter. There was a yellow five-gallon can and some tools under the fuselage. Ryderbeit said softly: 'Your gun loaded?'

Ben nodded. 'What are you planning to do, Sammy?'

'I'm not sure yet. It rather depends on what those boys down there are planning to do. What do you think?'

Ben looked down again through the binoculars, at the same moment as the big bald man came out of the tent; he was wearing a shirt now and carrying a machine gun. Ryderbeit gave a low growl and smiled: 'Huh-huh! Here's trouble!'

One of the other men was himself now watching the volcano through binoculars. Ryderbeit had lowered his own night glasses and was screwing the telescopic sights into focus. 'They must have heard Mel shouting to us,' he said. 'The best thing we can do is move around a bit under the edge of the crater and wait for them to come up.'

'And then what?'

Ryderbeit turned and grinned: 'What would you say, soldier? With that lovely piece of machinery down there and those boys touting machine guns at us?'

'They've only got them for the same reason as we have,' said Ben uneasily.

'Sure they have! For self-defense, I suppose?'

'What else?'

Ryderbeit shook his head, still grinning: 'You want to go down and find out?'

Ben said nothing for a moment. He looked again through the binoculars and saw the four men were again talking excitedly; the big bald one with the machine gun kept turning and looking back up toward the volcano. Ryderbeit crept back behind the bulge of lava and said: 'Let's move along a bit. And keep your head down!'

Mel was behind him, peeping over the edge. 'What are you going to do?' she said, looking quickly at each of them.

'You'll find out, darling,' said Ryderbeit quietly. 'Just do as you're told.' He turned to Ben and pointed up along the rim of the crater where it projected over the precipice. 'We'd better move round there — they may not be expecting us so far up.'

He began to lead the way along the narrow crumbled ledge just below the summit. Ben let Mel go on ahead, following close behind her, his eyes averted from the drop below.

Once his foot slipped and he heard the dry slithering sound of pebbles under his boot, then the silence, and at last the small echoing splashes far below. He crept on with eyes closed, one hand on the lava path in front of him, the other gripping the Winchester — like a blind man with a white stick.

About a hundred feet on, Ryderbeit paused. Several great humps of congealed lava had been thrust up above the summit, and between them was a parapet that reached just above their shoulders and made a useful platform for the guns. The ledge between that and the precipice was less than a yard wide. Ben crouched close to the parapet, his head below the summit, while Mel remained half standing, looking nervously at Ryderbeit. 'But what are you going to do?' she said again. Ryderbeit said with a hiss, 'Sit down and keep still!'

Ben moved his head round and glanced quickly down at the lake. It was just a huge pit now, full of darkness beneath the smooth orange sunset beyond the far rim of the crater. He looked down at the foot of the caves, and for a moment he thought he could see the body of Hitzi Leiter — a small, gray slug below the waterline. He shuddered and turned away.

Ryderbeit had laid the elephant-gun down on the parapet; he then carefully raised his head and peered over through the night glasses. 'Hold it!' he cried suddenly. 'He's coming!'

Ben looked over too and saw the big man with the machine gun walking up the gentle lava slope toward the spot they had just left.

'He must be nuts!' Ryderbeit muttered, lowering his head.

Ben looked at him sharply: 'What do you mean?'

Ryderbeit was already laughing quietly and shaking his eyes: 'I mean he's a sitting duck! They're all four sitting ducks! It's a bleeding cinch, soldier!'

Ben said: 'Now look, Sammy, you just tell me what you're planning. That man's got a machine gun and he's coming up here to find out who we are and what we want. We want to get back out of here, so the sensible thing to do is go down and meet them and ask them politely to help us.'

Ryderbeit was already laughing quietly and shaking his head. 'Oh soldier, you really are a marvel, you know! How long have I known you? Not even two weeks, but in that time just look what's happened to us! Three dead bodies and every kind of villainy and treachery and you still believe in the voice of sweet reason.'

'What's wrong with reason?'

Ryderbeit chuckled: 'Oh nothing at all! In fact, I'd say those four boys down there are just panting to be chatted up with a little reason. They're not really interested in getting diamonds or anything comic like that. In fact, the whole thing's just a gag. I mean, if I was down there with a helicopter and had spent the last few days hunting for diamonds, I'd be just wild to meet up with a party of gatecrashers like us! Because that's what we are, you know, soldier. We've walked in. We've busted up a good party.'

'All right, all right,' said Ben. He looked again over the parapet and saw the big bald man was now about halfway up to the summit and still coming on. He was holding the machine gun at the ready; it had a stumpy barrel with a skeleton handle and a drum-shaped magazine.

Below, two of the men had disappeared again into one of the tents. The third man was again watching the top of the volcano through binoculars. Then one of the others appeared, also carrying a machine gun, only this one was a heavy weapon with a tripod.

'Now this is getting really cozy,' said Ryderbeit. He had picked up the .416 again, while Ben watched the man by the tent rest the big machine gun on the ground and lie down beside it, fitting in a scythe-like magazine below the breach.

'Where's the other bastard?' Ryderbeit muttered.

At that moment the big bald man stopped. He was about a hundred yards below them, and fifty yards to the left. There was no cover anywhere; he just stood in the middle of the lava slope looking up toward the summit.

Below, the man in the gray shirt now came out of the second tent and stood beside the man lying with the machine gun on the tripod. He seemed to be talking to him; then he nodded and walked over to the helicopter. He opened the cabin door, climbed inside and came out a moment later with a rifle. He went back toward the other two men and went on talking. Through the binoculars it looked to Ben as though none of them was unduly worried.

The man on the slope had not moved. Ryderbeit whispered: 'Well, how does it look to you, soldier?'

'I'd say they were being careful.'

'Careful!' Ryderbeit cried: 'Soldier, they're out there in the wide open. They're going to be massacred!'

Ben said: 'They probably think we're Xatus — don't you realize that? They heard Mel shouting just now and thought it was some war cry. And I can hardly blame them. If I was one of them I wouldn't expect to find a girl out here, would you?'

But Ryderbeit was not listening. He was watching the bald man who had started to walk on up the slope again; and Ryderbeit suddenly made an adjustment to the sights, slipped off the safety catch and said: 'Right, this is it! Are you ready?'

'Ready for what?'

Ryderbeit glanced at him, then back through the sights and whispered: 'I'm not going to argue, soldier. Those boys have got machine guns. That's war you know. You don't argue with machine guns — you just fire and pray you don't miss.'

Mel cried behind them: 'You can't just shoot them! They're our only chance.'

'They're our only obstacle. Now stuff it, little girl, or I'll have to get rough with yer!' He glanced back at Ben and patted the stock of the elephant-gun: 'You just leave it to me. When I fire at this near guy, you blast off at the tents. Don't worry if you miss — just keep 'em busy and worried. But for Chrissake don't hit the helicopter.'

The bald man with the machine gun had stopped again. He was now only about fifty yards below them, still looking up at the spot they had been at earlier.

'He hasn't seen us yet,' Ryderbeit whispered.

Ben said: 'Sammy, we can't do this! It's murder!'

Ryderbeit jerked his head round, his eyes glaring: 'Now listen, soldier!' — and his voice was scarcely more than a hiss through his teeth — 'We're nearly at the end of the line, so don't upset me! There are three boys down there with guns, and two of us. If you like the odds, you go down there and meet them.'

Ben looked into those narrow yellow eyes and saw that Ryderbeit was ready for a shooting match and that no amount of persuasion could now stop him. He was back in his element where neither moral values nor plain reason would reach him. For a moment Ben thought he could smell the stench of the corpse still clinging to them both, and he wondered if he could manage to take Ryderbeit here and now — club him down with the Winchester before he had time to swing the elephant-gun round in the short space between them.

The bald man with the machine gun was now less than thirty yards below, but beginning to walk slightly away from them. They could hear his boots crunching on the lava, and Ben could hear his own breathing, loud and fast, and felt the wood of the Winchester wet under his sweating palms. Behind him Mel suddenly shouted: 'Oh God, this is ridiculous! Why don't you go down and talk to them?'

Ryderbeit turned: 'Because I don't want to talk to them! Now will you be a good girl and keep quiet, or do I have to get really cross with you?'

'But what do you want?' she cried, almost in a sob.

'I want that helicopter, darling.' He lifted the elephant-gun and watched the big bald man again through the telescopic sights.

'It's still murder,' said Ben.

Ryderbeit didn't move. 'And what do you think those boys down there are playing at? What do you think that white-haired lad was up to? You talk about murder! Well, I'd say we were up against a whole gang of murderers! They started with Stopes, then they sent out the little white-haired guy to fix us, and now they're down there with machine guns ready to finish the job off properly, if they get the chance.'

Ben realized the only thing to do now was play for time. The big bald man had turned and begun to walk further away around the side of the volcano below the crater. Ben said: 'You mean, it was the helicopter the white-haired boy was heading for?'

'I'd say it was a pretty fair guess, wouldn't you?'

'Not fair enough to shoot those men in cold blood without even giving them a chance.'

Ryderbeit glanced up from the gun, his face darkening into a snarl. 'Soldier, you're beginning to worry me. I'm not fooling, you know. You better be careful.'

But as he spoke, Mel leaped up round them both and with a quick graceful vault was over the parapet and standing above them waving and shouting something that was lost in the noise that followed. There was a shriek and swish of air and the rapid knocking sound of a machine gun. Then the .416 roared twice and Ben saw the bald man swing round and the gun at his hip gave a puff of smoke, as Mel dropped backward over the parapet and fell beside Ben. At first he thought she had been hit. 'They're shooting!' she screamed.

Then Ben ducked down and felt splinters of lava flying into his hair and face. The elephant-gun roared again, and suddenly both machine guns stopped. Ben looked quickly over and was just in time to see the big bald man stumble and kneel down, dropping his machine gun, then roll over and lie still. At the same time there was a flurry of dust near the tents. The man lying on the ground behind the gun was moving sideways in a curious crab-like motion. The other two men had disappeared.

Ryderbeit fired again and the man on the ground jerked suddenly, then was still. Mel was murmuring hysterically: 'Oh my God, they're shooting!'

'You bet they are!' Ryderbeit cried. 'And you deserve to be the first to get it up your shirt. Now shut up or I'll do it myself!'

She cowered back behind them both, as Ryderbeit looked again through the telescopic sights. 'That's two of the bastards! The other two look as though they've taken cover in the tents. They'll probably try and make a run for it. They obviously weren't expecting us to be armed. Bad mistake, that!' He looked at Ben and grinned: 'Satisfied now?'

Ben said nothing; he was stunned and deafened, and felt slightly sick with the smell of cordite that came seeping in on the lingering stench of the putrescent corpse.

Ryderbeit was saying: 'It's going to be a dogfight from now on. If we let those other two get away we're in trouble. You take the tent on the left, then the one on the right. But keep clear of that stack of equipment. It looks as though there may be gasoline in it — and we're going to need that.'

Ben wiped his hands on his shirt, slipped off the Winchester's safety catch and pulled the rifle into his shoulder. Across the V-sights he thought he saw something move in the entrance to one of the tents. He put the sights just above the flaps and took a deep breath. Ryderbeit said: 'All set?'

'O.K.,' Ben said in a hoarse whisper

'Let 'em have it!'

Ben squeezed the trigger, taking the sharp kick as he swung the sights over to the second tent and fired again, a little higher this time, and watched the tent cloth shiver. The next second there was an answering crack of a rifle and a bullet whined away across the lava many yards wide. Then the flaps of the first tent opened and a man came running out, bent double, carrying the rifle he had taken from the helicopter. He was heading for the pile of equipment.

Ben fired simultaneously with the elephant-gun and the whole horizon seemed to wobble, as the man jumped with his hands in the air, the rifle spinning down beside him, then sat down abruptly. Ryderbeit fired again and the man seemed to shrink to half his size and did not move again.

'Three,' said Ryderbeit. There was a sudden silence. Ben realized that one of the .416 shells was lying smoking against his trouser leg.

'One more to go,' said Ryderbeit. 'We're doing beautifully, soldier. And it occurs to me that it may not be just the helicopter we're winning in this little shooting match.'

Ben looked at him, trying to think clearly: 'What?'

'The diamonds, soldier. You forgotten the diamonds?'

Ben realized that he had; he had forgotten everything, even the helicopter, besides those tiny figures of men jumping grotesquely under the terrible blow of the bullets. 'We're still going after those diamonds?' he asked vaguely.

'That's what we came for, soldier. Only I've got a hunch we may not have to go after them anymore. I think we may be right on top of them — down there in that camp.'

Ben felt a spasm of excitement that seemed to have no relation to fact: it was like the first shock of seeing the helicopter.

Ryderbeit was saying: 'If those men helped to murder Stopes and sent that white-haired boy out after us, it seems reasonable to suppose that that helicopter's been out here hunting for the diamonds for at least ten days. And if those boys knew their stuff, and Stopes was right all along, I'd say there might be a very nice little horde of diamonds down their waiting for us.'

At that moment Ben looked down and saw a quick movement round the back of the first tent. Ryderbeit was looking through the telescopic sights and let out a loud obscenity. 'We missed him! He's behind that tent on the right. Just put one straight through it, and I'll get him when he comes out.'

'Do you think he's got a gun?'

'Probably.'

'I didn't see one.'

'Don't argue, soldier. Just shoot!'

Ben put the tent in the center of the V-sight and fired. He wasn't sure whether he had hit or not. Nothing happened.

'Again!' said Ryderbeit.

The next shot shook the canvas. Ryderbeit was watching through the night glasses. 'A little lower this time!' Ben aimed at the ground just in front of the tent and fired again: and again nothing happened. 'You're putting them in there nicely, soldier! Keep it up.'

Ben went on firing into the tent until the Winchester was empty. Ryderbeit put one bullet through the canvas privy and his last shot into the other tent, which caved in sideways and collapsed, and he cursed: 'Where is the bastard?'

'Could he have taken cover inside the helicopter?'

'That's what I'm afraid of. He might have sneaked out while we were firing. These telescopic sights give a very restricted view. Unless, of course, we've already killed him inside one o' the tents.'

'That's what he's probably hoping we'll think,' said Ben, as they both began to reload.

Ryderbeit fired once more at the tent that was still standing, then picked up the night glasses and studied the target carefully for several seconds. 'It's the helicopter that worries me,' he said at last. 'I can't see in below the controls. He could be lying on the floor.'

'Anyway, how do we know there are only four of them?' said Ben.

'I'm guessing. There are two tents and a helicopter big enough for four. If there was anyone else, I reckon he'd have shown himself when the others did. I'm betting on four.'

Ben nodded and looked down again at the helicopter. There was no movement anywhere.

'We'll give him five minutes,' said Ryderbeit, 'then we'll go down and get him.'

Ben felt a looseness in his bowels and a growing sickness from the smell of the corpse that persisted even through the burnt cordite. He was not looking forward to running down that naked slope towards the camp. One man with a gun in that helicopter would be quite sufficient.

'Can't we wait till he shows himself?' he suggested. 'He'll have to some time — if he's still alive.'

'Sure — in two hours' time, when it's dark. He'll make a run down those slopes to the left, then try to double back into the crater. I don't know if he's got a gun or not, but stalking a man at night with a poor moon in a place like this could get awkward.'

'He might give himself up.'

Ryderbeit laughed unpleasantly: 'And then what? Take him prisoner? Don't be silly! We'd have to shoot him anyway — I'm not having a witness to this. I want it nice and clean. And knowing the old English hypocrisy, I'd say you'd prefer it done in the heat of battle while he's still game? Eh?'

Ben said nothing. In a way Ryderbeit was right; for he realized with a shock of guilt, that as soon as the shooting had actually started he had begun to enjoy himself. With three men dead below he had no real sense of having killed. They were just untidy shapes huddled across the empty lava field. He avoided using the binoculars on them.

A couple of minutes later Ryderbeit pulled in the gun and said: 'Right I'll go over first. You follow in twenty seconds. I'll take the slope down here — you go down that way. And if he starts shooting just lie flat and watch for the flashes. Don't shoot back if he's in the helicopter — leave that to me.'

He jumped over the parapet, head down, the elephant-gun held with both hands at the hip and began to race down the slope in a zigzag, covering perhaps fifty yards before Ben climbed over after him.

For a split second he looked down at the tents and the helicopter, and nothing had changed. Then he began to run wildly, waiting for the shots. None came. He passed close to the big man, bald as a stone, lying with his black eyes wide open. He had no time to be scared, watching the black slope closing between him and the tents. He could now see that the half-covered stack of equipment consisted of gasoline cans and wooden crates; the tarpaulin had come loose at one end.

He was now less than twenty yards from the helicopter. The only sound came from his boots on the lava.

Ryderbeit was approaching round the back of the helicopter. Ben saw the man in the gray shirt lying on his stomach outside the first tent. He had cropped black hair and wore leather gloves smeared with oil; Ben guessed he had probably been the pilot. There was oil on his shirt and his trousers were dark with blood. The other man lay a few feet further on, twisted round on his back with one knee in the air hooked round the tripod of the heavy machine gun. He had glossy black eyebrows and his head had been almost severed by a shot through the throat.

Ben stepped round the bodies, up to within a few feet of the helicopter. Ryderbeit was creeping along under the metal struts of the tail, up beneath the belly of the cabin till he was within reach of the door. 'Get back!' he yelled. 'Down!'

Ben ducked round the nose of the machine with his back to the tents. He watched Ryderbeit lean out and pull down the handle. The door swung back, pressing him against the side of the fuselage. There was a moment of absolute silence. The sun flashed like fire off the edge of one of the rotor blades above Ben's head and he had time to notice the markings on the silver fuselage: *LV777* in squat black figures. The tarpaulin flapped lazily behind him. The lava was too dark to show any clear shadow. It was the fuselage that caught it: a darting movement against the sun, and Ben saw Ryderbeit spring out from behind the door with the elephant-gun jumping in his hands.

He saw the white flame spurting from the muzzle, and Ryderbeit's eyes seemed to be squinting at him as he fired. The air was ripped open and went white as the flame from the gun, then burst into blackness. He was falling, down and down, through an endless tunnel; and there were cold waves breaking over him and a gentle peace, and then nothing.

He crawled back up very slowly, every movement sending a rush of pain through his body that exploded somewhere in the side of his head. The higher he crawled the worse it grew, until he was trying to scream, but all that came was a metallic roar all around him, and he felt the ground shaking under him. He tried to move, but something held him across his stomach. His hands were resting on the greasy arms of a chair.

He had his head forward and tried to open his eyes which seemed to have swollen up and gone dry inside their sockets. There was an acrid smell everywhere that flooded his lungs and made him want to vomit. A voice called wearily: 'Give him a drink!'

A hand touched his face, eased his head back. The side of his head, away from where the hand touched him, was a raging ball of pain, as another voice said: 'Try and drink this.'

A plastic cup touched his mouth: the liquid was cold and burned. He swallowed hard and recognized the smell now as gasoline. He was sitting in what seemed to be a cell with round glass walls. A webbing belt held him firmly in his seat. Through the glass on his left he looked into a velvet sky and saw mountains with snow on them. Mel was leaning over him, holding the cup to his mouth again. It was brandy. He drank more deeply this time and the pain began to contract into one violent area just above his right ear. He touched it, and it felt sticky and soft like a plum.

The floor and walls went on vibrating through the noise, and he realized that Mel was shouting at him when she spoke: 'You're all right now?'

He tried to speak, to look at her; he felt very sick. Above the noise, a shrill rattle like a grasshopper started up in the wall beside him. There was a hot film across his eyes. He could see Ryderbeit sitting with his back to him, hunched over a panel of dials and knobs. Beyond the window in front of him the sky was blood red.

After a moment Ryderbeit turned round; Ben couldn't see him very well, but he heard him shout: 'You're all right now, soldier! Just you wait till we're back!'

'Where?' The brandy made him choke. 'Where are we?'

'We'll be over Benisalem in an hour.'

The film over Ben's eyes began to clear and he could see Ryderbeit beaming at him with a wild happy look. 'You bloody nearly didn't live to see the day! I got him just in time. He was hiding among the gasoline cans under the tarpaulin behind you. Didn't have a gun, but he came at you with a bloody great monkey wrench. He caught you on the head as he fell. I got him through the middle.' He leered: 'Blew most of his guts out through his back!'

The floor lurched violently, the engine rising to an unhealthy scream, and the brandy bottle crashed over on to the floor beside Ben's seat. He had just enough strength to lift it and drink. Dry blood was flaking off the side of his face when he moved and his head was still slamming with pain. If only the noise would stop and the floor keep still. There was another lurch and the belt dug into his stomach; he was beginning to feel sick again.

He tried to concentrate. Ryderbeit seemed very happy. Mel was happy too. That was wrong, somehow. They didn't like each other. Or perhaps that was a long time ago. He looked round at her and saw her sitting forward with her palms pressed together and a bright quizzical look in her eyes that he had never seen before. He picked up the brandy again. It seemed to ease the pain.

Ryderbeit turned to him again and chuckled: 'Hit it, soldier! That's genuine French cognac.' He looked at Mel and winked. 'A lovely drink for a lovely day!'

'What are you both so damned happy about?' Ben muttered.

'We're all happy, soldier. It's all over. We're rich.'

'What?'

Ryderbeit gave Mel another wink. 'Shall we show him?'

'Why not?' She leaned over the back of her seat and picked up a leather carryall and took out an oilskin packet about the size of a woman's handbag which she began to unroll across her lap. Inside lay about a couple of hundred small brown pebbles like coffee sugar.

Ben gaped at them. He felt drunk. The pebbles began to tremble with the vibration of the cabin. Mel looked at him, and her flat expressionless face suddenly broke into a fierce smile. 'There are five more like that!' She began folding the packet up again. 'We found them stowed in the locker back there. All we had to do was count them. Isn't it marvelous?'

'How much?'

It was Ryderbeit who answered: 'Some of the stuffs not very good grade. And there's a lot of dross. But a few are real beauties. I'd put them between eight hundred and fifty and nine hundred thousand dollars. I don't think they quite top the million mark.'

Ben began to laugh. There are some odd effects from concussion, he remembered. Mel had returned the oilskin packet to the carryall and put it back behind her seat. Ryderbeit was still turned, grinning at them both. The engine had changed pitch again, the cabin bumping and sinking wildly.

'How did they get here?' said Ben.

'Brought up from the river by our much lamented friends back there, just as I said. They must have been pretty well organized. Couldn't have left a day before we did because they had to wait for this.' He picked a sheet of paper up from beside the control panel and handed it to him.

At first Ben thought it was the map they had taken from the body of the white-haired boy in the desert: a little more creased and thumb-marked perhaps but covered with the same intricate markings and drawn in the same neat ballpoint. The only difference was the one Ben had predicted: instead of running due south into the swamp, the dotted line curved to the west, following the lava flow he had seen from the volcano.

Ryderbeit gave him his crooked grin: 'So we were right, eh! That little white-haired fellow was heading for the helicopter to help his friends pick a nice little fortune off the river.'

'But who was he?'

Ryderbeit shrugged: 'Just one of the gang — probably hired because he'd known Stopes or Hitzi Leiter. It was a clever idea sending him to impersonate Hitzi. It struck me at first as a bit too elaborate, but I now see why they did it. Because one of their big problems, once they had murdered Stopes and got the map, was to make sure no one else knew about the plan. They probably had had Stopes under some sort of watch — as you said, the white-haired boy was up at the club that night and saw us — but they didn't know exactly who we were, or how many of us we were. When they did know, they could hardly try to knock us all off in Parataxín — and even if they did, they could never be sure they hadn't missed someone. On the other hand, if they'd risked letting us chance our luck, even without the map, we might have got through to the river — just as Hitzi did — and that could have been very embarrassing for them, especially if we had guns.

'No, they wanted everything smooth — a big helicopter to the volcano and a flight each day to the river to collect the diamonds. So they devised the idea of sending the white-haired lad off to Benisalem to wait for anyone who turned up, then pull the Hitzi Leiter stunt. The plan had two advantages, you see — it found out the exact opposition they were up against, and by planting the false map with us it provided a means of getting rid of us without too much fuss. A bit oversubtle perhaps, but it might well have worked — if it hadn't been for the moon snakes.'

'Then why did they shoot at us on the volcano?'

'That I don't know,' said Ryderbeit. 'The bald guy may have panicked, or just been trigger-happy, or perhaps he really did think we were Xatus. Whatever it was, we'll never know now.'

'But how did they find out about the river in the first place?'

'Probably the old Captain blabbed too much when he was in his cups. Discovering a river full of diamonds isn't an easy secret to keep. I don't suppose we'll ever hear the whole story — at least, I'm not hanging round Parataxín long enough to hear it.'

'Are we going back to Parataxín?'

'We are! We'll be hitting the city bang in the middle of the Carnival, which means the police'll be too busy dealing with riots and rapes and murders and about a hundred thousand drunks to bother about three little innocents like us.

'I'll put this down just outside Benisalem, and we'll pick up Mel's car and drive like the damned all night to be in Parataxín by morning. And if dear Danny Berck-Millar is ready and available, we should be able to dispose of the stuff within forty-eight hours.'

Ben helped himself to more brandy. 'Nine hundred thousand dollars!' he breathed.

'Four hundred and fifty thousand,' said Ryderbeit: 'after the discount. A hundred and sixty thousand pounds.'

'Divided three ways.'

Ryderbeit was watching the mountains in front as he repeated, almost inaudibly above the noise: 'Three ways. Over fifty thousand a piece.'

Ben turned to Mel. She was staring out at the falling darkness with a small secret smile.

'What are you going to do with fifty thousand quid, Mel?' he asked, offering her the brandy.

'Buy a big house in the country with a walled garden,' she said, drinking from the bottle. 'It should be enough, shouldn't it?'

'It should if we ever get it.'

She looked at him quickly: 'We'll get it. Why shouldn't we?'

'No reason at all.' He called to Ryderbeit: 'Do you think you can put this thing down in the dark?'

Ryderbeit yelled over his shoulder: 'In the mood I'm feeling I could land it on my head! It's not the dark I'm worried about — it's this wind over the mountains. If we hit it really bad it can blow one of these crates around like a piece of thistledown.' As he spoke, the machine dropped with a roar, and shriek of metal. Ben watched him bending over the controls, and felt strangely uneasy. They had killed four men. In self-defense, perhaps? — or just in order to steal nearly a million dollars? His half-forgotten puritanical upbringing was beginning to nag at him: to warn him that these things are not done with impunity. He felt obscurely afraid.

'Did you bury the bodies?' he asked Mel.

'We didn't have time.'

'And the mule?'

'We left it. It'll probably die. We couldn't take it with us, could we?'

'No.' He watched Ryderbeit ease up one of the levers by his side, moving his hands delicately like a surgeon. The red splash of sky ahead was shrinking into purple darkness. He was a good pilot: he liked flying almost as much as he liked killing, and he did both well.

They were now swaying and rattling down past the craters of the Hiarra, with the lower slopes lying bald between seams of vegetation like a rumpled, molting carpet. Far below were the lights of Benisalem.

Ryderbeit pushed the lever further forward. They were going down fast now.

CHAPTER TEN: DELIRIUM

The lobby of the Hotel Fenix was full of unshaven men in black suits and alligator shoes, asleep in armchairs along the wall. It was cool and dark here after the roar of the streets. The Carnival of San Jose de Montecristo had now reached noon on its third and final day, and the tempo in Parataxín was running high.

Ben followed Mel through to the reception desk, each carrying an identical Panagra overnight bag. She wore a lemon suit of rough silk and her hair was shining, almost blond. She looked very conspicuous; even the exhausted police outside had turned to watch her.

There were two men at the entrance to the bar selling black-market tickets to the bullfight at five o'clock. Ben and Mel pushed past them up to the desk. The clerk had silver braid on his shoulders and sleep dirt in the corner of his eyes. They asked for Ryderbeit's suite and he motioned wearily to an Indian pageboy who led them over to the elevators. The doors hissed shut, cutting off the sounds of the Carnival that boomed into the lobby like a heavy sea.

They started up to the fifth floor. There was a mirror at the back and Ben looked at his gray reflection, with the bandage Mel had wound round his head like a grubby turban. He felt rundown and nervous. In both the Panagra overnight bags were two of the oilskin packets. It had been agreed between the three of them that each would carry his own share until the diamonds were finally exchanged for cash. And now, after all they had been through, that moment was very close. Ben was nervous, but not for any specific reason — simply because so far everything had been going just a little too well. Something had to go wrong.

It was two days now since they had landed the helicopter outside Benisalem. No one had seen them, and when they walked into the town and collected Mel's car from the hotel, no one asked any questions. They had driven all night as planned, and had not even been checked by a patrol. In Parataxín they had gone straight to Mel's flat, had bathed and shaved and eaten a huge breakfast; then Ryderbeit had gone to his usual hotel, collected his luggage, and with the money he had taken off the body in the desert, had booked the last suite in the plushest hotel in Parataxín.

Ben had stayed in Mel's flat and collapsed on the sofa where he had slept for nearly fifteen hours. He was drained of all desire for her, and there was not even a pretense of affection between them now. They were in business together, and the business was almost completed, and then they would go their separate ways.

He regretted nothing, although he was still beset by a lurking sense of guilt over the men they had killed. He wondered how long it would take for the condors to come down from the massif and devour all trace of them. But now there were other things to worry about. Yesterday evening Ryderbeit had come over and told them that Danny Berck-Millar would meet them at the Fenix at three o'clock next day. There had been no news of Stopes or of the helicopter or of the four dead men on the volcano. All normal life in Parataxín had been paralyzed by the Carnival.

The elevator stopped and he followed Mel out, along a deep carpet. The door of the suite was opened by a huge man in a pleated white shirt, cavalry-twill trousers and cream moccasins. He stood about a foot taller than Ben and smelt of aftershave.

'Mister Morris? Mrs. MacDougall? Come right in!' He spoke like a Midwestern American, although he did not look like one. His enormous brown face had slanting eyes and a little button nose, and his hair grew in tight black curls that ended below his ears.

Ryderbeit was lying behind him full length on a sofa, his shirt open to the belt, with a golden tumbler standing in the middle of his flat naked stomach. 'That's them!' he yelled. 'Let 'em in, Danny Boy! Children, meet Danny Berck-Millar, otherwise Mister Fix.'

The big man shook hands; his grip made Ben wince. He held on to Mel's hand for several seconds longer, with quite a different touch, smiling into her eyes: 'So you're Mel, huh? You must be a very tough kid, Mel!'

'Hard, Danny Boy — hard as coffin nails,' Ryderbeit growled from the sofa.

Her face remained impassive. Danny Berck-Millar released her hand, but went on smiling: 'I've heard a lot about you, Mel — and I must say, you're a lovely girl!'

She smiled politely and walked round him, while Ryderbeit shouted: 'You got the goodies, you two? Show 'em to Danny Boy.'

They went over to a table in the middle of the room, put down their overnight bags and took out the four oilskin packets. Danny came up beside them and watched them unroll the packets in four neat rows, then he nodded slowly and stared at the heaps of pebbles for a long time. The fan hummed on the ceiling; Ryderbeit drank his whisky; and through the windows came the monotonous rhythm of the Carnival.

Berck-Millar turned and smacked his huge hands together: 'Six packets — that the lot?'

'It's enough,' said Ryderbeit.

Berck-Millar walked across the room, rubbing his hands together with a sound like rice paper. 'What are you drinking, you two? Whisky? Bourbon? Bacardi?' There was a cabinet behind Ryderbeit's head that was as well stocked as a miniature bar.

They both asked for whisky. Berck-Millar did not appear to be drinking. Ryderbeit leaned back and hauled down a nearly empty bottle of Johnnie Walker Black Label, holding it upside down over his glass. 'O.K., Danny Boy, what d'yer say?'

Berck-Millar poured Mel and Ben their drinks, then stood staring at the carpet. 'I need a second opinion, Sammy, before I can let you have an exact figure,' he said at last.

'Shit!' said Ryderbeit: 'I'm the expert — I've given you the figure. Not a cent less than nine hundred thousand dollars before the split.'

'I'll give you four hundred grand after the discount,' Berck-Millar said, and looked up with a beautiful square-toothed smile.

Ryderbeit drained his glass off and his face had that hooked dangerous look that was not quite drunk, and certainly not sober. He spoke in a careful voice, watching his toes at the end of the sofa: 'Give or take a few thousand, you got nine hundred thousand dollars' worth of diamonds there, Danny Boy. I told you I'm cutting you in fifty-fifty. I don't have to say it again.'

Danny Berck-Millar gave a pleasant, throaty laugh: 'You're an old rascal, Sammy! How long did you say you worked down there on the Rand?'

'Long enough. Four hundred and fifty thousand — in low-denomination U.S. currency.'

Berck-Millar stood in the middle of the room, smiling and shaking his head. 'You got one helluva nerve, Sammy! Trying to call the game against an old hand like me? — that's a crazy thing to do! I've got you just where I want you.'

Ryderbeit slid his eyes around, without moving his head, and leered at Berck-Millar. 'O.K., Danny Boy. So what are you going to do? Call in your boys? Have me and Ben and Mel here given the old Mafia treatment — a last drink with time to say our prayers, then have our bodies smuggled out in laundry baskets? You can do better than that, Danny Boy!'

Berck-Millar chuckled. 'Sammy, you lie there guzzling your booze, and think you're home and dry, don't you? Well, let me tell you something. From now, it's me — old Danny Boy, Mister Fix, the tired old middleman — who's going to be taking all the risks.'

'What risks?' Ryderbeit growled.

Berck-Millar paused, and his smile was suddenly gone, as he stood and studied Ryderbeit lying prone on the sofa; and as he watched them both, Ben felt a tight lump in his stomach. For the first time since they'd met he began to wish that Ryderbeit had a gun. Both the rifles, along with the rest of the equipment, had been abandoned with the helicopter. He glanced at Berck-Millar and wondered whether he could be concealing a gun under that close-fitting pleated shirt or the immaculate cavalry-twill trousers.

Berck-Millar was looking gravely at Ryderbeit. 'Sammy,' he said at last, 'I haven't inquired too closely into just how you got these diamonds — or even how you got to know about them. I just know you turn up one fine day in Parataxín, in the company of one young Englishman and one hell of an attractive English girl, and say, Danny Boy, here's a few hundred thousand dollars' worth o' crude diamonds. Change 'em into cash and we'll all be rich and happy.'

'You done worse things, you bastard!' Ryderbeit muttered. 'What do you want to know, anyway? We got the diamonds — that's all that matters.'

'Oh sure. Providing there was no one else after them.'

Ryderbeit twisted his head round and glared at Berck-Millar. 'What the hell does that mean?'

'Just what I said. You live in Parataxín, you get to hear things. Like stories about diamonds lying around on a river. Why should you be the only people to hear about them?'

'Just tell me who else heard about them.' Ryderbeit's voice was a hard whisper, and again Ben felt that tightening in his stomach. There were four dead men lying out on that volcano. Even in a country like this, that could still count as murder.

Berck-Millar was saying, 'O.K., so maybe I'm wrong. Maybe there isn't anybody else who knows about that river. Maybe it's all just between these four walls.'

Ryderbeit nodded. 'That's it, Danny Boy. Just the four of us. Three of us doing all the sweat, and you taking fifty percent at the end of it — you ungrateful bastard.'

Berck-Millar gave his throaty laugh again and cried, 'Fifty percent for having to go on living in this crumby town!'

'You don't have to,' said Ryderbeit.

'I work here. So do a lot of other people — some of whom might get to hear about these diamonds.'

Ryderbeit closed his eyes. 'What's this all leading up to, Danny Boy? You going to start asking for seventy-five percent?'

'I'm just explaining my position,' said Berck-Millar, with sudden portentousness, like a bank manager reluctantly agreeing to an overdraft. 'I'm sticking my neck out on this deal, and I just want to make it clear that if you're not being frank with me — if you're holding something back…'

'You're getting your bleeding cut, aren't you?' Ryderbeit yelled, and suddenly swung himself off the sofa, landing so close to Berck-Millar that they almost touched. 'You bloody dago!' he whispered. Berck-Millar laughed: 'Four hundred thousand, you drunken Yiddish Fascist!'

Ryderbeit put both hands on Berck-Millar's shoulders and pulled him down in a swaying embrace: 'Who's the other fifty thousand for?'

Berck-Millar broke away and said seriously: 'Don Ramaq-Gomez at the bank. He won't touch anything involving dollars for less than fifty grand. That's what he'll ask, and it'll come out o' my cut. Hell. I'm not breaking fifty-fifty on this deal!'

'You're doing all right. How soon can you get hold of this Don Gomez?'

'Not before eight this evening — nearer nine. He's got a seat in the President's box at the bullfight this afternoon, then there'll be a reception for the matadors. I won't be able to get him till after that.'

'Will he be able to get into the bank?'

Berck-Millar laughed: 'For two hundred thousand bucks he will!'

Ryderbeit opened a fresh bottle of Black Label and poured his glass three-quarters full, sipping it neat. 'Will he give you your cut tonight in cash?'

'You bet your arse he will! I'm not allowing any credit on a deal like this!'

Ryderbeit cackled over his drink: 'I suppose this bank of Don Gomez has got that many dollars on tap? In small, used denominations, remember. '

'Don't worry, it's the biggest bank in the country. They've got 'em.'

'You've talked to Gomez already, eh?'

Berck-Millar grinned: 'I gave him a couple of hints. He should be ready to deliver tonight, or tomorrow morning at the latest.'

'O.K. We'll say here in this room at ten?'

Berck-Millar shook his head, his eyes again on the carpet: 'Won't do. Old Gomez's got a reputation. He's not going to drag a suitcase full of hot cash right across this city in the middle of the Carnival and hand it over in a public hotel. C'mon now, Sammy, don't be dumb!'

Ryderbeit sat down again on the sofa. 'O.K., so you carry it across.'

'Gomez wouldn't hand over the cash until I'd given him the diamonds. Would you trust me with them? Hell, I wouldn't trust myself!'

Ryderbeit examined his drink and belched: 'O.K., what?'

'I'll have to talk to Gomez after the *corrida*, then I'll call you here. Well meet up somewhere private. It won't be before ten.'

Mel finished her drink, put her glass down on the table beside the diamonds and without a word began rolling up her two oilskin packets.

'Hey, whattya doing, honey?' Berck-Millar cried.

She put the two packets away in her overnight bag and said: 'It's only just four o'clock, Mr. Millar. I'm going home. Ben or Sammy can ring and tell me where we all meet.'

Danny Berck-Millar looked confused for a moment, then bared his teeth at her like a row of piano keys: 'Sure! Perhaps I could walk you some of the way? You'll never get a cab anywhere today.'

'Before you go, give us a hundred dollars on account,' Ryderbeit called from the sofa.

'I said no credit on this deal,' Berck-Millar replied, turning to the door.

'Call the deal off then, you mean dago! You get Mel — I get a hundred dollars. What d'yer say?'

Berck-Millar took out a roll of notes from his hip pocket: 'Two hundred pesos, and I want 'em back.'

Mel was already outside. When the door had closed, Ryderbeit sat up and looked at Ben: 'Get yourself a drink.'

Ben poured a gentle Scotch and soda and said: 'Is that fellow really American?'

'Cuban. Sit down. Naturalized. Hell of a boy! Mister Fix, that's him. If anybody can make that bitch Mel, it's old Danny Boy. Six wives to his credit and four of them getting alimony. That boy must be paying more prick tax than any honest man alive.'

'Can he be trusted?'

'I trust him.'

'And this Don Gomez?'

'He's one of the directors of the Banco Hispaniola-Crédito. He'll take his fifty thousand and be happy. Have another drink.'

'I've got one. How do we get the cash out of the country?'

'Danny Boy's taking care o' that. The bastard's not getting his cut for nothing, you know!'

'What's his plan?'

'Chartered plane to a private airfield outside Caracas. Something to do with that American company I was telling you about that he's got an interest in. We pay the cash in there and draw it out later through one of the company's foreign accounts.'

'You sure they won't cross us?'

'Why should they? People do this sort o' deal with them every day. You worry too much. For Chrissake, have a drink!'

'Let's take it easy, Sammy. We got a long time ahead to get drunk.'

'Nobody said drunk. I said drink! Sit down, let's do a little celebrating. We haven't celebrated anything yet.'

Ben sat down and thought, *There isn't anything to celebrate yet, except a few piles of pebbles on a hotel table.* But he needed a drink badly. It quieted his nerves and made his head better. He also felt he owed something to Ryderbeit in the way of companionship: it seemed that he and Mel might have been very wrong about him — almost as wrong, perhaps, as they'd been about Hitzi Leiter.

Ryderbeit got up to give himself another whisky. 'It's getting gray in here. Storm coming. I don't like storms — they give me a tight feeling inside.'

Ben looked up and saw that the sun had suddenly gone. The curtains swelled sluggishly with the fan. Ryderbeit squinted at him over his drink: 'Here's to being rich, soldier! We deserve it.'

Ben lifted his glass, and they heard fireworks exploding down in the street like pistols.

The phone rang at 7:40. Ryderbeit got his foot tangled in the cord answering it. He gave several grunts, and banged the receiver down. Ten o'clock tonight at Danny's place. He'll pick us up and take us to old Gomez's villa.' He sat down heavily and began to chuckle. 'Lovely, eh, soldier! Think — just a couple o' days ago. Bloody swamp! Bloody mules! Nothing to drink, nothing to eat.' He picked up a cushion and flung it across the room. 'What say we go and eat now? Suckling pig at

Cuchuro's?'

'Just a sandwich for me,' said Ben. His head was aching again and he was beginning to feel slightly unwell. 'Where does Berck-Millar live?'

'Not far. We'll eat on the way.'

'Does Mel know where it is?'

'Danny already told her. In fact, knowing that randy bastard, I wouldn't be too surprised if she got there a good deal earlier than ten!' He stood up and began to walk unsteadily toward the door.

Ben realized he had almost forgotten about Mel. 'What about your diamonds?' he said.

Ryderbeit halted and laughed: 'I almost forgot!' He went into the bedroom, while Ben rolled up his two packets on the table and put them away again in the overnight bag. Ryderbeit came back with the leather carryall they had found in the helicopter. When they were in the elevator he said: 'Shall we put 'em all in together?'

'I'll take care of mine,' said Ben; he had already wrapped the strap of the overnight bag twice round his wrist.

'Cautious, soldier!'

'Nothing personal,' said Ben.

They had to press their way through a crowd that stretched from the hotel bar into the street, which was one rocking mass of people, most of them beautifully dressed, and most of them drunk. The Negroes were drunk on music: they shuffled back and forth shaking their hips, their arms raised, palms and faces turned to the sky. The men wore flaming shirts and the women bright bandanas, and for every ten or twenty of them there was a band with drums and maracas, all playing against each other in a strange, obsessive rhythm.

For a moment Ben thought he had lost Ryderbeit; then he caught him on the far side of the street near the corner, panting against the wall. 'Let's get out o' here!' he choked. 'I need a drink.'

They started down a side street which was mostly crowded with *mestizos* and Indians, and they were drunk on wine. Rows of them lay sprawled under the walls among the charred firecrackers. The crowds swept up and down like a relentless tide that had no direction. There were babies in arms and tiny children trailing hidden under the crush. The noise was terrific.

Ryderbeit found a bar full of men singing Spanish *Hotas*. Ben stood against the wall while Ryderbeit ordered, and was filled with a strange euphoric feeling as though none of this were really happening. A man with a flushed face came up and gave him a glass of wine, raised his own glass and shouted something, then disappeared into the crowd. The wine was purple and very sweet. Ben drank it down without effort. Ryderbeit returned with two glasses of Bacardi. 'They got no bloody whisky!' he cried, and suddenly they were surrounded by a ring of men dancing arm in arm. They both raised their glasses to them, and one of them broke from the others and sang a high passionate solo with his eyes closed and his neck bulging. The flushed-faced man came back and gave them both two glasses of the purple wine. Ryderbeit lifted his above his head and yelled something, and they all lifted theirs and yelled too. There was more singing. Ben sipped the wine and realized it reminded him of blackberries. Somebody offered him another glass. He tried to refuse and heard Ryderbeit shout: 'Drink it, you bastard! It's only wine.'

Ben sipped it and looked at his watch. It was twenty minutes past eight. He changed the strap of the overnight bag over to his other hand. Ryderbeit had the carryall on the floor between his legs. It was not easy to believe there was more than £200,000 worth in those two bags between them. Around £50,000 for each of them when the cut had been taken.

When he thought of it he felt a rush of panic. He didn't want any more of this sweet black wine; he wanted to get out of here. The crowd swayed against him; their singing tore against his eardrums; his head began to ache again.

Ryderbeit was singing too, his eyes a bloodshot orange, his voice a tuneless croak. Ben took him by the arm: 'Come on, Sammy, let's get going.'

'What time is it?'

'Nearly half-past eight.'

'Plenty o' time.' There was more wine being passed round. From outside they heard thunder. Ben drank half his glass, then put it down on the bar and asked the barman for a black coffee. An old man in a beret was standing next to him, jabbering excitedly over a glass of tequila. After a moment Ben realized that the man was talking to him. He tried to listen, and he could not understand a word. The coffee seemed a long time coming. He unwrapped the strap of the overnight bag from his wrist and put the bag down in front of him on the bar. The barman brought him a tequila.

'No, coffee,' Ben said.

The barman nodded at the old man: 'He invites you.'

Ben touched glasses with him and finished his drink in a gulp. A moment later he began to feel ill. He thanked the old man and hurried from the bar without waiting for the coffee. The crowd of *Hota* singers had gone. Ryderbeit was sitting on a chair by the wall, the carryall still between his feet. Ben said: 'Let's get something to eat.'

Outside, the first warm raindrops were beginning to splash down out of the black sky. The street ahead was full of papier-mâché effigies of saints and clowns and football stars, lurching above the heads of the crowd, some ablaze with colored lights, others hissing and crackling with rockets.

Ryderbeit walked as though in a trance. Ben tried to shout at him through the noise, but he didn't seem to hear. The street led into the Plaza Mayor, and Ben saw they had come out very near the Panagra building. It was closed up now behind steel shutters.

There were three bands playing in the middle of the Plaza, and it looked impossible to get through. Ben was exhausted, with a nauseous ache in his stomach. He now saw that besides the various bands in the square, there were several rostrums on which groups of singers and dancers seemed to be competing for prizes. The excitement grew feverish after every number, and above the gaudy headdresses of the *mestizos* and the Negro women, the white solar topees of the riot police surged ominously back and forth to the howls of the crowd greeting each new decision.

Ben thought vaguely, *The girls are lovely. What a city to be loose in! And here I am with a bellyache, drearily drunk and dragging round more than half a million dollars with a psychopath whom I shouldn't trust with a half-crown.*

The girls were wonderful, he thought again: over and over again, as he turned and saw a procession of pointed black hoods like the Ku Klux Klan moving slowly round the side of the square, bearing in their midst a great silver crucifix on which the pink plaster body of Christ hung bleeding brightly above the faces of the crowd.

The slow chanting of the hooded marchers reached him across the surging din of the *maracas* and *mariachis* and drums and cheers and screams, and the police whistles piercing through the night. Ryderbeit was beside him, cackling loudly: 'Oh isn't it wild, soldier! As wild as it comes!'

The grim black hoods with their glinting slits for eyes had passed on with their tortured Christ, and in their place there were now dancing men in scarlet dominoes and girls with flowers in their hair, and youths with oiled heads and the slack, gaping faces of the mob in ecstasy.

Ben struggled against the crush, swaying back and forth, feeling as though his stomach was a bucket of slops and was overflowing. Somewhere ahead there was a roar of applause for a band of guitar players dressed in trim cutaway gray suits with sequined lapels and waistcoats. Ben could vaguely hear the plodding rhythms of a pseudo-European pop number. The words were unintelligible.

Across the Plaza another Christ appeared above the crowd, this time in what looked like gleaming marble. The pop number died out into a slow deafening chant of '*Er-co-lo!*' Ben had seen the name on the bullfighting posters.

Suddenly this God-fearing barbarism began to terrify him. He groped round, clutching at Ryderbeit's arm, pushing his way toward a café with marble tables and gilt mirrors that looked as though it might have a serviceable toilet. There was a long bar in front of the mirrors, covered with plates — fried shrimps and olives and fillets of smoked herring.

He hurried past them toward the stairs. There was a cubicle with a lock and sheaf of paper. He sat for a long time with his head down between his knees, and came out feeling lightheaded and giddy.

Ryderbeit was at the bar talking to a man and a woman. The man was enormously fat, with a black waistcoat and pearl buttons; his face was vague and sweaty. Ryderbeit yelled in

Spanish: 'Carlos — Maria — this is Morris. The great Morris! Morris — this is Maria!'

Shut your mouth, he thought: *I'm B. Mors, seaman, wanted by the police.* He steadied himself against the bar. The woman was talking to him in Spanish. He shut his eyes and wondered where Mel was. He felt very sick. He pushed between the woman and the fat man, stumbled into a table, fought his way out into the street. The sky was streaked with fireworks exploding behind the cathedral. The crowds were looking up and cheering. The whole Plaza seemed to be rocking itself into delirium. Ryderbeit was coming out of the bar with the fat man and the woman called Maria. He leered glassily at Ben: 'Hey, where yer been? You look sick!'

The man and the woman were holding him by the arms, trying to lead him away. The woman muttered something, eyeing Ben narrowly, and Ryderbeit shouted: 'You're a rude sod, Morris! These are my friends! We're celebrating.'

'You've left your bag inside, Sammy.' But before Ryderbeit could shake himself free, Ben had slipped past him and retrieved the carryall from under the bar. He stuffed his overnight bag inside it and carried it outside again. 'You need a bloody nanny! I'll look after it from now on.'

They began to shoulder their way round the Plaza. 'Who are these two?' said Ben.

'Nice people. Carlos is a bullfighting critic here. Maria's his girl. You shouldn't't've run out like that, you know. They were very offended.' He turned into a doorway, down some steps into a stone bodega, their feet crackling on gamba shells as they pushed up to the bar. Ben came in last. The barman was putting up glasses of red wine in front of the fat man, Carlos, who began handing them out. He looked sourly at Ben who said: '*No, gracias!*'

'Drink up!' Ryderbeit shouted. 'This is a good wine.'

'I don't want any.' He could feel the nauseous churning again in his bowels.

'What's the matter with yer?'

'Go easy, Sammy. It's very hot in here.' It was nearly a quarter past nine. He heard Maria say in Spanish: 'He does not like the Carnival.' He drank his wine and said: 'Let's go, Sammy. We got to get through the crowd up there.'

Ryderbeit was swaying on one leg, red dribble on his chin. Suddenly he stumbled and knocked his glass to the floor. 'Give me a drink!' he croaked.

'You've had enough.' Ben put down his glass half full. The bar had become very dim and his gut was a lump of sickening pain. He pushed past Ryderbeit, toward the back of the bar. There was a passage behind a bead curtain leading into a dark stinking cell with a trough along the wall. He went down over the trough, sweating cold, eyes closed, wondering how long the pain could go on. His whole body seemed to be melting into a foul liquid.

He recovered slowly. People came in and went again. A dwarf in a Pierrot costume came and grinned at him and began jumping up and down and waving his arms about; then he went too. The pain gradually drained away. He felt an immense relief and for a long time he just squatted there staring at the wet stone floor covered in newspaper. He picked out three photographs of Dr. Romolo and one of Sophia Loren. Then he went cold all over.

He had left the carryall upstairs. He got up and back through the bead curtain, battling down between the crowd along the bar. Ryderbeit had gone.

Somebody tapped him on the shoulder. It was the fat man, Carlos; he was pointing toward the door. Ben followed him into the street. It had begun to rain hard and he suddenly felt very sober. Maria was waiting just outside under the awning. Ryderbeit was not with her, '*Dónde está* Sammy?' he yelled.

'*Su amigo* —' the fat man gestured up the street.

'What happened? *Qué pasa?*

Carlos shrugged: 'He is drunk. He was molesting people in the bar.'

'Where is he?'

'He was thrown out.'

'But where?'

'Down there.' He nodded down the street, at a wedge of masks and lights and crowds. Ben started off into the rain without even thanking him. The first place he came to was a milk and ice-cream bar. Ryderbeit was not there. He found him at the end of the street, outside a café with steel chairs lining the pavement. He was slumped forward in one, asleep. The carryall was not there.

Ben lifted him under the chin, shook him, shouted at him: 'The bag, Sammy! Where's the bag?'

Ryderbeit's eyes opened heavily. 'Huh?' He licked his lips, then glared round.

'The bag, Sammy! Where is it?' He began hauling him out of the chair: 'The bag of diamonds, you stupid bastard!'

Ryderbeit was suddenly alert: 'You got it! Have you got it?'

'No, Sammy, I haven't got it.'

'You got it! What happened?' His face grew wild, streaming with rain.

'I left it with you.'

'Oh Jesus!' They began to run down the street back to the bodega.

Ben went in first, hunting along under the bar. The carryall was not there. The barman, and another man in a green apron, came up and seized Ryderbeit by the elbows. He began to yell. Ben rushed up and yelled in Spanish:

'Leave him alone! What are you doing?'

The barman shouted: 'Take him out! He is drunk.'

Ben began to ask about the bag, then he realized he had forgotten the Spanish word for it. Ryderbeit was howling like a dog. 'Shut up, Sammy!' he cried. 'Ask them about the bag, for Christ's sake!'

The barman said something to the man with the apron and Ben caught the word *policía*. He took a last look along the floor, then grabbed Ryderbeit's arm and dragged him outside. 'Let's just try to think,' he said.

'You had it!' Ryderbeit shrieked.

'I left it in there.'

'You sure you had it?'

'Yes.'

'Are you bloody sure? You lost it, you flaming bastard!'

'Keep calm. Let's check the other places.'

'Yeah! Left it in the other place!'

'What other place?'

'Oh God! The place with the mirrors!'

'No,' said Ben. 'I took it out of there.'

Ryderbeit was staring round him again with a crazy glare in his eyes. 'We stopped somewhere else, didn't we?'

'No.'

'Where did we go with Carlos and Maria!'

'We came straight here.'

'They've got it then!'

'No. I saw them afterward. They didn't have it. What's the Spanish for bag, Sammy?'

'*Maleta*,' he said vaguely. 'We lost it, eh?'

'You wait here. Don't go inside again.'

Ben spoke to the barman and to the man with the green apron, and he went along the bar and spoke to each of the men drinking, and to others drinking in groups by the wall. Some of them didn't make sense, or didn't understand, or pretended not to understand. None of them had seen the carryall. It had been made of good leather, and someone would be pleased, even if they did throw away the pebbles inside.

When Ben came out again Ryderbeit was sitting on the pavement in the rain with his head in his hands, and from somewhere above the howl of the Carnival, the cathedral was tolling ten.

They searched every bar and *bodega* down the street, and in the next street, and round the Plaza Mayor, then started back through each of the bars they had been in earlier; and everywhere they questioned people about the *maleta de cuero* — the leather bag — describing it in every detail, with the Panagra bag inside and the oilskin packets of pebbles that somebody might have tossed away after opening them.

But no one had seen anything. The blank, twisted faces stared and shook their heads; and slowly, as the night drew on and the Carnival died with the heavy rain, the faces of the people they spoke to began to assume the appearance of demons and monsters — no longer human beings, but the nightmare augurs of their loss.

Just before midnight they returned to the *bodega* where Ben had been ill and had last seen the bag. The barman and the man in the green apron had gone; instead there was a very tall thin man with his nose eaten away, sitting in the middle of the half-empty room, staring at the door. His nose looked suddenly to Ben like the twin barrels of a shotgun, and as he began to question him, the man burst into a peal of laughter that came in a weird high-pitched whine through the naked cavities.

A big dark man lurched up, shaking his head and pointing at the laughing man with no nose: 'He is crazy! Don't speak with him.'

'Have you seen a bag?' said Ben. 'Did anyone leave one here? A leather bag with some packets of stones inside?'

The man shrugged and went over and spoke to a man at the end of the room who disappeared through the bead curtain leading to the toilet. He came back a moment later with a battered straw bag splashed with mud.

'*Si, es esto?*'

Ben shook his head and went outside where Ryderbeit was wandering miserably up and down in the rain, stopping people at random and receiving always the same answer.

'It's getting late,' said Ben.

'There's always Mel's share,' Ryderbeit muttered. 'About sixteen thousand quid a head after we've split it. Nothing to sneeze at, you know.'

'I suppose not. She'll be delighted though!'

'Screw her! We owe her seven hundred dollars, that's all. All the rest she owes us. You think she'd have made it without us?'

'No. But I'm not sure she'll quite see it that way.' He was feeling too depressed to argue. 'Let's go and call Berck-Millar first.'

They began to walk down the street where two priests were making their way carefully along the streaming gutter under huge black umbrellas.

'I don't care how she sees it,' Ryderbeit growled. 'It's us against her. And she's bleeding lucky to get even a third of it.'

Danny Berck-Millar opened the apartment door and yelled:

'Do you know what goddam time it is? Past midnight!'

Ryderbeit pushed past him and stood in the middle of the room, looking at the steel-tube furniture and abstract paintings under concealed lighting. 'You got a lovely place here, Danny Boy.'

Berck-Millar slammed the door. 'For Chrissakes, I gave you nearly three hours to get here. So the deal's off! You know that?'

Ryderbeit gave him a slow smile: 'Yeah, I know, Danny Boy. It's all off.'

'What?' Berck-Millar paused frowning. 'Are you drunk, Sammy?'

'Not half enough, I'm not.'

The American turned to Ben: 'What is this? What's happened?' He looked at their hands. 'Where's the ice?'

'All melted away,' said Ryderbeit.

'What!'

'Have you got a drink, Danny Boy?'

Berck-Millar looked desperately back at Ben: 'What the hell is this? What happened?'

'We lost the diamonds, Mr. Berck-Millar. That's all. I had them, but I got sick and went down for a crap and left them upstairs. I thought Sammy had them. He thought I had them.'

For a moment Berck-Millar did nothing; he didn't move and he didn't say anything. He just stood by the door and looked first at one of them, then at the other, while Ryderbeit moved wearily over to one of the low sofas and sank down into the black leather cushions. Ben stood and waited.

'You lost them?' Berck-Millar muttered.

Ben nodded. 'Where's Mel?'

'Gone home.'

'Well, she's still got her share,' said Ryderbeit. 'Fifty thousand quid after your cut of it — makes just over sixteen thousand, split three ways. Give us a drink, Danny!'

'Get the hell out o' here!' Berck-Millar roared. 'Both o' you! And don't come back!'

They reached Mel's apartment after walking for half an hour through the rain. The street door had been left unlocked. Ryderbeit pushed the buzzer and began to lead the way up the stairs. Ben said: 'She's going to be delighted to see us!'

'Don't take any lip from her, soldier. We got to be firm. Those diamonds are common property among the three of us, remember. If she doesn't see it that way she doesn't keep them.'

He stopped outside the door to her flat. A blue envelope had been tacked under the number plate. It was addressed in bold capitals, simply to 'BEN'. He pulled it down and ripped it open, his hands beginning to shake.

Inside were about a dozen lines written in her sloping script. He read:

Dear Ben

Sorry but I couldn't take it any longer. Nothing against you — I think you're a sweet man, but Sammy and that American were really the last straw. I simply don't trust them, and I'm taking off and going to try to sell my share on my own. I hope everything goes well. Good luck. Might see you on the Riviera or somewhere. Don't spend it all at once. M.

For some time, he stood there staring at the piece of paper and knew he had gone very pale. Ryderbeit read it over his shoulder and let out a shout of rage. 'Let's get after the bitch!'

'Where to?'

'The airport!'

'She's got a car.'

'She may have holed up in some hotel for the night. Or do you think she's really here and is just conning us?'

'No,' said Ben. 'She's gone. It's no good staying here.'

He began to lead the way wearily downstairs and out into the rain again.

The two of them now sat under the café awning at the corner of the Plaza Mayor and watched the crowds stroll past. The Carnival was finished and teams of men in blue overalls were moving round the square, sweeping up the wreckage of floats and firecrackers and broken glass.

Ben and Ryderbeit had come back from Las Tajas Airport an hour ago and were drinking tequila. They hadn't bothered with breakfast and had no plans for lunch. They had spent all night first checking the airport and the hotels, searching for Mel, then back through the bars and *bodegas*, asking the last decrepit revelers if they had seen *la maleta*; then finally, at dawn, back to the airport.

But there had been no trace of either Mel or the diamonds. The morning was bright and clear as they drove back by taxi on the road past the turning off to the Casa Sphinx. It all looked very peaceful in the early sunlight, and the road out to Benisalem seemed a long way away now.

When they got back into the city they rang Danny Berck-Millar. He sounded still angry at first, then worried: 'She didn't turn up this morning for the meeting with Gomez.'

'She wouldn't have done,' Ryderbeit told him. 'She's probably halfway to Mexico City by now. Went off last night leaving a note saying she didn't trust us and fancied she could make a better deal on her own. Perhaps you're losing your touch, Danny.'

'You owe me two hundred pesos!' Berck-Millar bellowed, as Ryderbeit banged down the receiver. Then he and Ben had gone to the café on the corner of the Plaza and began to drink tequila.

The Negro with no legs came pushing himself past on his trolley with his rolls of lottery tickets. There was no sign of the man who sold electric shocks; Ben could have done with a few at the moment. The two of them just sat at the zinc-topped table, and drank their second tequila each, and for a long time neither of them said anything. They were at the end of the line now. Seven men had died violently, and the two of them had come through alive, unscathed, and broke. Ben's body now felt loose and empty, and his mouth had a foul, flaky taste in it because he hadn't cleaned his teeth in twenty-four hours.

Ryderbeit was sitting with both hands on the table, fists clenched, and after a time he began muttering to himself, over and over again. 'The bitch! The little bitch! She's not goin' to get away with it. I'm not going to let her get away with it.'

Ben looked balefully across at him. 'You mean Mel?' he said, and Ryderbeit shifted his eyes from the Plaza and glared at him. 'Who else would I mean?' His voice had a dull miserable edge to it. 'We'll get her, soldier! I'm not just letting her walk out like that.'

'She didn't walk out. She had her share — we had ours. It's no good blaming her for what happened.'

'Oh, don't be such a bleeding little prig!' Ryderbeit yelled, opening his fists and smacking the table with both hands. 'Why should she get away with it? And after all we went through!' His voice cracked suddenly, his lips quivering. 'I'm goin' to get my share out of that bitch — and don't start on about any bleeding ethics, because at this particular moment Samuel David Ryderbeit is not very interested in ethics!' He leaned out and smacked the table again, splashing the tequila out of their glasses. 'I'm going to hunt her down and get my share, soldier! Understand?'

Ben nodded. 'Have another drink, Sammy. You won't find her. She could be anywhere. Where are you going to start? Mexico City, Miami, Monte Carlo? She was going to buy an old English country house with a walled garden — remember? So what are you going to do? Go through every ad, and every sale of every English country house over the next six months?'

'It might be a way.' Ryderbeit made a hopeless gesture and spat vaguely in the direction of the legless Negro. When he looked back at Ben, his jaw muscles were working away under his taut greenish skin. 'You don't give a damn, do you? In fact, I think you're even glad she got away with it! The little girl's rich now, and Ben Morris is glad!' He leaned closer to Ben, breathing hard. 'You wouldn't by any chance be thinking of joining her somewhere, would you? After a decent lapse of time, of course, when poor old Ryderbeit is conveniently out of the way, down on his uppers and drunk out of his mind. Is that what you're going to do, soldier?'

Ben smiled sadly. 'Don't be a damned fool. I don't know where she is. I don't even care where she is.'

'Don't even care!' Ryderbeit shrieked, and almost sobbed. 'Oh holy Moses! And after all we've been through, and getting nothing at the end of it, and you don't even care!'

'That's right,' said Ben. But he wasn't really listening to Ryderbeit anymore. *After all they'd been through*, he thought. The desert, the swamp, the black lake and the mad night of the Carnival — and getting nothing at the end of it. But that wasn't true. He had got what he came for. He had forgotten Laura. The pain had gone, along with those piles of brown pebbles in their oilskin packets, and in their place all he felt was a great sense of release. In a few more weeks he would be back in London and find a new job with a firm of architects, sitting at a drawing board from nine to five, with lunch around the corner at the local pub. And in a few more weeks there'd be other girls — or perhaps just one girl — and he wondered now, smiling to himself, if she would believe him when he tried telling her the whole story. But it wouldn't matter if she didn't believe him. He had nothing to prove it, except his suntan and a cut on the head.

He put his hand up and touched the still-raw bruise just below the hairline. It was as though none of it had ever happened. And yet it happened — in a remote, detached way that was not quite in touch with reality. Not even Ryderbeit, sitting across the table, seemed altogether real. Perhaps least of all, Ryderbeit.

Ben looked up and saw him leaning forward, his fists clenched again, his lips moving, and his voice held its slightly breathless hiss: 'Of course, there's another way, soldier! We know the route, and we know exactly where the river is.' His hand had sprung out and clasped Ben's, the palm dry and cold, although his face was damp with sweat. 'If we could get back out there quick enough — before anyone else could get there…'

Ben looked at him and began to laugh. Ryderbeit's hand withdrew swiftly, as Ben sat shaking his head and laughing till he could hardly see through the tears. He heard Ryderbeit shout, 'What's so damned funny? Are you going soft in the head or something?'

Ben stopped laughing and nodded. 'I think so, Sammy. I think maybe we're both getting a bit soft. We need a holiday.'

Ryderbeit's eyes narrowed. 'So you're packing it in, are you? After all we've been through together — giving in without even a fight.'

'There's nothing to fight about. It's all over, Sammy. We're all washed up — cleaned out. Why not forget about it — for a few hours, anyway? Have another drink.'

He turned to call the waiter, when he saw Ryderbeit suddenly grinning at him. 'You say we're cleaned out, eh?' The grin stretched into that cunning leer, as he put his hand inside his jacket and drew out a lumpy white manila envelope. Without moving his eyes from Ben he slit the flap open and tipped onto the table six big brown diamonds.

'See, I got a sense o' humor. After what you told me back there in the swamp I took the hint and did what you suggested — stashed a few of the little darlings away as a keepsake.' He began moving the stones around with his finger. 'And they're beauties, too! Worth, I'd say, at least a couple of thousand dollars, even after Berck-Millar's taken his cut.'

Ben looked at the diamonds and nodded. 'You're a lucky boy, Sammy.'

Ryderbeit frowned. 'What d'yer mean by that?'

Ben shrugged. 'Well, two thousand dollars. You didn't lose everything after all. It's just me who's cleaned out.'

'No, you're in this with me, Morris.' He pushed three of the stones over beside Ben's glass of tequila. 'That's your share. Enough to buy more guns and more equipment. We can do it, soldier! Trust me!'

Ben sat back and gazed out across the Plaza. It smelt fresh and cool, even though the sun was now high in the hard blue above the shaded white arcades. A breeze stirred the scraps of litter and pennants left over from the Carnival. He said slowly, without looking at Ryderbeit, 'I just want enough to get me back to England. I'll take the cheapest route — by boat. You keep the rest.'

'I said we were in this together,' Ryderbeit snarled. 'Morris, you're coming with me!'

Ben shook his head. 'I'm tired, Sammy. I need a holiday. We both do.'

For a few moments Ryderbeit went on snarling and frowning, and sipping his tequila, without saying anything. When the glass was empty he held it up to the sun, turning it slowly till the last drops at the bottom shone an oily yellow. 'You know, soldier,' he said at last, still watching the glass, 'maybe what you say's not such a bad idea after all. I mean, we got to get our strength back. A few weeks in the sun, and maybe we could pick up a bit o' loose cash on the way. You know, some o' those holiday places are full o' rich, randy old widows just waiting for a couple o' virile boys like us to come along and cheer 'em up.' He began to arrange his three diamonds in a triangle, round his glass. 'So where do we go? Hawaii? Honolulu?'

'Too vulgar,' said Ben. 'Let's go somewhere cool. Sweden. Look at the midnight sun and sleep with lots of nice, dumb Swedish girls.'

Ryderbeit sat back and cackled. 'That's a most beautiful idea, soldier! It's almost got rid o' my headache.' He stood up and shouted for the waiter. 'Let's just stroll over there to Panagra and make a few inquiries. Berck-Millar can get us the money before this evening.'

'You think he will, after what's happened?'

'He will — for fifty percent,' Ryderbeit said, giving the waiter almost the last of his crumpled pesos.

'Four thousand dollars and two tickets to Stockholm,' said Ben, as they began to walk across the plaza toward the Panagra building.

'Two return tickets,' said Ryderbeit. 'We're coming back, remember. Stopover Jamaica.'

Ben did not want to argue at this stage, he just said, 'That'll be more than a thousand dollars each, just on fares. It doesn't leave us a lot — especially if we don't find any rich old Swedish widows.'

Ryderbeit threw an arm round his shoulder, 'Let's worry about the money when it's gone. Live dangerously! Eh, soldier?'

Ben nodded. 'You think I'll get past Immigration? I'm still B. Mors, remember?'

'They'll have forgotten by now. Too busy nursing hangovers.'

They went into the air-conditioned hall and chose the prettiest of the girls behind the desks: a raven-haired *mestiza* with a mole on her cheek.

Ben looked up and down the hall, and saw there were no police here now. 'A hundred thousand quid,' he murmured, 'before the discount. If she's lucky she might clear seventy thousand.'

'Don't talk about it, soldier. Don't even think about it.'

Ben smiled: 'It's a lot of money for a young girl, don't you think?'

'Please, soldier! You're bringing back my headache.' He leaned against the desk and leered at the *mestiza* girl.

A NOTE TO THE READER

Dear Reader,

If you have enjoyed the novel enough to leave a review on **Amazon** and **Goodreads**, then we would be truly grateful.

Sapere Books is an exciting new publisher of brilliant fiction and popular history.

To find out more about our latest releases and our monthly bargain books visit our website:
saperebooks.com

Printed in Great Britain
by Amazon

27528526R00165